Apache Courage

—m—

Trumpets Around the Camp

Cynthia Hearne Darling

ISBN: 1495486621
ISBN-13: 9781495486623

DEDICATED TO THE MEMORY
OF MY DEAR FRIEND,

SHIRLEY JONES

FOR HER YEARS OF WORK
ON THE
WHITE MOUNTAIN APACHE RESERVATION

AND

TO

THE MEMBERS OF THE WHITE MOUNTAIN APACHE
TRIBE

WHOSE STRENGTH AND RESILIENCY AND BRAVERY
HAVE MADE THEM SURVIVORS

"LET IT BE FOR THY SERVICE I NOW SPEAK AND WRITE AND RECKON."

SAINT AUGUSTINE

I

There was a hot and heavy haze over the Capitol dome this morning. It was only spring time, but the summer heat was already trying to poke out, raising moisture up from the stagnant Tidal Basin, turning it into humidity suffocating enough to burn the just-born grass. He could see from his high rise apartment building that the early mist had not yet burned off. Funny, he thought, how the sun's rays had the power to destroy the fog, yet not burn the little people walking to work underneath its power. He slammed his coffee mug down on the table in frustration.

"You're in the fog; you're the one who needs to have his mind defogged." Tom suddenly recalled the night before. He had been trying to forget it, but, now, for some reason, he could remember everything that happened last night. He was in a club on Eighteenth Street. Music was coming at him from all sides, the kind where the beat won't leave you alone, sealing you into a place where you are protected from your thoughts. And the girl – Lou – was with him more or less. What a lie. Lou was never really with him.

She was clicking time to the music with the artificial nails attached to her right fingers, while she held a pink cosmo in her left hand, its liquid jiggling to the beat of the music. He was definitely drunk, but he remembered thinking that pink wasn't really her color; it was too innocent, too naïve. She had turned to him as if she knew what he had been thinking and said, "Drink your drink." Then she turned her back to him, raising her cat-like eyebrows at the guy on her left.

There was nothing he could do but drink. One sober thought escaped the music's barrier and got through to him. Why am I, at age thirty, sitting here trying to avoid figuring out my life? The next drink he took banished the thought, splintering it into pieces, like the glass he had just knocked off the bar with his elbow. Didn't mean to, he mouthed. Nobody noticed anyway, especially not Lou, whose strapless back was still turned toward him, and it couldn't see him.

"Whada you do, Man?" said the guy to his right who had reached the drunk phase when he would have conversed with a baboon and not noticed.

Tom's response was short. "I'm a phony. That's what I do for a living."

The drunk didn't care. "Me, I own a bowling alley. Should be there now. Should be there." He was chunky looking, and one line of salty perspiration was zigzagging down from his forehead to his cheek.

Tom was drunk enough to laugh at himself. "Phony, get it? I've got an expensive i phone.

I'm a phony." The other man didn't answer. He slid off the bar stool and wobbled out the door.

The next day Tom had a stinking headache, and it was a workday at that. Lou, however, Seemed to have no problem getting up and leaving his place. She sailed into her work in the back room of a department store as if she had never had a drink in her life. But, it was a different story for Tom who had to be on the front line every day in his job, communicating face to face with people.

He slugged down more coffee, intermittently lacing it with aspirin tablets. There was no question about skipping work; he had to go. When he put his head down to put on his shoes, he thought he was going to throw up. He pulled his head back to its upright position and stood still for a minute until the nausea went away.

Within the hour, though, he had gotten himself together and blown some of his personal fog away with a last cup of strong coffee. Now, in uniform, he was at his desk, opening the vertical blinds of his office window – his government-issued window that on good days gave him a picture of the tip of the Washington Monument. His eyes protested at the light, but he did it anyway. It was a form of deserved punishment for him. Outside, the early morning fog had burned off after all, leaving bright yellow rectangles deposited on the carpet of his office. Everything seemed calmer to him now, with the sun's rays neatly confined to their own spaces in orderly progression.

Thomas Gideon Collins, Captain, USA, Ph.D. Psychology, went around the corner of his desk and sat down. He said to himself that he was getting to the point where he had to concoct a big analytic deal out of everything, making a damn introspective analysis out of everything he saw, as if he had to interpret the whole world into his own mindset. Hell, a fog was a fog, and the sun was the sun. The rest of his gibberish was just a reaction to the alcohol that had creamed him last night. He didn't know what was going on inside himself. It was beginning to be difficult to get any reasonable thoughts out of his mind, and in this business, that wasn't going to pay off. Shortly, he was going to have to face a guy whose legs had been blown off. He had no answers for him, no pills that would ever replace what he had lost.

At thirty, he had suddenly looked at what he had been doing for a living and hated it. A dozen years before, he had taken the advice of well-meaning relatives who had been through the Great Depression: "Son, get your degrees and find some security in your life. You will never be sorry." All except Tom's mother -- That was not what she had told him. She didn't want him to enlist, but when he did, she said to him, "Do the right thing, Tommy. Don't be a shirking child in whatever you do."

Maybe that was just what he had ended up becoming, some kind of shirking child. He had to acknowledge that everything his family had told him was good advice. He did have a life of stable financial security; he was not rich, but he knew that each paycheck would arrive in the bank every two weeks. However, in his naivete, he hadn't expected that there were battles to be fought and situations to be faced by someone like himself who had the temerity to call himself a counselor.

No one had told him during his training that he might not be able to cure people or even help them with the educational tools he had been given. These useless diplomas on his walls, what did they mean but some kind of status? Granted, they did give him the power to refer people to others who could provide the magical pills that everybody seemed to want these days.

He couldn't understand what was going on inside him. It was like a mid-life crisis that had come upon him far too early. He shook his head as if trying to clear the damn fog that kept coming back. He had watched his friends and contemporaries. None of them seemed to going through this kind of inner rebellion – at least, if they were, he couldn't tell. The military guys, his contemporaries with whom he was acquainted, looked like they were trying to get ahead, get promoted and get laid. He had to grin. Well, maybe he didn't mind the latter. At least it made him human.

He had noticed his drinking pattern over a year ago. At first, he blamed it on not wanting to stay in by himself after work. He had few real friends. Well, he had a couple of guys in the military with whom he associated from time to time, but he hadn't wanted to mix his professional and social life, he rationalized. Mostly, the daytime acquaintances had either faded away or moved away. Except for Dempsey.

He had been around Tom for a couple of years. They both were Army, but Dempsey was a lawyer at the JAG office, mostly helping GIs write their wills before deployment. This morning, he called Tom after last night's bar scene with Lou. Dempsey hadn't been there. Too smart, probably, thought Tom wryly.

"Hey, Tom. What's up?" His voice sounded like a shriek.

"Tone it down, Dempsey, tone it down. My head's a mess."

Dempsey laughed. "You're the one who'd better tone it down on week nights."

"O.K., O.K. What do you want? I've got work to do."

It was Dempsey who was sober now.

"Nothing. Later." He hung up.

Tom had a momentary bad feeling about the conversation as he hung up the dead line, but he shrugged it off. He couldn't take on another bad feeling. A few moments later, though, he felt ashamed. He had treated Dempsey like a dog. He was somebody who had stood with him through a lot. He picked up his phone and punched in Dempsey's work number, asking to speak to Major Dempsey. In a minute he answered.

"Andrew Dempsey."

"Andy, Tom again. Sorry about this morning. I had a hell of a headache, but it's finally leaving me."

"Sure. O.K." He paused. "Listen, I'm saying this as a friend. Let up on that stuff. Your business is your business, but I'm telling you this as a friend."

Tom felt a surge of annoyance. He didn't need this right now.

"I know what you're trying to tell me, but a guy has a right to have a social life."

"Listen, I've got to go. Let's have dinner sometimes. We can talk later."

"Sure. Sometime. I've got a hell of a lot on my plate right now. It's hard for other people to understand."

"Maybe so. Maybe so."

The conversation ended uncomfortably, before Tom was aware of what he had done. He had pushed away his only good friend again. That left Lou to be with, and she had never been his friend. Dempsey was right. He did need to cut down on his drinking. He shouldn't have been so brusque with him. What's the matter with me, anyway? Maybe it wasn't the job after all. Maybe it is me.

His colleagues at work were observing him, he felt. What was it they were seeing? What made him different from them? He saw himself critically for the first time in a long time. He was standoffish; he didn't seek them out. He wasn't a water cooler kind of person. They had wives and children, and he didn't. It was as if they spoke different languages. He needed to make more effort. That's what he would do, and he would start right now.

He dialed Harvey Stein's number. He was only down the hall, but Tom wasn't ready for a face to face yet.

"Harvey? Tom here." A pause.

"Hi, there."

"Do you happen to have the latest APA quarterly that I could borrow?"

"Sure thing. Do you want me to bring it down?"

"No, no thanks. I'll pick it up from you this afternoon. Thanks."

"Any time. See you later."

After the conversation Tom felt more of a phony than ever. He had no interest at all in the journal and even less interest in Harvey.

He stared out of the office window again. They never changed, those endless graves that fanned out in orderly precision all over the hills of Arlington Cemetery, almost pushing themselves onto the highway that ran into Washington. There was something about the effect that those stones had on him – reminding him, he said to himself, " I'm only going to get to go around once, and I'm failing in what I'm supposed to be doing."

But if he had been completely honest with himself, he would have seen that it wasn't not being able to do his job that caused his frustration – that was only part of it. It was shame that was the greater burden, shame that he had let down these wounded warriors who came to him for help. He segregated his work life from his bar life for that reason. The clubs had nothing to do with his job.

It was even shameful for him to admit to himself that this was not the place for him. This was a job where he had accepted security and practicality while living in the shadows of the au courant, yuppie hangouts of Arlington, Virginia. However, as the years progressed, he realized that he was still young enough to find that he wanted adventure and freedom. He didn't want either the Army life or the sophisticated, metrosexual life of his contemporaries in Northern Virginia.

No, wait a minute -- that's not the truth – the fact was that he was doing a lousy job and he didn't want to face it. The truth was that when things weren't going right for him, he wanted to pack up, leave the job, and go on to something else. Coming into the Army had served its purpose; he needed the money for an education he couldn't afford. He had liked the life, the order, the friends who shared his views. He still liked all those things. He just couldn't take the job any longer.

Without thinking, he grabbed <u>TheDiagnostic and Statistical Manual of Mental Disorders</u> sitting on his desk and sent it flying across the room. It flew like a plane, low and horizontal, hitting the wall and flopping onto the floor. He stood up, not to pick up the manual but to open the blinds completely, to bring the outside further into his view. He wanted to see the real world. Outside the window the green field of graves lined up like a patchwork quilt, orderly, serving their purpose. They never changed. He had to face these graves; he couldn't ignore them. He hated being faced with these damn rectangular mounds of earth and grass headed up with their never-ending white slabs. They reminded him of the wounded who came into his office every day, each one fitting into his appropriate niche. He was getting paid to see that every broken one of them was repaired, like a piece of damaged china, and put back into its appropriate slot.

His rawest fears admitted, he found himself cooling off, moving into a stage of reminiscing in a less destructive way. At any rate, he said to himself, he had finished his degrees in psychology and had gotten momentary joy in being able to offer causes and solutions to difficult cases. He had liked the detective element of his field, the sense of satisfaction he felt when he could figure out the motivations of persons who were basically acting against their own good. But that was last year, not now. Ungrateful SOB, he suddenly thought. "The Army paid for my education, fed and clothed me. Why knock it now?" What had changed in him within a year's time?

He was supposed to be a curer of PTSD, of depression, of traumatic brain injury, and he was failing in all areas. He, the Great White Hope, was a farce. These guys looked to him for their well-being, and he couldn't provide it. During the first years of his Army practice - it seemed to him now - he had sailed along in a false honeymoon stage, where he and even whole families thought that what he was doing was helping them assimilate into some kind of normal life. Then, it had begun to happen: the longer these men and women were back at home from duty, the worse they got. More of them began to come forward to talk about their struggles with their lives and their thoughts of suicide. The realization that he had no ability to cure anyone burned a hole in his own skin, just as the numbers of wounded were growing like weeds in an unkempt field. Referrals began to come to him with increasing regularity. Now he wondered: How many broken guys and women lay line up ahead of him, waiting, their backs turned away from Iraq and Afghanistan, their faces looking toward him?

God, here he was, obsessing over it again. He turned back to his desk, staring into the computer screen without seeing it. A young Corporal entered the room and put a piece of paper into his in-box, walking out quietly when it looked as if Tom were concentrating hard on something.

Tom shook himself to get out of his funk, got up and retrieved the Diagnostic and Statistical Manual he had thrown against the wall and placed it on his desk.

"Got to get ready for my next appointment," he heard himself say.

He looked at his watch. Ten more minutes and his first appointment of the day would be here. He was nineteen, smooth-skinned and muscular in his upper arms and chest. Maybe his legs had been like that also. He couldn't tell; the one remaining leg was covered by his pants leg. The lower part of his left arm had disappeared along with the leg, gone somewhere, never to be used again. Whatever IED device that burst through his armored personnel carrier in Afghanistan was an equal-opportunity employer – it took off one left arm and one right leg, as if it were trying to be fair about the whole procedure, to create some kind of weird stasis or rebalance.

Here he was in an office with a window that looked out on the graves of dead people, waiting to see a GI who had more courage than he himself would ever have in facing death. And the irony of it was that he, Doctor Tom Superman, was supposed to know more than this young GI who had been maimed for life. How could he have the balls to think that? He, in a minute, would be forced to sit in this room, firing off therapeutic salvos into the haze caused by war, never fixing anything. He was supposed to fix something even when his own tools were broken.

During the last couple of years he had worked with alcoholics, schizophrenics, the depressed, and frightening psychopaths who weren't afraid of killing anyone. In his kind of profession he was supposed to be society's answer to depravity and horror, to interpret brain anomalies that no one could fathom. His tiny weapons of good talk and medication were pitifully small in the face of evil. He was nothing more than a barrier society used to keep these people away from them. Diagnose, label, medicate, separate them from us. He was the German Shepherd dog that was trained to guide people back into the mainstream, if possible; but sometimes there were those that just couldn't be herded back into the fold.. Tom recognized his own bitterness. It had been building up in him for a long time, all these doubts. How ironic that he had come into the

Army looking for personal glory – he the great fixer. He definitely had not been very modest at age twenty.

But the hoped-for cures never seemed to come; there were no magic bullets to replace the real bullets that had hurt them as fighting men. There were some steps forward, true, but the complete cure never seemed to come. There was one good thing he could do for them, he had to admit; it was a small talent he had been given. He sensed that people craved for someone to listen, for understanding.

Even at the age of thirty, Tom had figured out that time could the helper, but he was powerless to speed up the process. So, much of these spaces of time consisted in listening, responding and listening again. But time was kind of like a flirt – it would pull at you, promising help, only to tell you no, not now; wait a little longer. Wait until the fire in you is burned out, and, by then, you may be healed. Yeah, he and his colleagues had tried it all – cognitive processing therapy, prolonged exposure therapy, medication – did any of it work? He didn't know about the efficacy of the first two, and he had serious doubts about what medications actually did to patients – no, people. He was not going to call them patients any longer. It made them more distant from him. It was true, he had to admit, that there were miraculous 'clicks' when the wounded and some in the helping professions worked together so well that a guy made great strides. When he saw it happen, it made him feel happy, yet sad that he couldn't seem to work that magic himself. He never knew if it was the therapeutic technique these professionals used, or if it were their empathic ability.

Be honest, he said to himself. There were people who seemed to be achieving positive steps with these guys; there was a woman who had developed a manual for families and the wounded. He had read it and he liked it. It was practical; it told people what to do in each uneasy circumstance that came along. It had a lot to do with controlling anger. He could have used the techniques in her manual, and, in fact, he had tried that. But something was missing, something missing inside him. He couldn't seem to make that bridge happen between himself and the other person. It wasn't them; it was him.

He wasn't blind. He had watched his three older colleagues in the office. All men, they seemed to take this reality in their stride. Don Amisette, his next door office neighbor, checked off his lists, read books on the latest therapies, went to conferences and came in early every work day. He brought his lunch and ate at his desk. Don was a nice guy. He never showed signs of questioning his own abilities or the tools he used. He wasn't any better educated than Tom; he knew no arcane healing methods, so why was Tom the questioner, the one who was the doubter?

Maybe it was paranoia to think it, but Tom had also wondered at times if the others didn't have questions about him – maybe they saw him as untried, merely a kid who hadn't learned the ropes yet. They were always polite, but sometimes people, like herd animals, can sense things that are amiss. Maybe they could feel that something was not working right in him. Maybe they just happened to be the realistic, brave ones and he born to be the 'shirking child' of whom his mother had spoken.

Forget about himself for a change. The unfairness of it all for these patients was a burden Tom carried, but in his heart he knew there was a greater burden on him than that: he was a coward. He wouldn't have had the courage to join the infantry and get his limbs blown off; he would have never won an award or killed the enemy. Secretly, he knew that that was the reason he kept on with his education. He was afraid of dying out there in the field. He didn't even have the courage to face people who were brave.

As to the slowness of time being a healing benefit – that was something he actually believed in– he was also beginning to see that his own Type A restlessness was in conflict with the slowness of the passage of time, with what the healing process required, with his desire to run from his own cowardice.

It was when he was beginning to wake up in the middle of the night with the sharp realization that he could no longer set up groups, do cognitive therapy for wounded warriors, that he knew he had to do something different with his life. It was going to take a left-brained person to set up the steps for recovery, track the progress, check off each success and failure. It would take a patient person to note the failures and track the successes. He couldn't do it anymore. As he heard himself think, it hit him what a stupid excuse that was.

Tom presently had six individual patients, all under 23 years of age, with a total of six missing arms and legs, three wives and six children under four years of age. That didn't include the groups with whom he worked three times a week or the staff meetings he attended. For some reason, he saw them all -- the six families -- as a totality, total limbs, total wives, total children. Maybe it was less personal, less painful that way. Looking at them as individuals only incited more pity in him. He knew that two had PTSD and all feared what time would deal out to them, at least that's what the wives had told him. The men didn't mention it at all. One had traumatic brain injury, and they all were suffering from depression. Each time they met with him, he found himself dreading their appointment times more and more.

" I'm nothing but selfish," Tom told himself. "Maybe I'd rather spend time on myself, not having to face the months ahead seeing these families suffer or maybe split, or maybe never reach their potential. Maybe I'd rather go home at night and watch TV or go to a movie. You lie. You'd rather go to a bar." And, God forbid, there was the unspoken fear that someone might commit suicide, a fear that was always lurking around him. He didn't even want to admit it.

All this time he knew that he wasn't doing right by them, using the so-called latest techniques and meds that would be out of style in a few years. These techniques and their developers didn't acknowledge that it could be a flash of understanding in a brain that made success happen. It was as if the brains of these soldiers had been changed from this war, and no one wanted to acknowledge it. It wasn't the gimmicks of his trade that had the power to return these boys to their former lives, and that included what was inside the so-called diagnostic manuals. Maybe there was nothing ahead for them at all. He was disgusted with himself. All he knew was that this was all a battle he didn't want thrust upon him. In his more unrealistic moments, all he wanted to do was to be their friend, be there for them, but this would have been frowned upon by his professional colleagues.

Today, though, his hangover finally subsiding, he would do his duty. He would see the kid missing two limbs, wheeled in by his wife. Earlier, he had tried to encourage them by writing up a plan for what they could do. He listened, mainly to the wife, whose needs were huge, whose own life had been as shattered as that of her husband. After they left, he remained here, still at his desk, still wearing the same clothes, but inside of him, a flash of enlightenment hit his own brain – he needed, he had to be, somewhere else, somewhere that he didn't have to try to speed up time anymore. He wasn't worthy of the job that had been given to him. This was the patient with whom he felt the most connected. If he couldn't help him, how could he even think of helping the others?

Don Amisette's figure standing in the doorway interrupted Tom's trainload of thoughts.

"Hi, there," he said. Tom looked up.

"What's up?" he answered.

Don looked down to see the diagnostic manual splayed open on his desk where Tom had irreverently placed it. He grinned a great smile. His father had been a dentist.

"Oh, yeah," said Tom, noticing Don's look at the manual. "I dropped that this morning. I forgot to put it away before my first patient got here."

Don merely raised his eyebrows.

"I just dropped by to remind you that we have that training at 0900 tomorrow, for the whole morning. How about lunch off post after that?"

Tom tried to smile at him.

"But don't you always bring your lunch?"

Don nodded. "True, but if I plan ahead, my wife doesn't have to make it. I thought we could have time to talk for a change – what do you say?"

Tom's immediate feeling was that Don was trying to sound him out, or even figure him out.

Nevertheless, he replied, "Sure. Why not?"

Don said, "Great!" He gave Tom a mock salute and went back to his office.

The next day, after three hours of in-service training, the two men drove off post in Don's little car to a place in Arlington that claimed to have the best hamburgers in the county. Parking was never easy in Arlington at lunch time, but they were in luck. Don was able to squeeze into a spot on Wilson Boulevard. They sat at a wooden table, with giant burgers, fries and shakes in front of them. Lunch with Don was almost worth it. The meat was tender, crisp on the outside, juicy on the inside. Tom bit into it hungrily. Don didn't seem to be noticing the taste of the meat like Tom. Between bites, Don opened the conversation.

"I think there were a couple of useful techniques they mentioned today. There's always something new." He put his perfect teeth into his burger. Tom had to reply.

"Sure. I guess so." He picked up his shake and sipped on it.

Don looked at him, almost quizzically.

"Mind if I say something?" He didn't wait for a reply. "You seem to have a lot of concerns about what you're-we're doing, right?" Before Tom could reply, he added, "Not that that's bad of course. We should always be asking questions."

Tom hesitated. He didn't know how much he wanted to reveal to Don. He decided to generalize to be safe.

"Well, it's just that I wonder how effective some of these techniques really are." That was all he was going to say.

Don smiled, as if he were relieved. "Oh, that's what's on your mind? Well, hell, it's a job. We do our best, go home at night. That's all we can do. Nothing to do but add this stuff to our repertory. It can't hurt." He looked down, realizing what he had said. "Sounds callous, I guess, but it's true."

Tom was at the point of no return. He got up and headed for the rest room, saying, "That's just the point. It can hurt."

He headed out of the room quickly. He was not going to open himself up any more to Don. Don sat there alone. "Weird guy," he thought to himself. "He could use some therapy himself. I could have let that happen to me – let the job really make me crazy. But, I knew I didn't have to. We've got to learn how to chill out in this business."

He couldn't help feeling somewhat more capable, more superior right now.

II

Tom's angular, skinny body was the perfect home for a sometimes impatient, quick-witted man. He drove in a hurry, dropped his clothes all over the apartment, and left his books in stacks by the bed. If he had been a smoker, he would have been addicted by now. His mother had always warned him that not too many girls would like to take on his habits. She was right. He was going to try to do something about that, sometimes soon. Get organized, clean up the place. The resolve usually didn't last long.

When he got to his apartment that night, he threw the remains of his Chinese carry-out in the trash. He had gulped it down along with a beer while sitting in the car outside his building. Might as well eat in the car and get it over with, he had said to himself. On second thought, maybe not a good idea to drink in the car. Somebody might get the wrong idea. Well, he had done it, and it was over. After throwing the remains in the trash can in the kitchen when he got home, his eyes fell on his computer.

"Well," he decided, "I'd better get started." He turned the thing on, and the eerie light wreaked havoc on his face. He'd bet he looked like Boris Karloff right now.

He had made the definite decision to leave his job. It had come upon him gradually in the space of a month, in the heat of the Washington summer, and the more he thought about it, the more the idea grew. It was a way out of his dilemma. He had no regrets about his decision at the moment. Now he had work to do. His profile, in reality, didn't look like Boris Karloff, but it was sharp and defined by the light as he searched for job openings. He had the kind of face one calls interesting, full of crags and declivities that the light couldn't penetrate.

"Maybe I'll look for some clinics somewhere in a warm climate."

He didn't like what he heard himself thinking. No, he said to himself suddenly. No computer tonight. Maybe he'd go to the gym and pound a punching bag until his hands couldn't take it anymore. He promised himself no more going to bars during the week, but it was harder than he thought. He wanted to fight someone, but he didn't have anyone to fight. How can you beat up the gray haze of war? Was it the politicians, the people in China who sold guns, was it –Oh, God, there was no one he could hit. If he hadn't been too cowardly to join the infantry, he could have captured the opposite regiment's flag.

Not anymore, he couldn't. It wasn't regiment to regiment anymore, like a chess game. The wounds his patients got came while they were in armored personnel carriers, on their way to guard duty or to a protest in a neighborhood, or......

His mind turned to yesterday. Sergeant Wayne Pasternak, age 22, had gotten up from his wheel chair on his own power and walked with one scissor- like leg and one human leg into Tom's office. At first, he left his wife Sandy and little boy Cody in the adjacent playroom. His gray sweatshirt read ARMY in big black letters. It showed off his broad shoulders and the muscles of his one remaining arm. He spoke quickly.

"Sir, I'm here for my 1500 appointment."

His salute with his right arm was perfect. Tom's momentary thought was, "Thank God, no one has taken away his military status. They can't take away his biggest support."

He made sure to call him Sergeant. Duty and honor – this guy had done it all; he had faced fire, survived it. That could never be taken away from him. Suddenly, everything around him seemed gray – gray Army shirt, gray government chairs, gray walls, even Wayne's eyes were a kind of gray.

Tom closed the door, and they talked. As Pasternak spoke, Tom found himself trying to think ahead, to find something to say. He had read his medical records over and over, but they didn't reveal the inner person. They had been doing some cognitive therapy, but it seemed simplistic to Tom to merely substitute positive patterns of thinking for negative ones. It wasn't that Wayne wasn't trying; in fact, he seemed willing to try whatever Tom suggested.

"Can I tell you something, sir, something that happened in the dining hall last week?"

"Sure," said, Tom, glad not to deal with the cognitive.

"I was by myself, wheeling myself in to get something to eat before my prosthesis fitting. I had my cap pulled down over my eyes –didn't really want to deal with anyone. It's hard when people stare at you, like I'm different from them, you know." He paused. "It's like the rest of my life I won't be the same as they are."

Tom nodded.

"So, I wheeled over to the place where they have the straws, napkins and junk like that. I reached over and picked up a plastic fork, napkin, other things. The damn things fell out of my hand and onto the floor. Can't even use my real hand right anymore, damn it. I was embarrassed, and I tried real fast to reach down and grab them, but before I could, an old man with a cap on his head – he had to be in his eighties- picked them up and handed them to me. Neither one of us said anything, but I saw that on his cap it said WWII veteran, or something like that."

He stopped for a minute, his eyes refusing to cry. "But, you know what, Doc? It was the best thing that has happened to me in a long time. I felt like he knew what I was going through. We didn't speak, but he knew."

After Wayne Pasternak left the office to get his family and bring them into Tom's office, Tom sat still in his chair for some time. It was that connection between kindred spirits that mattered. That was what everybody needed to get through it all. And, he wasn't able to provide it, somehow. It was then that Tom knew that he should be spending some time looking for a way to attacking the battles in his own life, his own enemies. He knew he couldn't stay here pretending to help. He was an unarmed man in the front line of battle.

The whole Pasternak family came in together, Wayne walking upright and out of his wheel chair, holding Cody's hand with his own good one. Sandy brought up the rear. She couldn't have been more than twenty, yet she no longer looked her age. There was something in her eyes that made them look like those of an old woman. She sat down next to Wayne, alert, as if ready to do something, whatever it was, if he needed it.

Tom spoke to her first. When she answered, the words came out more quickly than they had from Wayne, but that didn't make it any easier for the three of them. Wayne was not looking at her, but stared at the floor.

"How did you sleep last night, Sandy?" asked Tom.

He noticed that she had a Kleenex rolled up inside the palm of her hand, as if she were hiding it. She tried to smile.

"Oh, off and on. You know with Cody...."

Wayne interrupted.

"Not Cody, me. Every time I move, she's on the alert. I wish she'd cut it out."

Her eyes were now focused on the floor. For a brief moment, Tom thought that she would cry, but she kept the Kleenex hidden.

"I didn't mean..." If was as if she were afraid to speak more.

The hour went on. Wayne's anger bit into his wife. It didn't leave him even when Tom pointed it out to him. Wayne kept pushing Sandy away from himself emotionally, telling her to leave him, saying that he would be better off alone. She fought back the tears, and the more she tried to control her emotions, the more Wayne lashed out at her. Tom had to stop him by raising his voice. Little Cody, aware of it all, dropped the blocks on the floor, ran over and sat between his parents as if he were a wall protecting them from each other.

By the end of the hour, the feelings of Sandy and Wayne were as raw as if their bodies had been cut with knives. Cody, now back on the floor with plastic blocks, looked up at both his mother and father periodically. After the session was over and they had left, Tom himself felt raw inside, bleeding inside. It was going to take a big effort on his part not to drown it all with a few drinks.

III

A   t home that night Tom faced the computer again. It was like a form
of escape for him. He had to have a new job. Fingers jabbing at the
keys like a man who never learned to type, he pushed two fingers of each
hand onto the plastic keys, hitting the letters in rapid-fire succession. For
over an hour he searched, with no results, nothing that seemed to satisfy
his needs.

Sometime after eleven o'clock he was about to give up for the night,
when the Public Health Service looked up at him from the inside of the
computer. He clicked a few keys, and it came back with its demands, its
locations, with smiling faces on top of uniforms. He remembered that
the hey-days when some young men used the Public Health Service as an
alternative to military service, especially to get out of going to Vietnam.
This era had gone with the end of the draft. That didn't apply to him
or anybody else anymore. Maybe, just maybe, it would be a good fit for
him, continuing his government service but doing it out somewhere where
there was space, where he could kick his legs out without hitting a wall or
a door. He printed all the PHS information and put it in a stack by his bed.

Escape. That's what he needed. A place where he was his own man,
where he would have time to figure himself out. A kind of freedom.
That's what he wanted. He got up, brushed his teeth, showered, and fell
into bed. For some reason, he began to think of his childhood home,
its pink bricks and blue shutters, a place of safety. But the fog of sleep
overcame him, and he fell into it gratefully, a deep, deep sleep, with no
dreams and no nightmares.

IV

The next few months went like wild fire. His active service obligation was over. He opted not to re-enlist. There was a fairly drunken farewell party which he barely remembered in the ensuing years, and even hardly remembered the day after, but there were powerfully stacked emotions waiting for him when the time came to say good-bye to the six families with whom he had been working. One of the soldiers was angry, yet there was nothing comforting Tom could say this time. It would have been stupid and useless to assure them that things would get better with the passage of time. He tried to do what he could by referring them to the best psychologist he knew, but he still felt that he was a rat. He had deserted them officially, but they would never know that he had packed them inside a corner of his heart, like a burden of shame he would carry with him for a long, long time. Wayne Pasternak, the five other patients and their families would go with him, hidden inside him.

He made his decision. He had been accepted for the position of psychologist on the White Mountain Apache reservation in Arizona, operated by the Public Health Service. In all of his travels over the world, he had never been West of the Mississippi, except for flying over it on his way to California. Right now, he didn't care where he was going, just out of here.

He hadn't even bothered to check out the area on a map or to find out what Apaches were like. It might have been that if he had found out, he would have had some reluctance – he might have wondered if he would be repeating his old pattern of helplessness, working with people whose broken souls he couldn't heal. No, he had deliberately decided not to look into it; it was better not to research too much, to anticipate problems. It was a new life he was looking for; he wanted to be surprised.

When he stopped at the gas station on the post for the last time, he felt a momentary sadness at leaving the order of the place, the parade ground, the commissary that had provided him food, even the short-haired recruits who looked younger every year. But the feeling didn't last long. Ungrateful bastard, he said to himself.

His mini-van, crammed with clothes, a flashlight, cheese crackers, soft drinks and a newly purchased GPS system drove through the gates for the last time. He had a crazy momentary thought that the six families were hiding in his glove compartment and leaving the post with him.

The question to be answered was simple. Could he regain his lost perspective on life? And more importantly, could he regain his integrity? He had left, pretty shamefully, the uncompleted tasks behind him. Was this the first of many failed attempts in his life, or would he be able to use whatever strength and power he had for whatever was ahead? He was going to give it his all – to move away from his red rage and his stupid black fear. It was a new start, and he was going to go for it.

What he didn't understand, however, even with all his introspection, was that it wasn't his lost perspective on life that he needed to regain. His friend Dempsey had known but had never told him. It was maturity; it was his need to become a man. Dempsey was certainly a friend, but he never told Tom the truth. The once good beginnings of a friendship seemed to be left behind, fallen into the cracks. He was going to keep up with him, Tom thought as he left Virginia. He really was going to have to do that.

V

From then on, it was five days and nights to Arizona, a deliberately slow pace, slowed even further by one flat tire and a driving rain across the Mid-West. During one of the days the rain was so bad that It hit his van windows at a slant, giving his windshield wipers a workout they hadn't had before. The starting date for his new job was approximate. Nobody out there seemed to be stressing as to his exact arrival date. He had chosen not to get there at break-neck speed, but to let the days take their toll on him, to see if he had the capacity to accept what came to him. Good luck on that, he thought wryly.

The morning he had left D.C., he remembered, he had plunged his loaded van into the morning traffic of the Washington mess, and headed South for Route 66 in Virginia. The back-up on the Beltway had started long before he had left at 0800, forcing him to start and stop for a good half-hour. He had drunk a couple of cups of coffee earlier, and his body felt tense and alert, ready to combat the other cars that came near him. He waited impatiently for the traffic to let go of its grasp of him. This was one hell of a beginning to the new start of his life. It was as if there were ropes on him that he was trying to shake off.

Tom shot his eyes over toward the vehicle on his right, as he was forced to stop in the Beltway traffic. The man in the driver's seat looked young and was driving a white box truck. There was a plastic cup holder on his door, steam arising out of some liquid. He had his left hand on the steering wheel and his right cupping his cell phone that seemed to be propped against the steering wheel. He would text, look down, and then look up briefly. The truck waivered closer toward Tom's van, edging into the left lane. Tom tooted his horn lightly. The driver took his eyes off his cell phone. He looked at Tom sharply. He seemed to drop the phone into his lap, but there was no doubt about what he did next. He raised up his finger in a non-military salute.

Tom felt his face redden. He had a strong desire to stop the van, get out and shake the devil out of the man. No, just a few more miles, he said to himself, and he'd be out of town, off the East Coast and moving toward places where people didn't act like rats in a cage. They might even say hello, they might be courteous. He kept this fanciful thought in mind until he reached the turn-off for Route 66, where he was thrown into another line of cars. It was as if he had no control over any of it, as if he had no choice in the matter. He was in a bumper car at the carnival, waiting for someone to slam into him.

It must be about time for Don Amisette to be having his first patient of the day. He had offered to take over the Pasternak family, but Tom had done his best to see that it didn't happen. The idea of relinquishing them to Don brought up his worst fears. That had made Tom really uneasy, handing them over to a person who probably wasn't in any position to help them more than he had. Maybe he'd call Captain Jean Moran to see if she got the referral he had initiated. No, better leave it all behind.

He suddenly realized that his mind had not been concentrating on his driving. Popping up ahead of him was a new landscape, the first glimpses of the Blue Ridge Mountains, their smoky haze entirely different from Washington's miasma. He was leaving all that behind, but was he running away or charging forth? Gradually, the road was moving him into the mountains ahead of him, and the traffic had slipped away into exit after exit along the road.

It was as if these mountains were taking him into depths where he couldn't be seen, but just as suddenly thrusting him out and up to almost touch the clouds. His van seemed to be making it, in spite of this new form of driving on without stopping. Hope it holds out, Tom said to himself. The trees were still dark green and full, showing no sign of late summer dryness.

After an overnight's stay somewhere in Tennessee, he found himself leaving the motherly mountains and skirting towns that proclaimed proudly that they were so many miles from Nashville or Memphis. When he got out to buy gas – more often than he would have liked to in the big van – he detected the soft, nasal twangs of the clerks in the convenience stores. A boy of about fourteen held the door open for him as he was entering to buy some ice. He thanked him, and was almost taken aback by a cheery "You're welcome, Sir." Either he looked older than he was, or people were becoming more polite.

Now he was passing through rutty fields on both sides of him. There were fewer towns, and the mountains had departed behind him, blocking out what was on the other side. He was detecting a sort of change in himself; he could feel it, but he couldn't define it. The first thing he noticed was that his hands were not holding onto the steering wheel as tightly as they had done leaving metropolitan Northern Virginia. His shoulders didn't seem as bunched up as they were the day before.

That night, when he arrived at what looked like a suitable and inexpensive motel, he put his feet out onto the parking lot next to the late 1950's building. From this little town somewhere in a Mid-Western state, he stretched out his arms and took a breath, noticing for the first time the reality that the space between here and Washington was huge. The space spread out before him in miles and miles of towns and ribboned roads and fertile fields, going East. For one brief moment, he felt sadness about what he had done, a small ache for familiar faces and places he had known.

He cut himself short from this kind of pity – all those memories weren't about people he was going to miss; they were about things. None of that mattered anymore. The six were with him. All else was behind him. This road in front of him was going West as well as East, you dope. You can always turn and go back East, any time you want. Remember when you were a kid in your parents' car and you pretended some bad person was after you? You always knew they were behind you, but they never did catch you, did they? Same as now, chump. Keep going.

Tom slept well that night, in a bed that you could put a quarter in, and the whole thing would jiggle. He tried it once, laughed aloud, then went to bed. There was silence around him, except for an occasional semi's braking around a nearby highway curve. The beige phone between the single beds didn't ring, and even his cell phone stayed silent and unmoving, attached to it umbilical cord, its feeding tube for the night.

Before he fell asleep, Tom thought about his dad. He'd call him tomorrow. It was O.K. with Dad, this move of his. He was surprised about Tom's leaving the Army, but he was better about accepting it than his mom would have if she had been alive. Dad had found a wonderful older woman after the death of Tom's mother. Dad was all right, maybe better than his son. He'd make sure he'd call him again soon, anyway. He turned over once, then slept hard until the sun peeked in between the blinds of his room.

In their last phone call, his dad's parting words to his son were, "Tommy, I know you'll do the right thing. I don't say this very often, but all your mother and I wanted was to see you happy."

The next morning, sitting in the van after a fast-food repast of a sausage, egg and cheese biscuit and blindingly hot coffee, Tom looked at his GPS, his own personal line of fate that he had set for his final destination before he left Arlington. He knew that sooner or later this line was going to lead him in a Southwesterly direction. The red line was doing that a slight bit now, tracking slowly down the screen toward the bottom left. It refused to show him the end of the trip, and he didn't care.

He was content to follow the line, like the yellow brick road in Oz, through Kansas. He didn't want to look ahead any more than that. He rode through the flat land, stopping once at lunch for a gigantic T-bone steak at a diner. Country music was playing, and big chunks of cornbread arrived with the steak. He had always liked country music. He wondered if he would like it as much if there were no other choice. Would it make him feel trapped and out of place? Was the sensation of feeling trapped something he carried around with him, like an errant gene? He wiped his mouth with the paper napkin, removing the greasy residue of the steak. No need to start anticipating problems. He hadn't even gotten to where he was going yet. He hadn't diagnosed himself as a full-blown paranoid yet, thank God.

It had been seven days since he had had any kind of alcoholic drink, not even a beer. Of course, it helped that he couldn't drink and drive, but he surprised himself that he had not even asked for a beer with his meals. Funny, but he hadn't even thought about it once until now. Maybe he didn't have a drinking problem after all.

He put down his paper napkin next to his plate and headed for the van.

VI

He had never been to Arizona before. When he had once crossed over it in a plane that headed for LA, the pilot had gotten on the intercom and pointed out the Grand Canyon down below, but that was it. It looked to him as if the earth had cracked open from that distance. Then it had disappeared from view. Now he was driving, on the actual ground of the state, crossing into it from the Northeast corner. A couple of days out of Kansas, the land had changed radically; it was no longer flat. Instead, it looked dry and empty and scraggly, pinyon bushes and cottonwoods cropping up near creek beds that must at some time have held more water than they did today.

He had a feeling that he must now be higher up in elevation, but there were no signs to tell him that. In fact, the signs seemed to get fewer and fewer. Boring and dried out was the first thought he had about the area, but some time later he began to think of it as surprising after a road runner crossed his path. At least, that's what he thought it was, since he had never seen one before except in cartoons. It walked in the same funny, rapid pace that used to make him laugh when he watched TV on Saturday mornings. Road Runners were real after all. What a hoot.

Next, a few miles later, another oddity appeared out of nowhere. He began to notice that the fence posts on his right were topped with what looked like old boots. They weren't on every post, just some. Maybe this was a game played by drunks. They say that's what happened to all those stop signs perforated by bullet holes, shot by guys drinking beer on a Saturday night. Kind of free. Nobody to stop them. Guess I'll find out about it all some time, he thought.

He was alone out here. He hadn't really thought of it before. And no cell phone usage. Probably there would be none until he could pick up a signal somewhere closer to a town of some size. One of the few signs, a wooden one, announced that this land was some kind of national forest. It didn't look like a forest to him. Boy, he was prejudicial already, comparing every new thing to what he had known before, as if that were the gold standard.

He drove at a steady rate, not pressing the van too hard. If he broke down out here, it would take a coon's age for a new part to come from somewhere to where he was now. It was early September, the sky a color of unending blue. It wasn't the soft gray-blue of the East, but a vibrant turquoise blue that seemed to have no end. He had to admit it was something he could get used to. It had a way of clearing one's mind.

He put his left hand outside the open car window, steering with his right. No moisture stuck to his hand, no gunky humidity. He let the wind whip through his fingers, forcing them to open, widened out like an old broom. He must be going pretty fast, because the power of the wind was trying to make his whole arm move backwards. He decelerated and brought his arm back inside. Watch your speed out here. You never know what these Arizona sheriffs are like; maybe they're like the ones in movies.

He looked over at the GPS. Early on in the trip, he had silenced the bossy woman inside it who kept telling him what to do. For some reason, he had named her Georgette. He knew he could always call on her if he needed her, kind of like an old girlfriend. No, not true. Lou had never been as available to him as Georgette had been. Wonder what she was up to. The same old thing, probably.

He drove on now, veering down South and toward a town called Pinetop, lying near the border of the reservation where he was heading. But, he still felt the need to slow the trip down, give himself time to be by himself. It wasn't that he couldn't have made it into Pinetop that night, but his mind wasn't ready for it yet. Instead, he chose to spend the night in another 1950's style motel, comfortable bed, television news coming in from Phoenix. He had gotten to like these places where you could pull right up to your front door. And, you used a real key, not a plastic card. That night there would be the same little bar of soap, the little black TV, and a coffee maker with little Styrofoam cups on a brown tray. It was easy to check out in the morning, and nobody bothered you by sliding the bill under your door during the night. It was all pretty simple.

The next morning he felt ravenously hungry, eating three eggs and a burrito and drinking two cups of coffee at a fast food restaurant next to the motel. He noticed that the more he drove, the more he seemed to eat. This was the first time he had ever had a burrito for breakfast, but there it was on the plastic-covered menu on the table. The beans went down surprisingly easy and filled him for the whole of the next hour. He'd have to try that again soon. A waitress with hair down to her hips, broad Indian shoulders, silently served him. He left a good tip. No response from her. Maybe she was shy.

He went outside and revved up his van. Earlier, at the motel he had banished the slight frost on the windshield with a paper napkin from yesterday's restaurant. The frost was a surprise. It seemed early for it, but how was he to know that? This part of the country was all new to him, even the weather. Tom flipped on the GPS without Georgette in order to get his bearings on the map. Next. he searched for a local radio station, wondering what kind of music it would be playing. To his surprise, however, it seemed to be in Navajo. At least, he could pick up the word 'Navajo' from the announcer who was definitely not speaking English. It wasn't Spanish either. The man now began to speak English, talking about a trading post and all the goods they could provide. He was quick at switching back and forth from English to Navajo, interspersing words from both languages, enough so that Tom felt that he could actually understand what he was saying.

Tom became suddenly exhilarated. Here he was, actually listening to an Indian radio station, half in English and half in Navaho. It sounded small town and personal, reminding him of his childhood, carrying him to a place where everybody knew you when you walked down the street. Once, at home, when he had thrown his empty coke can into the gutter from the basket of his bike, a neighbor had called his mom to tell her. He smiled to himself.

The Navajo radio station was fading out now, leaving nothing but static and bits and pieces of Navajo words. His thoughts moved back to Lou whom, he had to admit, he had dropped like a hot potato in Virginia, Lou with the frosted hair and the frosted nails and icy frost in her manner. When he told her he was leaving, she had replied that there were plenty more fish in the ocean, and there were, too, for her. She did wish him good luck before she hung up, and, she added with a parting jab, "You'll need it." He had always known their relationship wasn't permanent, but right this moment he missed her. It would have been nice to have someone sitting next to him in the car, someone he cared about. God knows he had had his chances in Arlington, but nothing seemed to last. Besides, all the women he knew would never have taken off for Arizona with him. He couldn't picture them leaving the metropolitan area. Well, there was one he knew, but she had been deployed to Afghanistan, and the chances were not great that he would ever see her again, anyway.

Now, here he was, out here, having deliberately made choices that would cause him to be alone, cut off from everybody he knew, and for what? Because he couldn't hack being back there, working with the most deserving people he had ever known. Maybe he was making a mistake. Someone would be taking his job permanently before long. His job. What a jackass you are. It's not about you all the time; you are the problem. You couldn't tolerate it, and you don't know why. You stink.

This confession hurt, but it was the truth. Well, at least he had admitted it to himself. "Damn coward," he mumbled aloud.

Suddenly, he found himself driving Southwest on a high plain. Funny how you could think on one level and be driving on another. He looked out at the landscape, and it seemed to go on without end. There was probably no town around here for miles. He had the urge, for some reason, to stop suddenly on this long stretch of road bounded by scrubby brush. He could look ahead and behind him almost a mile each way. Nothing. Absolutely no cars on the road, only a vulture with a red wattle lazily keeping an eye on any moving creature. He would do it. He slowed the van, pulling it over to the side of the road, onto the dust and bumpy holes. There was nobody out here to care whether he did it or not. He laughed to himself. Sounds like the old question, what was it now? If a tree falls in the forest with no one to hear it, does it make a sound? No, that's not right. He was here, and he knew what he was going to do.

Tom opened the door and slid his legs out of the car, keys jangling in his hand, and walked over to the tarry pavement of the highway. He stretched out completely on the road, just for the hell of it. It was rough, scratchy on his skin. A rock dug into his head. He felt brave, unafraid of the approach of any cars. He lay there a minute, interesting the vulture, and then he got back up as the pebbles began to eat into his skin. He could smell the pungent odor of the tar. It was a clean smell on this dirty road; it was soft, made pliable by the sharp rays of the hot sun. He dusted off his clothes and walked back to the van.

He got in, closed the door, put the key in the ignition, and fed the car a spurt of gas with his foot. He found himself driving slowly, now watching things on the side of the road. There lay a dead and rotting squirrel or something a hundred feet ahead, and there was what looked like the same vulture, now ahead of him, smiling an evil smile, circling around. Thought he was going to get me, didn't he? Well, he got what he wanted in the end, even if it wasn't me. This place might not be so boring after all.

VII

The town of Pinetop was not his final destination, but it was a necessary step toward Whiteriver, the center of the White Mountain Apache reservation, where the hospital was located. The hospital was to be his new center of activity; it was administered by the Public Health Service for tribal members who often lived far away from a hospital of any kind. The town of Pinetop lay abutting the border of the reservation, where his new life lay ahead of him. A woman named Roxanne Smith would be waiting for him there, according to the hospital administrator who had offered him the job on the telephone. He was to meet with her, a nurse, before going down to Whiteriver. So, he might have one more night to spend before he got to his final destination. More than one night, actually, in the Pinetop motel, since they had told him that his quarters, a newly refurbished trailer next to the hospital, had not yet been cleaned up from its last inhabitant. That was O.K. by him; he didn't mind this hiatus from routine at all.

He tried his cell phone again in order to reach Roxanne Smith. He must be somewhere near a cell tower now, for they connected on his first try. He was surprised that he could pick up a signal, since everything around him looked void of buildings, people and especially a tower. She was at home on leave in Pinetop, she informed him. He told her he was bumping around someplace where the trees were getting bigger and bigger, but he wasn't exactly sure where he was. She laughed. Roxanne sounded pleasant.

"Maybe she's supposed to check me out," he had thought at the time he had learned that he was to meet with her. "Maybe you're too suspicious, as usual. Don't always look for the worst."

After Tom had spoken to Roxanne, he was somewhat relieved, he had to admit. She sounded O.K., direct but nice. Everything seemed kind of simple. She told him where to meet up with her at the restaurant she had chosen and she also told him where the motel he would be staying in was located. In fact, it was the only motel in Pinetop where he could stay until his trailer was ready. She didn't tell him he had to do anything, but suggested he might want to follow her down to the hospital that day to take a look at where he would be working. The hospital had made a reservation for him at the motel, and he could drive back up to Pinetop after seeing his new work location in Whiteriver.

After he got off the phone, one thing puzzled him that she had said: This 'down' to Whiteriver and 'up' to Pinetop that she had mentioned in her conversation with him – what was that all about? It could be elevation, or it could be referring to a North-South destination. He couldn't think of any other reason why Roxanne Smith would use those terms. Well, anyway, so far, so good. His van had actually made it across country, and things seemed to be slowing down in time for him – not even any worries right now about what his next appointment with a patient would bring.

Some miles before Pinetop, he went through a town with the odd name of Snow Flake. There must be a story behind that, he reasoned. Maybe just the cold weather. As he got closer to Pinetop he noticed that the landscape around him was definitely changing. He saw now why this town had gotten its name. Bit by bit were appearing the biggest trees he had ever seen, ponderosa pines, with pine cones sometimes looking as big as coffee cups. When he took his eyes off the road briefly, he could see them lying on beds of needles, under the umbrellas of their mother trees. He remembered that old TV show – he had watched the Ponderosa ranch, the father, the sons. He had loved to watch the re-runs with his own father. The father and sons always did the right thing eventually; they were free and independent and made up their own minds. He found himself smiling at the old memories.

He didn't know how he knew what kind of threes they were. He remembered that ponderosa meant big, of great weight, in Spanish, and that was exactly what they looked like – overpowering and straight up, tall, dignified, darkening the needley forest around them. At first, there were single trees, and then came whole families of them. He had the feeling that they would be overpowering if you had to walk alone through them. Silly talk, you city dweller. Big high rises were probably potentially more dangerous than these trees. The road he was on was a bold strip through the trees, with the buildings in Pinetop flanking each side of the road in front of the giant trees. This definitely must be a higher elevation than he had been driving in up to now. The town looked like it might have been in Alaska, not Arizona. Bet there'll be hard winters here, he said to himself. He should have looked up the geography before he left Virginia. Somehow, he had just taken it for granted that Phoenix was hot, therefore all Arizona was hot and desert. But this day wasn't hot at all, in fact, it was quite cool. He could have used a sweater, but he didn't want to stop and pull one out of his bag.

This place was beginning to feel good, different. He was noticing that the asphalt strips in front of the stores were filled with trucks and SUVs. Most of the people he saw seemed to be wearing boots. Most of the men were wearing big hats or caps. What did he think they'd be wearing, anyway? Uniforms or three-piece suits? That was the trouble, he thought, remorsefully. He hadn't thought about it at all. Talk about not being prepared.

It was cool now. Would all these people still be here in a month or two, as fall came on? A lot of the cars had logos on them indicating they were from Phoenix, Tucson, and a lot of other places. Some license tags even read California. Were they going to head back down to the warmth of the lower elevations? Well, it didn't matter. This wasn't his final destination anyway.

He'd better start watching for the restaurant where he and Roxanne were to meet. She said it would be on the left side of the road for him, and suddenly there it was, a white building on an incline, fronted by a wooden sign that announced 'Croziers' in letters burned into the wood. He pulled in, hearing the crunch of his tires as he left the asphalt. The parking lot was full of small rocks that were a pinkish, gray color, as if they might have had a volcanic origin.

Roxanne had said that she would be sitting by the door of the restaurant, and she was, or at least a smiling, dark-haired and middle-aged woman wearing pants and a jacket seemed to be waving at him. It was as if she had known him before, no Eastern hesitation or fear.

"Welcome!" she greeted him as he walked up to the door of the restaurant and entered. "You're Tom, right?" He said yes.

"How was the trip?"

"Pretty good, thanks. I hope you weren't waiting long for me?"

She assured him she hadn't been there long and motioned to him to sit down opposite her. They both ordered hamburgers and cokes. He had already eaten a big breakfast, and it was still early for lunch, but he wouldn't mind eating again. Besides, it would make the conversation more relaxed, he rationalized.

Before the food came, he took advantage of the time to look around, as Roxanne was explaining was Pinetop was like. His first impression was that everything in the room was made of wood – the chairs, tables, bar, the ceiling and the floor. Well, nothing extraordinary about that, up here in the forest. The male diners all seemed to keep their big hats on as they ate.

Roxanne smiled at him. She started a new subject, telling him about the hospital.

"We're really glad you are here. There's so much to do down in Whiteriver. We sure can use you. The guy who was here before you left three months ago. He and his wife went down to Phoenix – said he needed to live in a bigger city. As for my job, I've been a nurse at the hospital for twenty years, and there never seems to be much outside competition for it!" She laughed. "Nobody seems to beating the doors down to take my place. We did have a little, run-down clinic before this one was built. The hospital isn't the most up to date place in the world, but it serves its purpose. If anything really serious happens that we can't deal with, we fly the patient down to Phoenix to the Indian Medical Health Center."

She was easy to talk with. He asked her some basic questions, the size of the hospital, the number of physicians, what the weather was like. After the hamburgers, Tom asked her, somewhat embarrassed, if they had ice cream here. He suddenly wanted sugar.

"Sure." She called out to the waitress. "Martha, bring him the chocolate chip ice cream. " The waitress nodded. "We all love it. That O.K.?"

He said yes. While waiting for the ice cream, Tom filled Roxanne in on the bare details of his background, and she in turn gave him what she called 'a reality check' on the needs of the White Mountain Apaches. Born and bred in Arizona, she told him she was frankly always nervous when Easterners came out to work for the first time. He looked surprised.

"No offense intended. I'll explain in a minute. I guess I have to tell you you're getting into something real different – I hope that doesn't scare you off?"

"No, I'm looking for something different," he answered. He had made up his mind not to go into great detail to anyone out here about his prior job.

"Sorry about that comment of mine about Easterners," she said, "but out here, we sometimes wonder where you guys from back East get your ideas about Indians," she grimaced. Tom had a quizzical look on his face.

"What do you mean?"

"Well, I'll give you an example, one of many. We had one young Public Health doctor who came out from Philadelphia. He had this idea that Apaches belonged on a spiritual plain somewhat higher than Jesus. He thought everybody was carrying around crystals, or something. Funny, but he wanted to give the tribal council some cartons of tobacco if they would pray for him. The council members weren't sure what to do, but they decided to keep the cigarettes and invite him to the Lutheran Church on Sunday. This same guy would go around looking for things to buy like Kachinas and rugs – we aren't Hopis or Navajos down here –we don't make those kinds of things – so, people thought he was kind of a dumb guy to be a doctor."

Tom was quiet. He wasn't prepared. He changed the subject. "Roxanne, tell me about your cases."

"Okay. Here goes."

She folded her arms across her breasts. She had a way of looking straight at him as she talked.

"But, first, I've got to tell you that I've lived up here in Pinetop since I was born. My mom was half Apache, my dad worked as a logger. I live off the rez because I want to keep a distance between my job and my home. Pinetop is over twenty miles from Whiteriver, you see. The reservation line, though, is just outside of Pinetop."

She took a final sip of her coke, pushing it away from her, before she went on.

"I don't know if you realize how high up in elevation we are here in Pinetop, but it's a couple of thousand feet lower down in Whiteriver. I'm not exactly sure of how much, but I know that it makes the winters worse up here. And, believe me, there are lots of other differences besides elevation between Pinetop and Whiteriver. My job is community health nurse. I don't think I've really ever wanted to do anything else since I got out of school. What I do sounds simple: I get in the car-- snow, rain, shine --and go out to find those who can't or won't come in." She looked at him. "I hope all this isn't too boring."

"Go on. I'm interested. Really." Maybe he wasn't looking interested, he thought. But he was, really interested.

"Well, just last week I had to find Molly DeClay down by the river at East Fork. That's a part of the reservation. She's about fifty, worn out from taking care of six grandchildren. She's on commodity food and she's a good Lutheran – more about that later – but she's got hypertension off the charts. If anything happened to her, those kids wouldn't have a chance."

Tom noticed right away how much she cared about the people and her job. It was all hard for him to picture what she was describing – did the woman live in a teepee? What was she wearing? Nevertheless, Roxanne seemed to have an affinity for Apaches as he once thought he had had about wounded warriors, that is, before he deserted them.

Roxanne motioned to Martha, the waitress, to refill her coke. Martha smiled inquiringly at Tom. He declined the refill as Roxanne continued talking.

"Then there's George Dewakuku. He's Hopi but kind of ostracized by them, because he's got some sort of screw loose, people think. I don't do much more than check his diabetes, see if he's got food and a blanket. He lives in a shack by himself. He believes that somebody or something is out to get him. If he tries to sell you a Kachina doll, buy it. It's all the income he has. He does a real good job of making them, and it kind of makes him feel a part of his people that he can't live with."

She stopped and waited. Tom didn't know what to say, so he continued eating his ice cream. He wasn't even sure what a Kachina doll was. Getting no response from Tom, Roxanne seemed apologetic, as if she had said too much for him to absorb.

"I'm just trying to tell it to you like it is. It's a lot of information to absorb on your first day here. Just stop me if you want."

"No. Keep going, please, Roxanne," he said.

"Call me Roxy. Everybody does." She smiled again. He smiled back.

"The truth is that we've got a crime rate that is fueled by alcohol and is turned in against the people —the N'dee —especially the women and children. Most people seem to accept that beer drinking is an unchangeable part of life. And, maybe it is. Everybody up here in Pinetop accepts it, too. But the sad thing is that child neglect, sexual assault, domestic violence, they all rear their ugly heads as soon as the beer cans are opened. As far back as we can remember, the Apaches have always had beer – tulepai – for celebrating victories, harvests, everything. But there was never as much alcohol content in it as good old American beer has today. It is definitely the drink of preference."

She pushed back a little from the table.

"It doesn't sound as if I love them, but I do. They're part of my own blood. You're going to meet so many really good people, people who have survived so much. I figured you didn't know this, being from the East and all. It's a lot to put on your plate the first day. But, if you don't mind, here's my own personal warning: Don't idealize us; we're not magic, just good people with a lot of needs."

She stopped talking for a second, then added: "Just remember about that part I said – We're not magic, we're just people like everybody else."

Tom was confused about her repetition of the magic part. Maybe she emphasized that to make sure he wasn't going to do any of the New Age kind of things she thought Easterners did.

She took a sip of her refilled coke.

"O.K. My sermon is finished. She still looked serious but went on:

"I'm pretty sure from meeting you that you'll find a way to do some good. There is so much that has to be done."

This time he looked serious. "I hope so. I'll give it my best," he found himself saying.

"Do you want to go down now to the rez?" It was like a challenge.

"Yes, I do," he said emphatically. "Let's get going, unless I need to check into the motel first?"

He found that he had a real curiosity to get down there, a curiosity that was getting the better of his old grinding fear of failure.

"No. That's taken care of, unless you want to drop off your things first?" He said no.

"Then, let's get going. Follow me down to Whiteriver."

He got into his van and she into her Jeep. It had warmed up a bit outside, but it was still cool to him. He noticed people coming and going from a little hamburger shack next door to the restaurant. There was a Dollar Store across the street which seemed to be very popular. Nice little town, he thought to himself. Everything looked good so far, but we haven't even gotten to the reservation yet.

VIII

They were leaving the morning coolness of Pinetop and the darkness of the Ponderosas, as Tom followed Roxanne's Jeep down the road, lower and lower in elevation with the passage of each mile. Tom was wearing his Army boots. He began to notice that his feet were sweating as the temperature climbed bit by bit. He actually felt as if he were back in the Army, in another country, maybe the Mid-East. But he felt no anxiety. For some reason, he felt at ease with Roxy leading the way down the hill. It that way, it wasn't like the Mid-East at all; now he had someone in front of him on whom he could rely. He checked himself. Just forget all that; slow down and enjoy the ride.

His van wasn't going to survive much longer out here; he was going to need some kind of four-wheel drive, a tougher car. It wasn't the potholes; the roads were smooth enough, but he had the feeling that, on a daily basis, his vehicle was going to get a lot rougher usage than it was used to. Well, his van might suffer from hard use, but at least it didn't look as if anyone were going to try to cut him off in traffic anymore, thank God. The old van had been through a lot in city traffic, but it had never been exposed to really bad winters or muddy, dirt roads as it would be out here. Yeah, a new kind of vehicle for a new place. He grinned wryly. Maybe he'd have to change also.

The road down was really good, too, bounded on the left by a steep, sloped hill rising upward. The right side of the road didn't have enough guard rails, in his Eastern opinion, and the hill jagged down steeply to sharp rocks and trees below. Not a good place to lose control. They had descended maybe as much as two thousand feet, he estimated, when the road began to level off. In the distance in front of him small wooden houses began to appear, often surrounded by trucks or cars, piles of wood, branched ramadas, plastic toys and trees. Roxanne kept going, not slowing down.

They seemed to be coming into a more populated area, yet the houses were still apart from each other. Finally, Roxy slowed down, motioned to him with her hand out the window, and turned in at a sign on the right that said Indian Health Hospital, U.S. Government, White Mountain Apache Tribe. It suddenly hit him, the reality of it all, the word Apache, the whole concept of this new job. It had lain dormant somewhere in his head until now. But, here it was, a place rooted into the soil of this scraggly, irregular land. New territory to be reconnoitered.

The building they were heading toward looked to him to be about thirty years old, solar panels rusting on the roof, with a big parking lot on the left side of the building's front. Trailers were visible behind the building. Tom parked next to Roxy's Jeep in the lot, brushing off his trousers as he got out of the car. Dust had accumulated on him as well as his van. The hospital was a flat building of a sort of adobe color, made of bricks. Funny that one of those trailers visible behind the building was to be his future home. They didn't look bad from here, pretty new, and the surrounding areas well kept up.

As they got out of their cars in the parking lot, Roxy led Tom to a side door. They entered the hospital, walking past cubicles of offices that looked like thousands of other cubicles provided by the govern- ment. So far, he hadn't seen any people, patients or employees. All was quiet as they continued on down a burnt orange carpet toward a bigger office with a glass door. There sat a woman behind a desk who appeared to be a receptionist. Carla looked up at them, then she looked down briefly, as if she were embarrassed, before she greeted them. She spoke in a soft voice.

"Welcome. Hi, Roxy. You're Tom?" He smiled an army smile, brief but friendly. "Please go on in," she said to him, pointing to the Administrator's office on the right of her desk. Then she looked at Roxy.

"Can I talk to you a minute? As Tom turned to go into the office where he was directed, the two women put their heads together and spoke in low voices.

He heard Roxy say, "Sure. I'm on my way out there now. I have my bag in the car." Roxy turned to Tom. "You know how to reach me if you need anything. It looks like I've got somebody to check on. Think you can make it back up to Pinetop on your own today?" She laughed. "There's only one road. Just make sure you go up it, not down!"

"No problem. I think I can handle it. Thanks so much, Roxanne. I may take you up on calling you."

He instinctively squared his shoulders and walked toward the Director's open door, entered, stopped and greeted the two men standing waiting for him. One was the hospital director, Ben Altaha; the other Jim Springfield, chief physician.

"Welcome!" said Ben. His voice was deep; it actually sounded like the Indian accents he had heard in movies. His Tony Lama boots were shiny, his pants creased. He was home after being away thirteen years in Phoenix working in a clinic. His shoulders were broad, his chest wide. He must be Apache, thought Tom. Jim, the other man, was white, in his thirties, turquoise bolo tie and his equally shiny belt accentuating his already growing stomach.

"Anglo," thought Tom. "That's what they call us out here." He had no idea where he had picked up that stray piece of information. Maybe from the movies. Kind of pathetic that his only store of information about Arizona came from movies.

The men went through the opening conversational rituals.

"How was the trip? I'll bet the climate is a big change from Virginia, huh? You're going to like it here," said Jim. "I'm from Delaware, and there is no sky like this back East!"

Ben was the quieter of the two men. He described the location of Tom's new office, discussed the trailer that was being repaired for him behind the hospital, and had Tom sign papers brought in by Carla. He said no unnecessary words, but what he did say was pleasant. Jim was definitely the more expansive one.

"We've got a tour lined up for you, Tom," said Ben. "It's pretty good – gives you an overview of the place. Ronnie Kane's a tribal elder who knows the history of this place better than most of us. He'll be your guide for a day or two."

"Good. I'd like that," replied Tom.

"Oh, by the way, weekly staff meetings are at 10:00 on Tuesdays," said Jim. Tom nodded.

Ben spoke once more. "Tell us what you need for your office, and we'll try to get it. You have two psych-aides and a secretary who's having some marital trouble. Just so you know. And, Carla, out front, will see to your I.D. Come see us if you have questions."

Everything seemed pretty straight forward to Tom, no big scenes, not much talk. He liked what he had seen so far. Ben reached over to shake Tom's hand, and Jim followed Ben's lead, ushering him out the door to Carla who was to guide him to his new office. Tom thought to himself,

"Not as much red tape as I'm used to. Good sign. But nobody I used to work with would mention that part about the secretary's problems. Wonder what that's all about."

As he walked out of the office and down the corridor, he noticed that his shoulder muscles were not bunched up tightly as they had been so often before. Carla walked before him to take him to the Mental Health Department. He twisted his neck right and left; it seemed pretty good in spite of the drive.

Carla said quietly, "We hope you will like it here, Tom. I know Ben will help you in any way he can. If you need anything, let me know."

"Thanks so much, Carla. There is one thing. Is there a government car available that I could use to make visits to people? I'm not so sure how long my van will hold up."

"Yes. One is assigned to your department. Come and get the keys any time you want. It would be great if you could go out to meet some people. A lot of us have a hard time getting into the hospital for appointments."

"Great. I like the idea of not being tied down to a desk every day."

She laughed. "You won't have to worry about that here."

IX

The office to which Carla brought him to was not far away from the administrative area. It was also not far from the door to the side parking lot where he had originally entered the building. When they had reached a fairly large open space, she pointed to a locked cubicle with a glass door panel ahead of them. It had been assigned to him. It looked, in fact, like other government office cubicles throughout the country, except that it had the luxury of a door. The burnt orange carpeting that covered the whole outside area seemed to continue on into his office, however, the color was not something he had seen in Washington, where gray was the color of choice. There were two adjacent offices with no doors next to his. Carla handed him the keys to his office. He had the sudden realization that he was free, on his own.

Two women, upon seeing Tom and Carla, came out of their cubicles, as if they knew who he was. The carpeted area outside the offices was marked by a sign on the wall that said Mental Health Department. It was placed over what seemed to be the secretary-receptionist's desk. On it sat a prickly cactus, a computer, and a picture of two chubby children. Sitting at the desk was a petite woman who was peering into the computer screen, shawl on her shoulders. He couldn't see her face. Shirley John, for so the sign on her desk said, had a biblical verse printed above her computer – John 3:16 – "For God so loved the world that he gave his only begotten son, so that everyone who believes in him may not die, but have eternal life."

That surprised Tom. He hadn't thought much about religion, but he had vaguely assumed that Apaches would have shamans and such things, not Christian ideology. Most people he knew had told him that Native Americans were very spiritual people, aligned with nature. From these comments, he had somehow gotten the feeling that they were closer to God in some kind of way than the rest of us. He suddenly remembered what Roxy had told him. She had been warning him not to stereotype people out here, to forget what he had heard from other sources.

Carla introduced the three women to Tom. Shirley stood up, her back to the computer as if trying to hide the screen.

"Oh, you're here," Shirley said, looking embarrassed. Tom held out his hand. She took it.

"Hi, Shirley. I'll bet business is kind of slow right now?"

She looked down. "Yes, it is."

Carla said to the two other women: "Arlene, Ina, this is Doctor Collins."

Ina smiled and came toward him. She was plump, dressed in blue jeans and tee shirt. Arlene, the last to acknowledge him, took her glasses off and held them, coming forward a step. She was small and angular, the opposite of Ina. Tom spoke, making the first move.

"Call me Tom. When we have time, I'd like to hear from all of you, to let me know what's happening, just as soon as I get settled."

He stuck out his hand to Ina first, intuitively feeling she was friendly. Ina giggled and took his hand. Shirley looked nervously at the government-issued clock on the wall, as he shook hands with Arlene also, who gave him a limp handshake. She seemed quiet.

Shirley looked first at Carla, then Tom. "It's time for me to pick my kids up from Head Start. Do you mind--?"

"Sure, of course," said Tom. "I'd forgotten that this must be lunch hour. Roxy and I ate early; we had some food up in Pinetop, but I can always use more. Anybody want to come to lunch with me? You'd need to give me directions to a place to eat."

Sitting down to lunch with them might be a good way to break the ice.

Ina and Arlene looked at each other. "O.K."

"My van is pretty full of junk, but I'll throw most of it in the back. There should be plenty of room. Where shall we go?"

"Well," offered Ina, "there's only one place." She laughed.

Shirley had already scooted out the side door. Tom and the two women left Carla, and they pointed him toward the same side door from where Shirley had left and where he and Roxy had entered earlier. It looked like all the staff used that door. He'd have to check out the main entrance and the waiting room later. He didn't think he had seen a patient yet.

They walked out to the parking lot. Roxy's Jeep was already gone. He unlocked his car doors, wondering quickly if he had needed to lock the doors at all. After all, though, his stuff was in it. He pushed his things toward one side of the back seat. The rest of his belongings were stacked into the rear of the van. Arlene got in the front, her long black hair clinging to the back of her seat, as if it were electrified. She didn't speak. Ina directed them to the Pinyon Restaurant.

Tom's first impression was that the restaurant had seen better days. One window was patched with duct tape where a long crack had been made in it. Ina looked embarrassed, but said, "Somebody threw a rock at the window a couple of months ago, but nobody has fixed it yet."

Arlene looked unhappy at Ina's comment. A dozen or so customers could be seen eating inside eating big plates of food and listening to Waylon Jennings' music piped through the air, even to the outside of the restaurant.

It had taken all of a minute to reach the little commercial area. A post office sat next to the restaurant, its door wide open. He noticed clods of dirt on the sidewalk in front of the restaurant as he opened the restaurant door for the women. For the first time, he saw a large number of Apache people, or at least a dozen of them. He had an instant positive feeling. It wasn't their faces, brown and broad; it wasn't their straight, black hair. It was something about the way they were talking and acting with each other. Above all, it was the laughter arising from time to time as they waited for their food.

The three of them entered, found a table by the window, and ordered. The Indian taco looked good to Tom; Ina had pointed it out to him. It looked like a big piece of fried bread covered with toppings of all kinds. After all, he said to himself, he hadn't eaten much in Pinetop. After they got settled, Tom opened the conversation with,

"How about giving me a run-down of a typical day for you both? Or, even better, tell me what you think we should be doing that we don't do now. I'm really going to need your help in filling in all the blanks for me."

They seemed to relax at the use of the term 'we.' The food came quickly. The waitress smiled at the two women but didn't speak. Tom began to eat the refried beans on the taco. He liked it. He was going to gain a lot of weight if he kept eating like this. But he felt that it was almost mandatory for him; right now he felt the need to fill in the conversation lulls with food. He wiped his mouth with his paper napkin. Still, the conversation wasn't exactly off to a flying start. He was wondering if they were wary of him, if he looked too army, too military.

Finally Ina spoke first by answering his earlier question. "Well, we do a lot of things. The doctors and nurses make referrals to us, and we see people like, like Billy Lupe who got kicked by a horse, can't walk. He has a lot of anger problems."

She stopped speaking and looked around as if to make sure nobody was listening. After all, it was a small town, thought Tom.

She went on, almost embarrassed. "We got some anger management training last year. Also, there's a report form on each patient that we fill out – it helps to keep the funding coming. Things like that." She giggled nervously.

"What could we do, if we had the chance?" Tom asked. Ina quickly decided to tell him more. Arlene still kept silent.

"Well, there's a lot of distrust around here. Everyone is afraid to tell about problems or secrets, because everyone is related to somebody else. That's what keeps us back, I think. Just my opinion," she said, looking at Arlene.

Arlene frowned at her, but finally spoke.

"We're a private people. We mind our own business. Some N'dee believe that white people have more power than we do. They laugh behind our backs to think that we can be trained in mental health issues. We don't get a lot of respect. Ina here is too trusting. Things get back to other people, and that can work against us."

She threw out the last phrase like a dare. Tom watched the two women interact. He didn't know if Arlene were jockeying for a top position, or if the two just didn't get along. It sounded to him like Arlene might have taken some psychology classes and wanted more. She acted as if she might be angry with somebody, maybe even him. Maybe she resented the fact that he came from outside to fill the job. Bad way to start off, if that's true. At any rate, he wasn't getting good vibes from her. She had begun speaking again, though. He listened.

"Then, there's Shirley, you know, back in the office" said Arlene. "She's got a bad husband. He's got no job, always nagging her for money, and her with the two kids. She's got other things on her mind. When I – we – ask her to do things, she gets kind of edgy." She was getting wound up now, not holding back her words. "You said how can it be better? We need more education like classes, training for us, so we could be respected."

She suddenly stopped talking as a new waitress came to clean off their table.

"Hi, Arlene," she said. Arlene nodded.

"My husband's sister," she explained to Tom, after the waitress left.

The rest of the lunch went peacefully, and the conversation had resorted to the weather, his new quarters, and what it was like back East. Ina said she had heard that Washington, D.C. was surrounded by water, even when you flew in. Tom laughed, and said, yes, he guessed that was so, but he had never thought about it. Must seem like that to them, he realized, after living their lives in Arizona. Just like me assuming that they all had shamans.

They left the restaurant, and he drove them back to the hospital. Both women were quiet on the way back. Did they have negative feelings about him, or was this the way they usually were? Well, he thought, this is the first step. But, I have the feeling that I'm going to have to prove myself before the Mental Health Department can really function well. Let's see what happens next.

X

When they got back to the office, Tom spent the rest of the day going through the files that Shirley showed him. They still used the old metal kind of file cabinet for their records, with a little key dangling from the keyhole. There had never seemed to be a good enough reason to keep them locked up more safely, said Shirley. Most people in the community knew everything that was in them, anyway. No records appeared to be computerized either, but Shirley did tell him that a list of available resources on the reservation had been put on the tribal web site. He spent some time looking at them, then set up a time for their own weekly departmental staff meetings, which was something, Shirley told him, that they had never done before.

He went into his office, sat back in the pseudo-leather chair, and surprised himself by yawning the kind of yawn that encompasses one's whole body. He must be more tired than he realized. He stretched again, then got up and walked to the administration office to get a pass to enable him to drive a government car. He needed to shake this sleepy feeling away. The walk didn't work. By four-thirty, the end of the day, he felt physically exhausted, but the tensions of the past few years that had been his daily companion – well, either they were dissipating or they had taken a vacation, he thought. He was nothing now but just plain exhausted, and that's not so bad, he considered.

He locked up his office and drove his van back up the hill to Pinetop, to the motel where the hospital had reserved a room for him, where he would be staying until the trailer behind the hospital was ready. He wasn't going to mind the drive back and forth for a few weeks, he thought.

There weren't many cars on the road, and the rounded hills of pine trees were all around him. He noted the subtle differences between East and West, little things that attracted his attention. He wasn't going fast. It was as if he were looking at everything with new eyes.

Within a half-hour, he pulled into the graveled parking lot of the motel and checked in. In twenty minutes he had placed his valuables and essentials safely in the room. He looked around his new quarters. He had usually been somewhat suspicious of new surroundings, but tonight he didn't feel any alarms going off in his head. He decided to open the window. There was something about the crispness of the air that he wanted and needed, like an ice cube on a hot day. He didn't know if it were his imagination or not, but he thought he could smell the green, antiseptic smell of the pine trees. As he had been doing recently, he fell asleep quickly, the key still in the inside keyhole of his door. With only the dark mesh screen of the window separating him from the outside, he fell asleep before he had a chance to wonder if there were wild creatures outside or not.

At exactly this same moment in Whiteriver, Arlene was putting dishes of stew in front of her three children. Her husband Sammy was drinking down a warm beer as he sat on the sofa. Arlene was quiet, but she was busy with her thoughts.

"He looks O.K. on the surface, but you never can tell people like that. That Ina, she always has to act the fool, like a dog who wants affection. Well, that won't be me. I'd better keep Shirley in line, too. They're both too trusting."

"Mai, can I have some fry bread?" called out little Big Boy from his seat at the table. Silently, she passed it to him.

"That kid," said Sammy. "He'll eat us out of house and home."

"Just leave him alone, Sammy. He's got one of those headaches again. He needs to eat something."

"Just wants attention," mumbled Sammy under his alcoholic breath.

XI

The next week went quickly. Tom called his dad in Connecticut twice, got his van checked out, and bit by bit began to learn the territory, both in Pinetop and on the reservation. He wasn't at all unhappy to find that Miss GPS Georgette didn't know her way around here any better than he did. He resorted to an old-fashioned map of the reservation that he bought for a dollar in a little shop in Pinetop. There were no street signs on the rez (he liked saying that now), but he was learning his way by going out either with Ina, Arlene or Roxy.

Carla had followed through with Ben Altaha's directions to set up a day for him with Ronnie Kane, a former tribal chairman, now an old man, who gave tours over the vast expanse of the reservation. He made a little money from taking hunters to where the wild turkeys were hiding or where the elk could be seen from afar, Carla had told him. She said that he knew more than most people about what was in the museum they had built near Fort Apache. He noticed that Carla spoke of Ronnie Kane with respect in her voice.

Before the present museum had been built, Carla said, there had been a wooden building that had housed many ancient treasures of the tribe. It had burned down, and they had lost irreplaceable parts of their tribal history. So, she said, they had to begin again, raise money and build another one. Tom said he was sorry, but she just raised her shoulders and dropped them, saying,

"When bad things happen, we just have to shrug it off and move on. That's life."

Tom had heard that Ronnie had married an Anglo woman, and they lived away from town in the woods. He was looking forward to meeting him. Carla said that being a guide was a perfect job for an older man with lots of stories to tell and time on his hands. She looked at her watch and said,

Carla looked at her watch and said, "Sorry. I've got to get back to the office. Come see me if you need anything."

"I really appreciate your help, Carla." Said Tom He thought about her comment about moving on after trouble. It sounded so easy to do. How could they really do that out here? No, wait. He didn't know these people at all yet.

At the end of the first week of Tom's new job, Ronnie Kane appeared for the tour an hour later than he was expected, coming directly to Tom's office to introduce himself. Tom was still in Army mode, and was surprised that Ronnie didn't come on time.

Ronnie held out his hand to Tom. He was tall, with a thick mane of white hair that fell back from his forehead.

"Howdy! Ready for some sightseeing?" No explanation for his lateness.

Tom smiled. "You bet. Thanks for taking me."

"No problem. The hospital pays me for my services," he chuckled.

"Good idea," said Tom. He didn't know what else to say.

He followed Ronnie out to the parking lot, to his Chevy Tahoe, and waited while the old man spat a wad of tobacco out onto the pavement before he got into the driver's seat. He cleared his throat as if he were preparing to speak. He did.

"Thought we'd go out to Fort Apache first. You guys seem to like that. You seen the movies about it?"

Tom said no, he hadn't.

"Well, that's good, because they weren't right anyway."

His arms and his hands holding on to the steering wheel were wiry and brown, with thickset veins. What looked like an expensive watch was on his left wrist.

He drove past the tribal building and seemed to be heading out of town; at least it was the opposite direction from Pinetop. Tom noticed that several people waved to him as they drove through the area. During the whole day that became the pattern. At every stop they made, everybody with whom they spoke gave deference to Ronnie. It seemed to be more than his age, but almost as if he had some kind of power. Tom found that he was learning as much while they drove to a destination as when they arrived at a site. Ronnie was giving him a personal feeling for what Apache people were like. His stories, Tom hoped, had been captured in a book somewhere.

"Funny world, if you live long enough. My grandfather was a scout in the Army for General Crook, so he and my grandmother got to live in a wikiup at Fort Apache. Special treatment."

He smiled. He laughed a unique Apache laugh Tom hadn't heard before. A laugh with a tinge of irony in it. And, what exactly was a wikiup? Almost as if he had heard Tom's question, he said,

"In case you don't know, a wikiup was what we used to live in in the old days. They've got a model one out at the Fort. It starts with long, curved branches tied together at the top and to each other, filled in with a lot of wood and branches. Don't see anyone living in them anymore, since we got the Great White Father in Washington to give us houses!" He laughed again and continued.

"People say my family was privileged. Maybe that's how I got elected tribal chairman." He laughed the Apache laugh again. "My grandfather said they chased Geronimo all the way down to Mexico. Geronimo was the leader of the Chiricuhua Apaches, not from here. He was Apache, but not our tribe. We got a lot of Mexican names up here. Maybe that's why. Them Mexicans kept coming up here for our women. Or maybe it was for the horses."

He was enjoying the story, and so was Tom. "Nobody could beat us riding any kind of horse. We still love our horses. That's why we let'em run free to this day. Horses, a good beef barbecue, a little beer —boy!"

Tom grinned, but Ronnie had abruptly stopped laughing and now had a grim look on his face.

"But this beer —guess you know what liquor has done to us?" Tom nodded. "Well, that's another story. Something's got to be done about that. People have to pay for what they do."

Ronnie went suddenly silent and dropped the subject. He drove on without speaking. Loosened soil, picked up by the wind, shone in the sun and whirled in tornadic circles in from of the car.

It was getting dusty in front and behind them. The particles of dry soil seemed to be following them, touching the car. The road was rough now. Ronnie slowed down, finally stopping the Tahoe in front of a building, or what had once been a building. It was now a shamble of pieces of wood, with vines growing around it.

"Big lightning bolt hit here, they say. Who knows – maybe it was really somebody who didn't like our keeping all this stuff. A lot of our history, the things we kept from our ancestors were in there. The building was old, maybe an old boarding school. Gone in a puff of smoke."

Tom said he was sorry. "Gone now. No need to be sorry. We're pulling together more things we got and putting them in the new museum. We just move on. Sometimes the Creator gets mad, and some say he has a lot to get mad at with us!"

He turned the car around and headed in the direction of the flat land that lay before them. The dust devils had disappeared. Tom acknowledged to himself that Ronnie was a more complicated man than he had originally thought.

"Wait until you see what's ahead," said Ronnie, looking at Tom out of the corner of his eyes while he kept driving.

The two men forged directly toward Fort Apache on what had originally been an old military road, explained Ronnie. Tom had no idea where they were, but it suddenly hit him that he was, once more, treading old Army territory. When the realization sunk in, he actually had a lump in his throat. This fort was moving him more than he realized. They stopped. Ronnie said nothing, as if to give Tom a chance to reconnoiter the territory.

Finally, Ronnie said, "Thought you'd be interested. I bet this is what you want to see -- Fort Apache, up ahead. They say there was a Colonel Green who wanted to make this area a fort. Said it would make our Apache people live on the reservation, that it was a good place to build because it had timber and limestone, and even had places where they could irrigate with water from nearby."

Tom watched Ronnie's expression while he was speaking. He had to ask. "Does it bother you that the Army was used to keep your people in one place?"

Ronnie laughed. "My people, as you call them, were here from the beginning. We chose to be here. My grandfather was a scout with the Army, the good old U.S. Cavalry. Just like in them movies. He was real proud of that. They used fifty Indian scouts at this post to find out about the hostile lands on either side. My grandfather said they had a good supply depot for scouting expeditions. So, where were my people, over there in the corn fields on the reservation, or here with the Army? As long as we are in the White Mountains, we're home. Life's not as simple as some people like to believe."

He shrugged. "Come on. Let's go see the layout."

In front of them was a view that suddenly made Tom feel that he had been transported back to an Army post, back to his past. What he saw before him bore the outlines of a post, only not as well kept up anymore. There was a still a well-defined parade ground, roads on either side of it, flanked by a row of what looked like limestone and wood houses, no doubt where the officers had lived or where the supply depots were located. Far beyond was a drop-off into a canyon or arroyo below and to the right the hills jutted up, jagged peaks like the tips of cones. A good spot to place a fort for defense, he thought. Whoever did this knew what they were doing.

They stopped briefly at General Crook's headquarters, the honest-to-God general who chased Geronimo up and down from Mexico to New Mexico and Arizona. It was a log building, well kept up. The few tourists who were inside the simple edifice were standing around, saying nothing, maybe using the time to get out of the direct sun outside. A portrait of Crook on the wall revealed an ample beard, short haircut, and a dark blue uniform that looked wrinkled, the brass buttons sagging toward the uniform material. A few pamphlets on a table below the portrait were the only sign of commercialism.

Neither man wanted to remain inside. Tom and Ronnie moved on quickly back outside toward the old adjutant's office, which now apparently served as a post office where tourists could mail their postcards.

There was a commissary building, officers' quarters, barns, a guard house and four barracks made of adobe, all flanking the parade ground. Tom felt at home. He had been in this kind of configuration many times before.

He stood still for a few minutes. He could almost hear the horses outside, even martial music from a little band. Were there wounded here? Did they have a dispensary? Some of the Cavalrymen must have been buried around here somewhere.

Ronnie waited patiently, but what he really wanted to show Tom was the exact spot where his grandparents had placed their wikiup, a round wooden construction of branches. His grandfather had taken him here many times when he was a boy, he said. A sort of model of one was visible that day near that same spot. When he saw it, it was hard for Tom to imagine two people, maybe even children, surviving in what looked to him like a wooden beehive. They would have lived in it winter and summer. Generations must have survived in structures like these. And, he reasoned, they probably didn't stay in one place all the time. They must have had to make many of these wikiups in their lifetimes.

"Did your grandfather have any feelings about chasing down a fellow Apache?" asked Tom. Ronnie shook his head.

"No, that's not the way it was. He was proud to be with the Army, proud to help General Crook. You got to remember that Geronimo was Chiricahua, not White Mountain. He belonged over in New Mexico, not here."

As they walked around, Tom didn't say much. Something was happening inside him. He was almost experiencing flashbacks – he might be hearing a military band off somewhere in the distance; there even seemed to be a strong smell of gunpowder in the air. Even his vision seemed to change- he was no longer seeing dust. Now, he noticed the orangeness of the soil, the little sparks coming from rocks. Now, there was a hush, like before battle, as if someone were out there in that canyon ready to attack.

He shook his head as if trying to get rid of the images. They went on until Ronnie, noticing that Tom was very quiet, said, "I see you got the Army in your blood."

"No," said Tom. Not me. It's the history of the place. Come on. Where are we going next?"

Ronnie looked at him, saying nothing for a minute.

Then, he said, "The next place is for fighting men also, only they ain't living any more. It's where we bury our dead, the ones who were fighters."

Tom raised his eyebrows questioningly, but he didn't ask any questions this time.

XII

Back in the car, Ronnie and Tom drove on a few miles further until they turned onto a dirt road and into dense, squat undergrowth – at least it seemed dense to Tom. It bore little resemblance to Ponderosa territory. The landscape was spotted with scraggly vegetation; the hills at a distance were short and rounded. The living growth on them looked like little balls of shrubs in a Georgia O'Keefe painting. Ronnie told him no more about where they were going, and Tom didn't ask.

"This here is what we used to call a washboard road," laughed Ronnie.

To Tom's eyes, it wasn't at all like the view he was used to when he drove up the hill to Pinetop, but full of occasional tumbleweeds and coarse, tough plants that seemed to be able to take all that the rough terrain could give them. Tom couldn't see any structure ahead of them.

Ronnie cut off the engine, and they sat in the quiet for a while. Tom was finding that Apaches didn't need to fill each moment with conversation. He liked it. It was a welcome relief. As they sat there in the quiet and the minutes wore on, a lean coyote carefully crossed in front of the car, his ears pricked and his nose up. He was gray, tough and scrawny, a real survivor. Tom had never seen a wild animal up that close before. The coyote completely ignored the car, as if smelling for something else. Just as quickly as he had appeared, he left. Ronnie spoke in a low voice.

"That coyote, he can never rest as long as his belly is empty. He looked mighty skinny to me."

After the coyote had gone, Ronnie motioned to Tom to open the car door. Both men walked toward a painted sign that read "U.S. Veterans Cemetery." Behind the sign lay graves with plastic flowers of indeterminate age on them and what looked like sad mementos of a past life as well. There were a few dozen graves ahead of him that he could see, some covered with rocks, some with wooden crosses atop them. Little plastic toys guarded some of the graves; on one there was a round, plastic teddy bear sitting at the bottom of a wooden cross. A lot of memories were resting here. As he looked around further, he saw that there were many more graves, not defined by a fence, just spreading out into the undergrowth.

A veterans' cemetery. Again, it took him back to Arlington, and the mathematical arrangement of the graves there, the sameness of them all. But this was different. Each grave was individual, many bearing loving mementos, the graves at times defined by rocks circling the rectangular space that was the sacred ground for a body that once had been alive. A new grave that must have recently been filled bore the name of a woman buried next to her husband. It wasn't so much military order here; it was something else, and the something else was Apache. Yet, these had been warriors, wounded warriors that belonged to a proud tribe of fighters. He owed them respect.

Ronnie pointed to one grave: "Lookee here. He was a scout with the Cavalry, and over here's one from World War One. Got a lot from Korea, World War Two, Vietnam. We make sure we keep these graves up. Don't want no critter disrespecting them. You can say a lot bad about us, but we are good fighters, and we are proud of our warriors. Maybe the Navajos have the Code Talkers, but we've got the fighters. It's in our blood. Nobody can really capture us."

He made what Tom took to be a gesture of respect as they left, bowing his head and touching his hand to his hat. Tom silently wondered if Ronnie was inferring that not even Anglos could beat them. Better not ask, he thought. They got into the car again. Ronnie's mood had changed back to the jovial laughter stage.

"Good name they gave those helicopters, eh? Apache!"

Tom had to reply. "The best. They do unbelievable work."

"Just like us," Ronnie replied.

Ronnie seemed to be able to switch quickly from the solemn to the funny, Tom thought, whereas he, he was still overwhelmed by the Army ties to himself that he had encountered today. He hadn't realized until now how much a part of the Army remained with him, how comfortable the structure of it all had been to him.

Back in the car again, Ronnie drove slowly back down the rutted road, saying, "I'm going to take you now to meet Bessie Baha down at East Fork. She's of the old way, still wears camp dresses and can tell some good stories. She needs the money, if you can see your way to buy a basket from her. I'd kind of like to see what you think of her." He turned to look at Tom. "That is, if you can take any more today."

He looked at Tom shrewdly, as if in some way he had figured him out. Tom didn't like it. He threw his words back at him.

"I don't know what you mean. Let's get out of here and on to the next place."

Ronnie was riling him. He was trying not to show his anger. Ronnie seemed not to notice it. He merely shrugged.

Within fifteen minutes they stopped in front of a small, HUD-built house, and Ronnie tooted the horn. All the houses that the federal government built, Tom was noticing, looked about the same, basically wood and adobe brick, small and now aging. Only the grounds of each house differentiated one from the other. Some families had stacks of wood next to the carports; others kept all kinds of rusty vehicles around the premises. Made sense, he thought. There wasn't exactly a junk yard nearby.

This particular house was badly in need of paint. Instead of rusty cars, there were two or three plastic items that looked like they had once been tricycles, maybe scooters. Attached to the carport was a shaky look-ing wooden structure consisting of four poles attached to each other by more pieces of wood placed laterally at the top. Dried branches were slung across the pieces of wood, making a branched covering, a ramada. Underneath the ramada sat a big wooden bench.

A stocky, short, older woman came out of the house when they drew up. She walked slowly toward the car, wiping her hands on her long camp dress. Her long gray-black hair was braided and fell down her back. Two little faces appeared behind her as if they were afraid to be seen. Bessie and Ronnie greeted each other in Apache, she laughing in a kind of 'aiyee' sound, Tom noticed. Ronnie turned to Tom, introducing Bessie. She nodded. Bessie motioned to the little boys to go under the ramada, and for Tom and Ronnie to sit on the benches under the sunlight that was slipping in through the ramada branches. Everybody did what she said.

Ronnie and Tom now seated, Bessie turned to face Tom directly. There was no sign of embarrassment with her.

"Welcome, Dr. Tom. I heard about you. I got to come up to the hospital some time soon. My legs don't hold out so well any more. You got any medicine with you?"

Tom tried to explain that he was a psychologist and didn't have medications. She picked up on it quickly.

"Oh, you read people's minds. We've got some of those around here, but they only come out at night." She laughed again, and so did Ronnie. Then, her expression changed.

"But I'm a good Lutheran. Nothing bothers me," she said, looking suddenly very pious. Tom was confused by her remarks, but he left it alone. She walked away from them, saying nothing, and returned in a few minutes with several burden baskets, as Bessie called them, their tinkling metal decorations blowing in the breeze. He did what Ronnie had suggested earlier and bought a small one for his office, handing her two ten dollar bills. He liked the looks of the baskets, tightly woven with strips of something and conical shaped. These ones of hers were small, with a sort of rawhide string attached on two opposite sides of the rim, probably so they could be carried on one's back. He surmised that these baskets had once probably been good for carrying nuts or berries or anything, sort of like the backpack kids use today..

They stayed a few minutes more, but it appeared to Tom that the purpose of the visit had been completed. They said their goodbyes, the little boys trailing them to the car, staring at Ronnie's Tahoe. Tom got into the car first, while Ronnie and Bessie stood outside, speaking quietly to each other, she tucking the money Tom had given her in a pocket hidden somewhere in the folds of her dress. They seemed to have a close bond between them, thought Tom.

As Tom waited in the car, it suddenly hit him — where he was and where he had been a few short weeks ago. What was he doing here? Was this going to be any better than Arlington? Could he handle this any better than back there?

His thoughts were interrupted.

Ronnie climbed into the car, turned it around, and said,

"Think you'll be surprised at the next stop. Better get going. That sun is going to beat us home if we don't hurry."

He laughed. Tom didn't respond. Ronnie hadn't cared about being late this morning, and it looked like he didn't care about being late going home. He wondered why Ronnie bothered to wear that expensive watch of his, if he wasn't going to pay attention to it.

It was going to take Tom another month before he was to realize that time didn't play as important a role here as in the Army.

XIII

The last stop for the day that Ronnie had planned was real punishment to his car. They turned back toward Ft. Apache and off the main road to a rutty stretch of ground that could barely be identified as a road, driving toward a place called Kinishbah. Ronnie pointed ahead of them.

"See here. Some ancient people built these stone buildings. Pretty big stones. Don't know how they could have done it back in them days."

Tom was surprised at the buildings and the size of the dwellings. Looking beyond them, he saw a steep drop-off into a canyon.

Ronnie saw Tom looking at the canyon.

"It's dry now, but I figure it must have once held some water, or these people would have never settled here." He slowed the Tahoe down until it was barely moving.

"This was before the time of our people; they weren't one of us. They say it was those ones like the Hopi or Zuni." He gave a wry grin. "Funny. Because our story of creation says we were made for this place. So how come there were others here before us?"

Tom was getting to the place where, when Ronnie posed questions, he merely nodded to show that he was listening. Ronnie was lecturing, not conversing.

As they approached the building along the pock-marked road, Tom saw a cluster of stone squares ahead of them that must have once been strong and securely built buildings. The people who built them must have been advanced enough to shelter themselves with permanent structures, and they must have made their home here for some period of time. These kinds of stone buildings could have been made as late as one hundred years ago, if archaeologists hadn't determined differently and dated them to a much older time period. It definitely didn't look as if the inhabitants were nomads. Ronnie certainly didn't seem to tie these people to his own Apache tribe.

It was hot out here, sitting in the car with the windows rolled up. Tom looked around, shielding his eyes from the glare coming through the windshield. They really were buildings, not forms of temporary dwellings. He had no idea that there had been ancient peoples in Arizona who lived like this. There seemed to be rectangular holes for what once had been doors, and he could make out spaces inside for what looked like rooms. He wanted a better look. His Army boots were hot – he was going to have to buy some Western kind of footwear up in Pinetop. He was definitely not the type to go around wearing sneakers or sandals. It just wasn't him.

As he was getting out of the car, Ronnie said, "Better be careful where you walk out here. Them rattlers love this place – they like to lie out here in the sun."

He said it casually, almost off-handedly, as he himself stepped out of the Tahoe and moved away from the car quickly.

"There's those who think they are evil – maybe back to the time of Adam and Eve. Not me. I just see them as doing the jobs they have to do. They respect those who respect them, and when they mean to get even, they do it fast."

Tom, who had gotten out of the car also, stood next to the open door on the passenger side, looking at the stones making up the buildings in awe. These had once protected living beings, people who chose to live here, who knew how to build solid living quarters some hundreds of years ago, maybe even thousands of years. How had they been able to cut the stones and move them to the right places? The sun was lowering itself into the canyon about a hundred yards from the dwellings, painting the stones a pink-gold color. Life goes fast, he thought, sometimes too fast to do anything worthwhile, but not so fast that one couldn't make mistakes. These people had lived and died and were gone. But, how do I know what their lives were like? They may have done more worthwhile things than we do today. What does it mean – worthwhile – I wish I knew. His mind had slipped into another world.

Suddenly, and without warning, a dark whip-like thing darted out from a rock next to Tom's foot, bringing him back to stark reality. It wasn't a huge rock; he hadn't noticed it when he got out of the car. A tongue went out from the front of the whip and a rattle-like sound at his feet made Tom's instincts push himself back toward the car, jarring his whole body. He felt nothing, but the snake must have aimed for his right boot, perhaps hitting the top of his sturdy shoe.

In a flash it was gone. For a second, he wasn't sure he had seen the movement, or whether his eyes were playing tricks on him in the sun. The reality finally hit him, and he considered jumping back into the car anyway, to take no chances, but he didn't. The snake was gone, and there was no reason to hide, whether it was real or unreal. His boots had probably saved him from the bite, if there had been one. He found that he was perspiring, but it was over before he could do anything. Ronnie, however, had seen it all. He came over, appearing unperturbed.

"Got your Army boots on, eh? Good idea out here. Guess we better be getting back anyway. Sun's getting lower, and I didn't bring nothing for snakebites."

He seemed to think it was all a good joke.

Ronnie got in on the driver's side and said no more about it. Tom had the energy drained out of him, but he wasn't going to tell Ronnie. For one crazy moment Tom thought that maybe this was a set-up, a test of Ronnie's to see if he were as good a warrior as his own people. He'd better watch his step, literally, from now on. No, that was ridiculous. No one could set up something like that. Had it all been an accident, or had Ronnie set it up to test him? Maybe Apaches were brave in the face of danger, but, hell, it wasn't Ronnie's foot that was the target! Tom had always, he felt, possessed pretty good instincts for self-preservation. Maybe he'd better start being more careful out here. There was just something about it all.....Maybe it was not going to be as easy to understand this place as he had originally thought.

Ronnie was in a happy, almost casual mood now, as if Tom were his best friend. As they drove back, he told tales about his mother-in-law, how mean she had been, how glad he was went she passed away. He put another wad of tobacco in his mouth, chewing hard on it, letting some of the spittle run out of his mouth.

Back at the hospital lot, Ronnie dropped Tom off, giving him what looked like a military salute and saying,

"We'll meet again soon, Dr. Tom. Sure did enjoy your company."

Tom thought he detected an undercurrent of irony in his voice. He nodded. He didn't feel like giving Ronnie thanks. He had come close to getting bitten by a rattler, and Ronnie didn't seem to care. Bet there'll be jokes told about him tonight, about the pasty-faced Easterner who was scared of a snake.

XIV

After Ronnie dropped him off, Tom climbed directly into his own car and went up the hill to Pinetop, with his mind somewhere behind him, processing what he had seen that day. It could have all been his imagination. After all, he was in a new world; there was a lot to learn. Maybe he was too anxious, too suspicious of everything, reading too much into everything that was said or done. He was supposed to be relaxing out here, not all revved up. That had been the point of his job change.

Soon, with the monotony of the trip back up the hill, he found himself relaxing at last. He was driving with only his right hand, his left arm out the window. But something was going on with his left arm. It seemed to be developing a dull ache as he climbed up the elevation, not painful, just a throbbing sensation that wasn't normal. Now what, he asked himself. Have you decided to become a hypochondriac out here? His mind was playing tricks with him. He had not been bitten by a rattler; the ache in his arm had nothing to do with Kinishbah – it had been over an hour since he had been out there.

It did worry him, though, when the slow ache kept on for over fifteen minutes. He was too young to be having a heart attack, he assured himself. It's just that damn scare about the snake, maybe a delayed reaction to what had happened. He drove slowly. The ache seemed to be lessening a bit during the next few minutes. He tried to gauge whether it was actually better during these last few minutes, or whether he was imagining that also. He put his arm back in the car. Maybe that's what was causing it, leaving it out the window so long.

He tried to take his mind off his arm by looking around. No one was behind him on the road to curse him or flick him off as in the D.C. area when they thought he wasn't going fast enough. There was just an empty road up the hill ahead of him and a steep drop on the left. No guard rail, as usual. Must be bad in the winter. Nobody behind him, either. Now he was passing a woody area outside Pinetop, when he saw movement out of his left eye that took his mind completely off his arm.

An ungainly looking creature was trying to get himself off the ground by flapping its large wings. Its body was so big in relation to the wings that Tom slowed to a halt, watching in amazement. He finally realized what it was: A wild turkey was struggling to lift its weight off the ground, finally making it to a low tree branch. It seemed to have been startled by something, maybe his van.

At least, it looked like a turkey to him – brown, big body and gobbling like the ones in cartoons. He stopped on the road, watching it. No cars were behind him. He had never seen anything like this before. He didn't see how a bird as big as that could get off the ground, but it did, finally perching on a limb of a pine tree. Cartoons – his whole idea of life in the West came from them. Pathetic. All of a sudden the turkey disappeared. It was gone from his eyesight. He drove on, but slowly.

His thoughts went back to his arm again, but the ache definitely had subsided as came near to the reservation line and into Pinetop. He asked Roxy about it later the next day, and she said that some people who weren't used to the changes in altitude experienced such symptoms when they went up the elevation between Whiteriver and Pinetop, sort of like a diver coming up from the deep waters. Well, thank God, Tom thought. I'm not having heart attack symptoms after all. He wasn't even going to tell her what he thought it was – a reaction to the near miss of the snakebite. He'd sound like a hypochondriac for sure. Later, when he thought about it more clearly, it didn't make sense that the symptoms would occur only when he was going up the elevation, and not down. Or did it? He'd look up what experiences divers have with the bends. Snake bites, arm aches, what a mess it was. Roxy had said that most of the symptoms went away as people moved down to lower elevations. Thank God for that. He'd keep an eye on this phenomenon in the future.

That night, back at the motel after his dinner at Croziers, he sat on the bed looking at the television but not seeing what was on the screen. What he had experienced during the day kept running through his mind. This was a habit of long standing for him; he couldn't help reviewing the day when he was home at night.

Usually, he was adept at figuring out people. That's why he went into psychology. But as for Ronnie, he couldn't figure if he were one of the good, the bad or the ugly. Finally, he brushed it all off. He was what he was supposed to be – a man honored by the tribe, a good guy. Let it go, he said to himself. Think about something else if you have to worry about something. They just have pretty warped senses of humor out here.

Lou came to his mind for the first time in a while. He was beginning to feel some guilt about her and the abrupt way he had left her. No, said Tom to himself. Face it. You're lonely. She hadn't been expecting or wanting any more from him than he had given her. She had never seemed to care that much. Maybe that's the reason he had hooked up with her – she required nothing from him. Nevertheless, he punched in her number still hidden in his phone. He let it ring eight times. No answer. Just as well. Might as well go to bed. He rubbed the upper part of his left arm. Everything seemed normal. The television was still sending out signals when he fell asleep. The next day, he remembered he had some vague dreams about somebody trying to cut his foot off.

After he got up the next day, he took a hard look at his boot where the snake might have attacked it. Nothing, no traces of snake venom, whatever that looked like, nothing at all but dust on the toe. It probably hadn't even hit him at all. Yawning, he got up and prepared some bad coffee in the motel coffee pot. His dream about his foot came back to him.

"Figure that one out, Dr. Freud. It'll give you something to do. Oh, screw it," he thought.

XV

Tom's routine had settled in as fall got colder. It surprised him that the snow started falling seriously in October, even with the aspen trees in the highest part of the reservation still a brilliant yellow. Their leaves were like nothing he had ever seen before – shining like little gold coins when the sun hit them and the wind jiggled them around.

By this time, Tom had traded in his van for a Jeep. The trailer behind the hospital had become available, and after he cleaned it to his satisfaction up to Army standards, he moved in. Clean but messy, that's me, he thought, justifying his life style. He had scrubbed the bathroom floors, the tub, sink and toilet, but by the time all his belongings were in and he had begun living there, pots and pans stayed on the drying board and clothes were both in and out of the closet.

By now, he was glad he didn't have to drive up and down to and from Pinetop every day. There were frequent threats of snow and some real snowfalls in the area as well. Most of the summer visitors from Phoenix and other places farther South had already left for warmer pastures. Pinetop's population had already decreased drastically; only the hardy remained and those who liked to ski more than bask in the sun.

The trailer was small, but it provided all the right necessities – warmth, room to fix meals, a small but comfortable bed. All he had to do was get up, eat and dress and walk a few hundred feet to the side door of the hospital to get to work. He found himself thinking that it was all too easy. Nothing to complain about the job either. His patient roster was growing. He hated to use the word 'patient' out here as much as he had back East, but it had been planted in his mind by the medical model a long time ago. It didn't seem right to call them clients either, or, God forbid, customers. They were human beings with needs, just people. There was no adequate way to describe them that didn't sound impersonal.

When he walked into his office one day – he had made the decision not to lock his forbidding office door after work hours – a man was sitting there, apparently waiting for him. Tom hadn't expected anyone this early, and besides, Arlene always tried to shoo away those people who wanted to wait for him. He was going to have to talk to her about that. But Arlene had not arrived yet.

This man had on some kind of knitted skull cap and wore elaborately embroidered but old boots. His face was lined by the sun and the dry air. The jeans and shirt he was wearing were tattered and faded. He didn't speak a greeting but nodded to Tom, who nodded back. A full thirty seconds later, the man spoke. By now, long silences in communication on the reservation didn't bother Tom. In fact, he was growing to like them more and more. He waited. The man spoke in a gravelly voice.

"They say you O.K. I'm George Dewakuku, born Hopi, here now."

Tom replied, "Thanks. He thought for a second. "I think Roxy mentioned your name to me. What can I help you with, George?"

Suddenly, George jerked his cap off, exposing his short gray hair, worn in an almost- like military cut. He grabbed Tom's hand and put it on his head. It happened so quickly that Tom didn't have time for his instincts to kick in as they had done with the rattlesnake. The man's hair felt bristly, his head knobby.

"Feel. Feel this scar. They cut my head open. Big, huh?"

Tom shrank back slightly at the touch of the bristly head, but he kept his hand where George had placed it.

"It's over now. Happened a long time ago. Not many have a scar this big on the head."

George was grinning. It was a battle scar of which he was proud.

"I come over to get some medicine." He paused to look at Tom, "And also I need your words to help me remember things. I hear you got words. Old Bessie Baha told me."

Tom remembered Bessie and her camp dress and her cryptic words to him. George lowered his voice and looked outside of the office.

"You close the door, please." Tom did.

"It's like this. I got two owls around my place every night. Can you do something for me?"

Tom was at a loss for words. Finally he answered.

"I don't know, George. Tell me more. Did you lose your memory after this surgery?"

"Maybe. Maybe too much beer. Ha! But I want it back. You got something to help me?"

Tom had told himself a long time ago that in this business he would never promise what he couldn't deliver.

"Well, I don't know, George, but let me check your medical chart to see what's going on."

"Then, how about this, Doc?"

He reached down and took off his big leather boots, exposing his bare feet, and thrust them towards Tom. "I got diabetes, my feet are bad, like they're gonna drop off. Hurt like I'm walking on fire."

"Tom looked. His feet definitely looked as if they had been through a lot. They needed to be bathed, and the nails cut, for starters. God knows what else was wrong. He gave him a written referral to Dr. Lang, the internist. Tom wondered how George could walk on those feet, especially while wearing boots without socks. And who knows how far he had to walk to get here. There was something about the man that Tom liked. He was direct and sounded truthful. He didn't have any need to compete with Tom, as Ronnie apparently had. What you see was what you got.

After Tom gave him the referral, George still sat there, seemingly content to stay with Tom, as if he wanted to say more. Time really is different here, thought Tom. There seemed to be more of it, more time to spend, more time to wait. He, too, was finding that he was learning to slow down his pace. He was discovering that people here often had something else to say to you, if you gave them the time.

While Tom had been watching George, George had been watching Tom's reactions as well. He seemed to be sizing him up. Finally, he asked for and got a referral for food and clothing from Social Services and a permission slip to allow him to be taken to pick them up in the hospital van. Tom realized later that George had not only checked him out as the new man but got what he needed at the same time.

He'd probably be back, Tom thought, as George still sat there. He made a mental note to check out George's medical chart. Come to think of it, he'd go out to see Bessie again, to see if she had more to say to him. He had a feeling that she did. His thoughts were interrupted by what George did and said next.

George scratched his head where the scar lay and looked at Tom.

"You got one of these?"

Tom was surprised at the question. "No, I don't have anything like that. Why do you ask?"

"They say you been in the Army."

"I was, George. Just got out a few months ago."

"Where was you wounded?"

Now Tom thought he understood. He felt his face turning red. It made him angry. He didn't know why.

"I wasn't wounded."

"Maybe you have a scar somewhere, like your back, somewhere you can't see."

"No, not me. Listen, I've got a call to make. Come back to see me again if you need to. Take this referral to Dr. Lang, and he'll see you about your diabetes. Better put your boots back on. Ask them to call the van for you to go to Social Services afterward."

George looked straight at him, but he did as he was told. He put his boots on, saying no more. Tom ushered George out quickly. After George left, Tom didn't like himself at all. He looked out the door and watched George walk on toward the clinic, slightly stumbling as he went down the hall.

George had been gone no more than a minute before Arlene, having arrived at work, suddenly appeared, running into his office with a can of Lysol spray, making a grimacing face. She looked disapprovingly at Tom.

"There's a terrible smell in here from him. That man's no good, Mr. Doc " – everybody's new name for him, it seemed. " They ran him off from Hopi. Don't encourage him or he'll keep coming back. He smells so bad. You need to get rid of him. Nobody can help him."

She probably thinks I should be run off, too, since I'm another outsider, he thought.

He asked her directly, ignoring her earlier advice, "Arlene, what about owls? George said they came to his house every night."

She stopped and put the spray can on his desk.

"Leave him alone, Mr. Doc. He's going to die. Let him be."

Tom made no answer. He found himself annoyed that she was telling him what to do. She didn't seem to want to answer his question. He wanted to know why she thought George was going to die, but he decided to drop the subject for now. He let her return to her cubicle while he sat in his own space and wrote a couple of reports. The smell of the Lysol kept reminding him of George. His mind kept going back to him. He had pushed him away without finding about him and what he needed. That was something he should never have done.. He had been threatened by George's questions, so he dumped him. An old pattern that he needed to squelch; he'd have to make up for that soon.

The day was passing slowly. Without access to a window, he was surprised when Shirley came running over to tell him that it had begun to snow hard. He'd better go out before lunch and clean off his Jeep in the parking lot. He was going out later in the day to check out a man who, his relatives said, was talking to himself and who might have a gun in his pocket. He went out to the lot and gave a quick brushing to his front and back windows, stamping his feet before he came back inside.

Later on that day when he went out a second time to get in his Jeep to go look for the man, he had to brush another two inches of snow off the windshield that had accumulated in a short time. As he was brushing off the snow for the second time with the broom he now kept in the car, he looked up and noticed a young woman and a toddler exiting the hospital by the side door. She had wide shoulders and her body tapered down to her small hips and jeans. Her black, silky hair swung back and forth. Neither she nor the boy were wearing jackets. Maybe they didn't have any, or maybe they noticed the cold less than he did.

The boy was running behind her, stumbling, calling something like 'mai, mai,' but she kept slowly walking, with no visible response to him. The snow was slippery, and the boy was having trouble walking. He was crying, but he kept running toward her as she walked slowly down toward the main road. It gave Tom an uneasy feeling. He didn't know anything about the people with whom he was working. He had never seen a mother who did not respond in some way to her child who was crying. There was so much he needed to learn. There had to be a reason, cultural or otherwise, why she was reacting to the boy in this way. He needed to find out more.

"Got to do something about that," he said to himself. Or was it just another commitment he wasn't going to keep?

He got into his Jeep and headed out to find the man who was supposed to be talking to himself. It proved futile. The family that he dropped in to see said that he had gone down to Phoenix with a girl-friend the day before. They weren't worried any longer. Tom wondered what would happen to the girlfriend. He'd probably never know the end of the story, unless the guy did something bad enough that would hit the papers. He looked at his watch. He'd better get back to the office before the snow got bad.

When he got back to the hospital, he found Ina there by herself. She liked to talk, and at times he liked to listen if they weren't busy. Her stories sometimes explained people's motivations to him. Maybe he'd ask her about the mother and boy he had seen earlier walking away from the hospital.

"Anybody here while I was gone, Ina?"

"No, but you just got a call from Social Services. Tina Oliver, she's the director, she wants to invite you to come down there and see how they operate. You probably know they used to be under the BIA." Ina laughed.

"Says she expects you'll do a lot of 'interfacing' with her. What does that mean? Getting in someone's face?"

Tom couldn't help laughing, too.

"Not exactly. I guess I'd better call her back. We want to keep all of our avenues of communication open."

Ina was laughing again.

"The thing is, we don't have any avenues here in Whiteriver!"

"O.K., O.K., I get it. Pretty good," replied Tom.

They really were bent on laughing at things around here, thought Tom. Better than crying, he guessed.

XVI

The next day Tom mentioned to Ina that he would like to learn more about the people here. He had been thinking of the mother and boy, but she had other ideas. Her face lit up. She suggested that he talk with Rev. Herz, the Lutheran minister, to get to know him and to hear what he had to say. She was very animated when she talked about the minister, her black eyes dancing back and forth.

"He's a really good man, Mr. Doc. He's got a lot to teach. Do you want me to take you down to visit him?"

Arlene overheard them and immediately jumped into the conversation, saying,

"I'm the one who knows Rev. Herz. My family has been close to him for a long time. I'll introduce him to you, Mr. Doc."

She stared disapprovingly at Ina.

The sparkle in Ina's eyes disappeared. She shrugged but said nothing. Tom reluctantly agreed, but added,

"Maybe we could all three go to see him."

"Oh, no, Mr. Doc," said Ina. "You go on down with Arlene. I've got work to do."

That same afternoon Arlene drove him in the government car to the main part of town, a cross roads that consisted mostly of a collection of frame buildings that had seen better times. It was only about two minutes from the hospital. He could have driven himself, but Arlene seemed to take great satisfaction in doing it, so Tom let her.

Since he was not driving, Tom was able to look carefully at all the buildings. He had, by now, driven past them many times, but he was beginning to look at things more carefully, to take more time than he had done before now. There was one building on the corner that seemed to have once been a grocery store or a trading post, Tom thought. It looked empty now.

On another one of the corners, however, sat an imposing building that seemed to be only a few years old. Tom had seen the big tribal insignia on the front of it before, but this time he made a note to himself to spend some time finding out what went on in there. The tribal seal was round, and inside it bore what looked like the colors of the rainbow, the sky depicted by a semi-circle. Beneath it was a mountain, and below the mountain, what looked like tassels or tails seemed to be hanging down from the earth to below it. He'd better check the tribal website again before he went down to talk with someone there. The universe around the earth was dark. To him, the tribal seal looked light and even hopeful. Several people were sitting around on the benches outside, as if waiting for something. Arlene explained that today was court day.

Arlene was driving carefully but determinedly. She turned into a driveway next to a big old white frame house that looked as if it had been built in the early 1900's. It had a screened-in porch and a big side yard that abutted the stone Lutheran church next door. Tom wondered if the stones had been brought from the same place that the Cavalry had obtained them years ago. They looked like the same type of limestone that General Crook's quarters had been made of. There weren't a lot of stone buildings around here, except for the ones at Kinishbah. Maybe the ancient builders had a system for getting the rocks out of the ground. It would have been pretty hard even today to build that church out here.

Arlene stopped the car and took off her glasses, putting them in her pocket. She, saying nothing, took Tom up to the front door where she tapped gently, as if afraid to disturb anyone. No Lysol cans this time, thought Tom. They didn't have to wait long. Arlene had made sure that Rev was available. She was looking smug, like an ambitious student who had done her homework.

The Rev. Carl Herz opened the door for them and took them into the dining room after Tom had been introduced. He said that his wife had gone to Phoenix to shop and visit patients at the home for the elderly. He was a lean, tall man, gray haired, with blue eyes lined on both sides by deep crevices. Anyone seeing Tom and the Reverend together might think they were related. It could have been the eyes or maybe the lanky height that they had in common. No, that wasn't it, thought Tom. Both of us have a way of moving our limbs about like we were impatient about something.

"Well, well, nice to meet you!" said Rev. Herz.

Tom felt like it was a personal greeting, though he knew Carl Herz must have seen dozens of young PHS employees come and go over the years. Arlene stood by them, suddenly very submissive. Her black hair hung down on both sides of her face, covering some of her expression. Tom noticed that she spoke in a softer voice here than she did at the hospital, when she greeted Rev. Herz. They were escorted into the dining room and offered chairs. Tom responded to the older man.

"Thank you, sir. I hope I'm not taking up too much of your time," replied Tom.

"Son, we don't operate on the same time schedule as you boys do up at the hospital. Have a seat. How about some coffee?"

Both Arlene and Tom declined.

"Everybody here calls me Rev. I've gotten used to it. I hope you'll do the same," he said.

He leaned the chair back on its two rear legs, his feet almost off the floor, his hands on the table, balancing himself. It looked as if he had been doing it for years. The chairs in the dining room were oak from another era, a deep honey color. A china cabinet behind him was full of Victorian-looking objects.

"I've got kind of an old story I usually tell new people. Arlene has heard it before." She nodded. "But it's not too boring. Would you like to hear it?"

"That's exactly what I'm here for –Rev." It took Tom a slight pause before saying the title, but he was beginning to feel good around this man.

"There's so much here to see on the surface, but I'm not sure if I'm interpreting it correctly."

Rev laughed and looked at Arlene. She smiled a half-smile.

"And you never will be sure, my boy, not completely. What you just said about seeing things on the surface was very perceptive. I'm sixty and my father was here before me, the first missionary. He's 86, and we're both still learning. My dad was sent out here by his Lutheran synod. He and Mom worked, built a church, grew to love the people. My sister and I were born here."

He paused for a minute as if he were thinking what to say next.

"Simplest thing I can tell you is, as I see it, there are two layers of things going on here. One is pretty open, Christian believing, pretty ordinary, full of people making mistakes just like the rest of the world."

He paused, putting his elbows on the table and placing all four chair legs on the floor. The china in the cabinet rattled in protest.

"But, I've got to tell you that running below all you see on the surface is something else, complicated, painful, and even dangerous. I get up in the pulpit and go after the devil. He hasn't hurt me much yet. But he's hurt a lot of lives around here."

It didn't seem to be a secret; he was saying it in front of Arlene, as if she knew all about it. Rev sipped his coffee. Apparently this was not a new subject for him, nor for Arlene, who said nothing.

"When the big Eastern churches divided up the tribes- pretty arrogant, but it stopped churches from fighting each other for souls – we got the Apache, the Presbyterians got the Navajo, the Episcopalians the Sioux, and so forth. Maybe God was trying to tame our German spirit by giving us a hard-nosed, enduring, warrior people just like we were! The Lord sure did know us well." He laughed again.

"I preach on Sundays to a pretty full house. There are about eleven thousand people on the rez. I'm never really sure how many are Lutherans, but we've got a lot more than most other churches. The Mormons are trying to beat us, the Pentecostals are a big attraction to some, and so on. So, I ask myself: Am I here because I was born here? Or what does God want from me, after all? Almost everyone has been exposed to the Gospel – maybe my job is over."

"Oh, no, Rev!" Arlene interrupted. "We need you."

He answered, looking at Arlene directly.

"Sometimes, Honey, I think that I've moved from being a preacher to a social worker. I've known your parents and your grandparents before you. But, then, it comes to me on some days: I've been called to fight whatever you want to call it – the devil, bad spirits, witchcraft, and that's my job here."

Arlene had shrunk back to her submissive self again. Tom thought he understood most of what Rev was saying, but this last part about the devil, witchcraft and so on, surprised him. Witchcraft? Was that possible in today's world? In the United States of America? Also, hearing someone wondering what God wanted of him, well, that had struck a chord in him. He had experienced some thoughts like that himself, but an answer had never come.

The conversation had gotten deep. Rev seemed to sense it and changed the subject to mundane things. They spoke about basketball in Phoenix, the casino up the hill, even the cold weather. As they shook hands to say goodbye, Rev said,

"Son, I'm here if you need me." He paused. "And let me tell you something: I can use all the help I can get, if you are ever interested."

Tom caught himself frowning. He wasn't sure what to say.

Rev patted Tom on the back and turned to Arlene.

"Arlene, I haven't seen your grandma for a while. Tell her I'm praying for her." She nodded.

"It's getting hard for her to get out in the cold," she replied.

They walked out the door and went toward the car. For some reason Tom felt good, as if a bond had been established between himself and Rev. Arlene would be proud to take credit for it, if he were any judge of her. Tom could see why she wanted to bring him herself. Brownie points. At any rate, this was a man who could explain some things to him, and he needed that a heck of a lot out here.

As they left Rev's house, Tom pulled his coat collar higher up around his neck. This was going to be a cold night. The next time he went to Pinetop he was going to get a pair of long johns. He sat next to Arlene, making no attempt at conversation. Rev had been very enlightening, but he wasn't sure what Arlene really thought of all he said.

Arlene, too, was quiet on the way back to the hospital, until she asked him a question that surprised him.

"Why did you come out here, Mr. Doc?"

He paused before answering her.

"I guess I wanted something different." That was all he was willing to reply.

She kept her eyes straight ahead on the road.

"Some of you guys seem to come out here to get away from something. We've seen that a lot."

"You must get tired of that."

His response was the old psychological delaying tactic.

"Yeah," she said. "We do."

XVII

It was getting colder. Tom was really glad now that he didn't have to climb up to Pinetop after work anymore, as the snow was coming down hard now and had been doing so with more and more frequency during these past few days. He was glad to be inside, in his cozy trailer. Tonight he had set up his laptop near his bed. He had made up his mind to do some serious research on the White Mountain Apache.

The first references he found were credited to Basse, Kluckhon, Goodwin and other anthropologists. A lot of the data seemed to be old. Maybe nobody studied them anymore; maybe it's no longer politically correct. Well, that wasn't going to help him one bit. He needed to find some more relevant information. Also, he really wanted to find out more about Geronimo, even if he wasn't from the White Mountain Apaches. There was something about him, his strength, his bravery, that fascinated him. It was Ronnie's stories about him that had stirred his interest. Sure, there was no doubt that he had killed a lot of people, but Tom had a desire to find out more about the circumstances.

In a few minutes, though, he accidentally came across a monograph on witchcraft that interested him, because of Rev's mentioning the subject. It was from back in the 1970's. How spells are cast, who's a witch, causes of illness, sorcery – He noticed that a lot of the cases took place in Cibecue, the most traditional and isolated part of the reservation. He guessed that if this kind of thing existed any more, it was probably only out there, and not in Whiteriver. He printed some of the information, setting it aside in the basket Bessie had sold him. There definitely were some puzzles for him to figure out around here.

"Well, I've got plenty of time ahead of me to do it. It's not like I'm hitting the bars every night."

Come to think of it, he hadn't had a drink since he had arrived here. He hadn't even had a date. Was he going to have to give up women if he didn't go to the bars in Pinetop? He had been so busy recently that he hadn't had time to think about a social life.

He decided to take a hot shower, turn up the heat in the trailer and read <u>The Maltese Falcon</u> again, one of his favorite books. Pretty good way to spend a cold night, he said to himself. He was alone, but at least he wasn't unhappy, was he?.

XVIII

The next day Roxanne called him at work.

"Hi, there. I haven't seen you for some time. How's your trailer doing?"

"Good, Roxy, and business is good, too. Seems like their curiosity about me is overcoming their fears." He laughed.

"We do like to find out about someone new," she answered.

"Well, I guess you could say the same about me. I've been looking up information on the internet. Trying to find out about customs, even about witchcraft, if you can believe it."

He laughed, as if to show her how ridiculous it all was. She didn't laugh back.

'Well, that sort of leads into what I was going to say. Tom, I thought you might like to take a trip around with me, if you have time. I'm looking for George Dewakuku, to see if he's taking his meds, and there's also a girl out by the canyon I'd like you to visit with me. You never know what odd things happen around here."

"Sure thing. When?"

"This afternoon, O.K.? How about two o'clock?"

"Good enough. I'll be ready. I've felt for some time I should be paying more attention to George."

Tom was glad he was wearing his heavy boots and thick jacket when he left to go out with Roxy. He never had bought those Western boots he had thought of, but his old ones were holding up just fine. They were kind of like a good luck charm – after all, they had probably saved his life, hadn't they?

He was curious about what Roxy had said on the telephone. She implied that there was something strange that she wanted to check out for herself. Only one way to find out, he said to himself.

She picked him up on time. A needling, icy rain that was dangerously close to sleet was coming down. She was driving her own Jeep, not the government car, and bits of rock pellets peppered the bottom of the car as they headed out to Canyon Day. It didn't seem to bother Roxy. She described the young woman they were going to see as she drove.

"Let me give you a quick run-down on Sheena, Tom. By the way, I asked her if I could bring you, and she said yes. She's twenty-one years old, chosen Miss Indian America three years ago, beautiful big eyes. She did a lot of travelling after she received the award, speaking to tribes all over the West, even got to D.C. to receive some honors. But she had a boyfriend here at home who didn't want her leaving him. He drank a lot, was seeing other women, and he even beat her up at times when she was back in Whiteriver. But Sheena said she couldn't get him out of her mind, said she couldn't let go of him."

Roxy paused, took her eyes off the road for a second to turn up the heater.

"Did anyone ever arrest the guy?" asked Tom.

"It's not as simple as that. Most times the women won't press charges, just like in other places. Sheena would never even get a protection order against him. "

Roxy drove on, but now she was paying more attention to the road, as sleet and hail the size of BBs started falling down on the car like the sound of machine guns. The roads hadn't iced up yet, and the wild horses had disappeared to some safe haven, but she didn't take anything for granted.

"Anyway," Roxy went on, "Sheena would never tell the police what her boyfriend was doing to her, so things kept going from bad to worse. Her mother knew it, and she was worried sick."

Now, both of them were watching the road, not talking. Canyon Day wasn't far away, past Blueberry Hill and the bar that was now closed, but even so, Roxy said, guys drank in pairs around the building. Roxy knew she had to be careful not to hit a drunk wandering out on the road. The bar opened only in the evenings. Better to leave the money here on the reservation than spend it in Pinetop and crash their cars coming down the hill on the way home. That was the thinking of most of the tribal council, Roxy had told him. Tom nodded to respond to what she was saying.

Suddenly Roxy pulled over to the side of the road as they neared the bar on the left hand side of the car. She had spotted something moving. It was a man who seemed to be dead drunk and curled up on his side. A man coming out of the bar had staggered over to him and was kicking the prone shape with his foot. Roxy got out immediately, bent over the man just as the kicker, seeing their car stop, disappeared behind the bar. Tom tried to go after him, but Roxy called out to him,

"No, don't waste your time with that. Call the Fire Department and get an ambulance to come out here ASAP."

Tom made the call with his cell phone. Roxy and he waited for the ambulance to arrive. He was unconscious and bleeding from the head and mouth, probably where he had been kicked. A line of drool mixed with blood escaped his mouth and fell onto his jacket. The ambulance seemed to take forever. Roxy pulled a blanket out from her car and covered him with it. There wasn't much else she could do out here.. Even in the cold, Tom could smell the man's fetid breath, the beer, the sour smell of vomit.

Within ten minutes the ambulance arrived, and the paramedics hoisted the man into it on a stretcher and drove off, siren screaming. He never saw the man again. Tom found out later that the man didn't make it through the night. It was a combination of the alcohol, his destroyed liver, and the kicks. Later, when the police questioned him and Roxy, they couldn't identify the kicker. That was all there was to it; the man was dead. Chalk another victory up for beer.

At last, they got back in their car and on the road toward Sheena's. There wasn't much to say about what had just happened. The sleet was still pelting the car. After ten minutes, they arrived, as Roxy stopped in front of a neat looking, sloped-roof house, with two cars parked out front, both covered with snow. She backed her car into the driveway, in front of the other cars, to make sure they could get out later.

She said, "Let's stop out here a sec before we go in. I didn't finish my story, and there are things you need to know. Sheena is really a nice girl. She's gained weight now from being in a wheel chair all the time, but otherwise she's as beautiful as ever."

Tom looked at her quizzically. Was this the person about whom Roxy had told him – the one that odd things were happening to?

"She's paralyzed in the lower half of her body. When her boyfriend finally left her for someone else, she ate a handful of aspirin, got into her pickup and ran it over the rim of the canyon. It's a wonder the aspirin alone didn't tear up her insides or kill her. Instead, she messed up her spine, all because of the no-good chump she thought she loved. They say he's with the new girlfriend now, down on the San Carlos reservation."

She paused and reached into the back seat for her bag.

"So, I come to see her every once in a while, to watch for skin sores, talk to her. It's a hell of a life for a young woman. I'd like you to get to know her, to see what you think about her mental state – give me some ideas on how to help her. She was glad when I told her you would be coming with me."

By this time, Sheena could be seen from the open door, in her wheel chair, waiting for them. She seemed anxious for them to come in. They got out of the Jeep quickly, the icy rain and sleet hitting them in the face as they ran toward the door. Once inside, Roxy introduced Tom as the new psychologist. Sheena smiled. Her features were delicate, her skin tawny.

"Welcome. Nobody here but me. Mom and Benji walked to town. They're scared of driving in this weather."

Tom shook the ice off his jacket. Roxy began by asking how she was and took various meds and bandages out of her bag. Sheena looked embarrassed, and Roxy noticed.

"It's O.K., Sheena. We'll just do all this in the other room." Sheena looked relieved. "And, by the way, Tom's a good guy at keeping things confidential, too. You can trust him. I wouldn't bring him if I didn't trust him."

Sheena looked timidly at Tom and sighed. "I know I really need to talk to someone. I'm trying the best I can to keep from getting down.

I'm just scared to tell anyone around here what's happening to me, even my mom."

"Would you tell me what's going on, Sheena?" asked Tom.

She responded, "Well, sometimes I think that maybe I'm just exaggerating, that it's all in my head. There are some good things going on with me also. Maybe I should just concentrate on that. For example, I can earn some money from sewing, I watch TV, even go out partying with friends, but" -- She looked at Roxy —"I feel as if I made all of this happen; I know it was my fault." She put her eyes down. "Then, other days, I think I'm just making all of this up."

Go on, Sheena, and tell Tom what you told me before," urged Roxy. "We'll do the bandages later."

Sheena pushed the wheelchair over toward the front door and locked it, looking at Tom.

"You're not from here. You don't know about some of the things that happen. Most of you guys who work down here, you don't understand, but it's true, all of it, everything bad that goes on. You are just blind to it. You have to grow up around it to know about it."

She shrugged her shoulders and held on to the wheels of her chair tightly. Tom could see the white of her knuckles.

"Before all the bad things began to happen to me, I got a warning from someone who we're pretty sure has a lot of power around here—you know, the power to make good or evil for people."

She shivered slightly. She looked at Tom as if to see if he understood. He was trying to remain open. Good and evil, she had said. Tom suddenly remembered something that Rev had said. Tom waited for her to speak again, but she had stopped talking and was sitting still. He took the opportunity to look around the room while Sheena got herself together. A fire was sputtering in the fireplace, and an intricate quilt with some kind of star-shaped pattern covered the sofa where he and Roxy sat across from Sheena's wheel chair. She really was pretty, he thought. What would become of her if she had to be trapped inside that chair all of her life?

Sheena finally was able to speak again, this time with more control.

"That person I was talking about – the one with the power -- came over to me one night while I was attending the wake of a friend. My friend Johnny had gone to high school with me – he was a good friend, not a boyfriend. A tree fell on him while he was working for the BIA. He was chopping it down, but he must have messed up and cut it at the wrong angle."

She looked down. "He was probably the kind of guy I should have been going out with, instead of Travis – but no use to talk about that now."

"Anyway, we were all drinking at the wake." She smiled briefly. "All of the men thought I was something then. I had been chosen Miss Indian America, gotten some good prizes and awards from just about everybody. The truth was that I got to thinking I was somebody special. Well, this person came up to me and said to accept what they were going to tell me as a warning. I was pretty drunk, but not so drunk that I couldn't hear what they said. They said I was going to pay for putting myself above all the others in the tribe. They said it real quietly to me. That this was not the Apache way."

She pulled out a tissue from her pocket, wiping her eyes, and then looked at them.

"I can't, I won't tell you who it was. I was warned not to mention the name of this person."

"A spell had already been cast, I was told. This person gave me a symbol, what you call a talisman, of the authority they had to make spells." She shuddered. "I don't want to describe it. But, I had been warned. I went out back after the wake and buried it out in a field, away from everyone, even as drunk as I was. I was scared, but I wanted to keep that thing from hurting me or anybody else. Then I drove home, still drunk, but I made it. But, in a week's time, this happened to me." She pointed to her legs. "And here I am." She put her head in her hands for a minute. Finally, she looked up.

Tom and Roxy said nothing, waiting. There were tears in Sheena's eyes when she went on.

"A few days ago, I got another warning, Roxy. I didn't tell you. I couldn't tell anyone. Another curse has been put on me. I am going to die." She turned toward Tom. "That's why I wasn't sure I wanted to say this in front of anyone else. Oh, I'm so scared I don't know what to do! That's why I'm telling you both now. I can't handle this!"

Roxy immediately tried to refute the threat, but her attempts weren't working. Roxy looked at Tom. He knew that she wanted him to come up with an answer. He had to say something.

"What about Rev? Do you ever talk with him?"

"Oh, no. He doesn't know I believe in all this. I didn't used to, but I do now. Too much has happened to me." She sobbed.

They tried to comfort her, but it didn't help. Roxy helped her into the bedroom, where she checked for bed sores, applied medication, and tried talking to her, encouraging her not to be afraid. Tom listened from the living room. After the two women came back out, Sheena seemed more composed, almost drained of emotion. The three of them drank coffee prepared by Sheena, and talked, Roxy and Tom trying to give Sheena time before they left to make sure she was all right. There wasn't much else they could do. Tom felt out of his element, as he had so many times before.

Finally, he and Roxy were forced to leave as the ice persistently hit at the windows and made the fire sputter even more.

Sheena said apologetically, looking at Tom. "I'm sorry I was so upset. Will you please come again, maybe with Roxy? Or could I come to see you at the hospital?"

Tom said he would come again, or it might be best if she could come to see him if she could. He was thinking about the rumor mill and what people might say if he visited her at her house while she was alone. He was surprised that she asked him, but he agreed immediately. He was afraid that she might try to take her life again. After all, she had tried it before. The more he found out about people here, the more respect he had for their ability to keep living in the face of adversity. He was going to do all he could to keep her hopes alive. How do you comfort someone in a case like this? Suddenly, he remembered all the people he had worked with before who had no arms or legs to use. Some of them had been close to taking their lives. Maybe they still were. Well, he knew one thing: he wasn't going to abandon Sheena as he had with the others.

XIX

O nce back in the car, Roxy started the engine and put on her seat belt. She said soberly,

"I'm pretty sure who's doing this to her, and to George, too."

"Who?" asked Tom.

She looked grim. "Let me do some more checking around. I'll tell you what I think when I'm sure of it."

"O.K. I'd like to help in any way I can, Roxy."

She nodded in the affirmative. They drove in quiet for a while until Roxy spoke again.

"Tom, you can say no because of the weather, but I still think we should go see George before it gets even worse on the roads. I'm concerned about him."

Tom said yes. He had been feeling as if he were wearing a brand of guilt across his brow for how he had responded to George.

They were both quiet again on the way to George's. Tom was thinking of Sheena. It was odd. Most people and animals, for that matter, move to safety when their existence is threatened. She didn't seem to be trying to find a safe spot. It was as if she were her own enemy, putting herself in danger by letting these thoughts of hers get to her. Where was it written – in some book that he had once read -- that described the soldiers on the front line that don't flee – the writer called those people "the imbecile line." The Red Badge of Courage. He remembered it from college. It had made a lot of sense at the time. People who didn't run from danger weren't very smart. Or were they?

"That's probably what I thought I was doing – unconsciously – when I moved out here. Getting out of the front line. But does it really work? This escape of mine may just have gotten me back into another battle with myself. Well, I'm not running this time."

He realized that he had been gritting his teeth during the ride, probably anxious about the weather and the driving conditions. Funny. He had never done that before. Roxy finally had turned off onto something that might have been a road. He deliberately stopped moving his teeth back and forth. He needed to keep his feelings under control.

It wasn't the weather that bothered him; it was that Sheena's feelings of inadequacy that she described so poignantly had opened up the old wounds inside of him. He thought sourly, how great he was getting at self-analysis. Everything was gray and white all around them. What may have been the road was white, and the surrounding air gray like the gray that transforms the air after ammo has been set off.

They crept along until Roxy finally spotted George's dwelling by the small orange glow emanating from the cracks of the closed door. How she was able to spot it, Tom couldn't figure out. Just years of doing it, he guessed. One couldn't call it a house; it had no windows. The only signs of life around it were the orangeness emanating from the cracks in the door and some pathetic plumes of smoke that crept out of a pipe in the roof but were soon beaten down by the atmosphere.

It was almost dark when they found the shack. Tar paper was flapping on the roof, making a slapping sound in the wind. Roxy tooted the horn a couple of times to alert George. After they got out of the car they could smell the faint, damp odor of wood burning. The dim light around the door was like a beacon for them as they walked up the rocky path to the hut.

As they neared the door, Roxy called out George's name. They could hear him make a grunting sound almost like a bear, then move something away from the door. Next, there was a scraping noise as if he were pulling back a board to allow the door to open. He opened the door slowly, motioned them to come in, and they did quickly. He closed the door and replaced the plank, settling it into its groove. The open door had removed all but the slightest bit of heat coming from the fireplace.

Tom looked around. The shack consisted of one room lit by a fire in a make-shift stone fireplace. By the dim light, Tom saw a wooden table in the center of the room and an ancient couch against the wood wall, with some sort of rug thrown on it that probably served as a bed. In one corner sat another, smaller table with what looked like an iron skillet and a couple of cans of food on it. A rickety chair was drawn up to the big table, on which there appeared to be some feathers and a partially carved piece of wood in the shape of a human figure. A knife lay next to the wood.

George saw Tom looking at the wood carving, the knife and the feathers.

"I been making these kachina dolls a long time, back to when I was with my people. I carried the knowledge with me, even when I had to leave. They say that these spirits come down from the mountains when it gets cold."

He shivered slightly. "And even if these ain't my mountains around here, it sure is cold enough for them to come down."

Roxy asked him, "Are you going to sell this one, George?"

"No, not this one. The others I sold, I did to make money. But, I'm going to keep this one and hang it up on that wall there. I'm going to study it, see if it can give me strength against evil."

Evil again, Tom noticed Here it was again. Everyone seemed to mention it, Sheena, Rev and now George. He must have been carving the wood recently, for Tom noticed wood shavings on the floor, but, then again, he thought, it wasn't as if George were going to sweep up the place very often. The figure's hands were crudely made, but George obviously had tried to differentiate the fingers instead of making simple fists. It looked like a human figure, a man. It was made to be stood erect, with one foot in front of the other.

Where the face of the kachina should have been was what looked like a mask, divided into different spaces and colors, with two squares at the top and one rectangle below them. A kind of fringe of orange yarn had been placed around the mask. It was around the orange fringe that George must have been working before they came. He had half-finished placing feathers around the fringe, brown feathers with white spots. The carving still looked as if it needed work.

"I call this one 'Found Face.' It's like he knows who he is -- he's got a face that he can show to everybody. But we can't see the real part of him behind the mask."

There must have been personal meaning in what George was telling them, Tom thought. He hoped George would keep talking. He did. He seemed to like to talk about the doll, to have people listen to him. Tom was going to have to learn what the symbolism meant.

"See, the thing is, well, the important thing is what's behind the face. There's God, the Sun Creator, back there behind the mask. He's so powerful I can't show him."

He put the doll down. The orange fringe around the head, when lit by the light of the fire, suddenly looked like the sun itself, rays coming out from all parts of the curve of his head.

"I look to him to teach me, to make me strong. He don't like being here, but he still has power."

Roxy said later that the dolls were George's only source of extra income, and that he must have felt that the Sun doll was something special, something too special to sell. Tom made a note to himself to buy a kachina doll from George, as he had done with Bessie's burden basket.

Tonight George was wearing socks, unlike during his visit to the hospital, with the infamous boots lying by the door. Tom looked around. The only pieces of clothing he could see were the ones George had on his back, his old blue jeans and flannel shirt and the cap that he was wearing. However, he did notice what looked like a wool-lined vest that was hanging on a peg on the wall. A fire in the stone fireplace made the room barely livable. There was no other lighting. The place was so bare of comfort that it humbled Tom. This man survived here, in the midst of poverty and loneliness. He was so much more resilient than Tom, Tom with all his degrees.

"Mr.Doc, and Miss Nurse – no good day for a visit."

He moved the old blanket from the even older sofa, making room for his guests. Tom sat down. Roxy had George sit next to him while she inspected his feet, checked his blood sugar, and even ran her hand over the scar on his head. Tom thought how squeamish he had been at touching George in his office. He tried to make up for it.

"George, I thought you were coming back to see me at the hospital. What happened?"

George avoided Tom's question at first and squinted around the room in the firelight. He coughed a raspy cough, and then he got up off the old sofa to put back on his socks that he had taken off for Roxy's examination of his feet. Standing on each foot, he managed to get them back on his feet without falling. He asked Roxy to sit in his place on the sofa and she did. George stood between them and the fire. It took him a long time to reply to Tom's question.

"I figured you was O.K., you being an Army man, and pretty good at keeping things private, too. You would keep things inside you that nobody should know about me."

He rubbed his big hands in front of the fire.

"That's honest-to-God how I felt. But I didn't come back, 'cause I got to protect myself. They tell me I don't belong here, that I got no business coming up to the hospital, so I got to be careful."

"Who told you that, George?" said Roxy. She looked over at Tom.

"Can't tell. Spirits don't like talk. Same spirit came to me one night. Left whiskey. Said it's a good way to kill myself. I didn't do it. Next time spirit come again, says stay away from Mr. Doc, tell nothin' or spirit will make me sick. So, I don't come. I had the power inside me not to kill myself, but not the power to disobey her."

He reached over to stir the fire with an old stick lying next to the hearth.

Apologetically, he said to Tom, "I sure am sorry, but that's the way it has to be."

Tom was flabbergasted. "Who would tell you not to come to see me? Who, George?"

George didn't answer the question. He turned, picked up a log next to the hearth and threw it on the fire.

"But I got my kachina now. Maybe he's more powerful than the bad spirits around here."

He walked abruptly toward the door.

"Big storm coming on. Time to go, I think."

He reached out and shook their hands, and led them directly to the door. They didn't seem to have a choice. But before he opened the door for them, he said to Tom,

"Maybe you don't want to talk about the wound you got in the Army. That's O.K. by me. Maybe you got the kind that don't show scars or nothin'. I figure you must be a brave man out there in the war, and you don't want to say it. That's all right with me."

He looked straight at Tom, who didn't know how to answer right away.

"I just want you to know that I woulda come back if I could. But I got to think about my own safety, too."

All Tom could do was grab him by the shoulders and mumble a sort of thanks, saying,

"You just may be right about me, George. I guess I have been in a war – but the bravery part –time will have to tell about that. I've got a feeling you're a far better soldier than most people. If you have the courage, and I know you do, come up to see me when the storm goes away. I haven't got the guts to ride back out here on my own!"

Both men laughed. He didn't know why he said what he did, but it was right. As Roxy and Tom went outside, they could hear the scraping of something being put in front of the door, as well as the big plank nestling back into its place.

Once back in the car, Tom and Roxy were quiet once more. There didn't seem anything appropriate to say after visiting Sheena or George, and the weather wasn't helping any. Snowflakes instead of ice now whirled in circles around them, and they concentrated on the disappearing edges of the road. For some reason, neither of them wanted to talk about George. Roxy looked non-commital when she dropped Tom off. She told him she would talk to him later to let him know what she found out about the drunk man who had been sent to the hospital. Funny, thought Tom. She had been very willing to talk about Sheena before their visit to her, but she hadn't told him much at all about George. Did Roxy think she really knew who was frightening George? Could it be the same person who was threatening Sheena? And why was he, Tom, brought into it? Why was he considered by some so-called witch to be a bad one to talk with? He couldn't think of anything he had done to turn anyone against him.

Back in the trailer, Tom thought all evening about Sheena and George. What could he do for them? None of his exalted training had prepared him to help them. Were they going to be more wounded warriors he had to carry around in his conscience? Not if I can help it this time. I'm not going to let anyone down again. But, how could he possibly be of help to anyone when this belief in evil spirits seemed to crop up everywhere? This was one thing about which he knew nothing except for the bits and pieces he had picked up on the internet.

The drunk, Sheena and George were whirling around in his mind like the snowflakes outside his trailer. How could his being here have provoked such emotions? It was going to make it doubly hard to do anything for anyone. There were problems enough waiting to be tackled, but somehow his presence here seemed to add another burden to the lives of people like George.

XX

The bad weather continued into the next week. Tom stayed mostly in the office or visited hospital patients, but his thoughts kept coming back to Sheena and George. After she had dropped Tom off that afternoon of their visits, Roxy had called him and said it would be better not to talk about what they had heard, for the safety of George and Sheena. She said she had some checking to do. It was a week later, and still he hadn't heard from her. Roxy's remarks made him decide to hold off on contacting either George or Sheena right away, at least until he heard back from Roxy.

Confined mostly to working in the hospital because of the weather, Tom was picking up the strong feeling that the mental health office still seemed to hold undercurrents of discontent. He could sense something, but he couldn't define it. He knew it had to be something coming from one or all of the three women. It was as if all three were very careful of what they said; there was a lot of Ina looking at Arlene, Arlene looking at Shirley, and so forth. They didn't trust each other, and he didn't know why.

Shirley had asked Tom for permission to come later in the mornings, saying she had to take her children to Head Start. He said yes and hadn't thought any more about it at the time, but the rez rumor, according to Ina, was that Shirley's husband had moved back in and wanted her to prepare breakfast for him. Tom noticed that she sometimes stayed on the telephone for a long time, tears welling up after she got off the phone. Tom thought it best to wait until she wanted to talk before approaching her. She asked for no help and offered no reasons. Tom did tell her she would have to limit her phone calls. She agreed, but still revealed nothing to him.

Somehow, he felt that the issue with Shirley didn't seem to be what was affecting the office. He thought about Ina. Ina seemed happy just to have a job. He didn't think the vibes he was feeling were coming from her, but he didn't know much about her, either. She told a few jokes occasionally, giggling in her lilting way, and when Arlene was out of the office, she told tales about her and gossiped about people in the hospital. Beyond that, he really didn't know her well. He had noticed, though, that she had the ability to work well with others. Everyone seemed to like Ina, even her own relatives.

Arlene was another matter. She came in one day, a few weeks after they had been to see Rev, went directly toward Tom's office, entered with his permission, and closed the door behind her. Tom had from the beginning sensed that she didn't like him, so he waited guardedly for her to speak. But, contrary to her usual manner in the office, she appeared subservient as she had in front of Rev. She sat in the chair usually reserved for patients. When she addressed him this time, she called him by his first name.

"Tom, I know you think I'm kind of mean and all, but I have a lot on my mind." He didn't protest, but waited for her to finish.

"I think I need to tell you what's going on with me. I don't want to be the butt of any more gossip around here." She looked straight at him, as if he had been talking about her.

"My boy, Bruce Lee, we call him Big Boy, has been having these real bad headaches for the last few months. He's five. Roxy got an appointment to take him down to Phoenix, to PIMC, the Indian Medical Center. Well, we did. He's got a brain tumor."

She stopped. Tom made real sounds of sympathy this time. How much more could these people take? He waited for her to continue. She remained expressionless.

"They say he's not going to make it, and I don't want him down in Phoenix, so far from home." No tears. A pause.

"I went to see Rev, and he prayed with me. You know I am one of Rev's most faithful church members." Tom nodded, still waiting.

"But I heard from some around here, believers in the old way, that a bad spirit is running around. That's never bothered my family before, because we're Christians. But I have heard of something that bothers me, and I want to ask your opinion"

Odd, thought Tom, for her to ask me. She went on.

"It's this: Do you think a bad spell could have been put on my boy? They say it can get in to him through another person -- like, what's the word? – a conduit, somebody who doesn't know what's going on, but he is helping the bad spirit do his work, anyway."

She paused. "So, what I want to ask you is this –do you have an opinion on this? I know you've read a lot of books. What do you think?"

Like so many other times here, he was at a loss for words. But he immediately sensed that she thought he was the one who was the conduit for the evil that was harming her son. His intuition was strong about this. Later, when he thought about it, he even suspected she had looked this word 'conduit' up in the dictionary, so to better make him understand what she meant to say. Pretty far-fetched, but she had that capability.

He spoke what he felt to her, expressing his sympathy for her and for Big Boy, but he didn't answer what she asked. He felt she was carefully watching him for his reactions to what she said. Instead of giving her an answer to her question, he said,

"I'm not able to give you an answer. I'll have to speak to Rev about this. It's out of my area." This wasn't the answer she wanted.

"No, no, don't go to any trouble," she replied quickly. "I'll talk with Rev myself. Sorry to bother you about this."

She had gotten what she wanted by talking to him, he thought. She let him know what she thought of him, what he was capable of. Tom wasn't going to let her go right away. He decided he needed to answer her in some way. He continued, as she was getting up to leave his office,

"I will say this: No, I personally don't think that there is an evil spirit that uses someone as a conduit to send harm from one person to another. This is more Rev's territory than mine, but if anyone asks me, I am in Rev's camp, not that of some evil spirit that has no power at all."

All the while he spoke, she was watching him, her head slightly bent down, but her eyes peering up at him, almost like the owls that George talked about. She left quickly as if she wanted to get away from him. Later that day she left a leave slip on his desk with a polite written request to use some of her annual leave to be with Big Boy.

Tom was determined to talk with Rev soon, not only about Big Boy but about George and Sheena as well. And he was going to look at that monograph on witchcraft more carefully. All he knew right now was that she was directly throwing out a challenge to him, and that if he were going succeed here, he would have to stand his ground. She was trying to define him as the enemy, and he was going to refuse to let her do so. She had accomplished her purpose in letting him know what she thought about his part in the illness of her son. That was going to make it hard to separate his personal feelings about her from judgments about her work capability.

XXI

The rest of the day was quiet compared to Arlene's opening salvo in the morning. He attended the hospital's weekly staff meeting, finding what new patients had come in, especially any who had mental health issues. It was also a way for him to get to know the staff better. When they knew what to expect of him, he thought, it made it a lot easier for them to trust him and to work with him. So far, the nurses and the doctors had been easy to work with.

He was seeing more and more people suffering from depression, physical and mental abuse, and especially alcohol addiction. Kids were using all kinds of substances.. Thank God, meth use hadn't hit here yet. He had even been called by Social Services to see a hyperactive little boy, eyes slanted, unable to connect emotionally with anyone. He was born a fetal alcohol baby, with a mother who never stopped drinking for the nine months he was in her uterus. Social Services wanted Tom to recommend drugs for hyperactivity. He said no, not until he checked with experts who knew more about this kind of treatment than he did. He never wanted to see children medicated in order to keep them quiet. What was wrong with this child would probably never be cured. He would need love and patience, and Tom didn't have a pill for that, he thought wryly. He had second thoughts about his refusal, but he stuck by his guns.

That wasn't good enough, making a decision not based on facts. He needed to find out more about fetal alcohol children, what worked for them and what didn't, before he, God-like, made any recommendations.

He asked Roxy to bring in Althea Begay, a young Navajo woman, and her son Willie. Roxy had been unable to stop her from drinking before Willie was born, because she had been up in Navajo and just recently moved to Whiteriver. Now, however, she kept after her like a hawk, making sure that the now pregnant again Althea got hold of almost no alcohol. She checked on her on a almost daily basis, until Althea decided to stay sober until after the baby was born.

Althea, when she came to Tom's office, confessed that she was scared of Roxy, scared that her three other children would be taken away if Roxy found out she had been drinking. Roxy was like a ferocious bear, she said. This was a side of Roxy Tom had seen, but he knew that what she was doing was right.

Tom looked at Willie. He was almost three years old, his face looking like it was smushed against the pane of a window. It was the only way Tom could describe it.

"Tell me about your son, Althea," said Tom.

She was nervous, clutching her hands together. He noticed.

"I'm not trying to figure if we need to take him away from you. I'm just trying to learn more about him, so we can figure out how to make your and his lives easier."

"Boy, do I need a beer!" she blurted out, then quickly said,

"But I'm not doing it. Roxy would kill me."

"What about Willie?"

Althea looked at him.

"You can see for yourself. He runs from place to place, grabs at everything. Don't seem to know I'm his mom. Don't seem to care. Just goes to anyone to comes along. Don't sleep much. The truth is, I get tired. How's he going to end up?"

"I honestly don't know, Althea. That's what I'm trying to find out. There are a lot of people out there who know more than me about children like your son. Your letting me see him to will be a big help in describing him to others who will know how to help him. When I learn what I need to know, I'll talk to you."

Willie suddenly grabbed Tom's pen and began to jab it into the orange carpet. Tom carefully took it away from the boy.

He watched them as they left his office after a few minutes. A pregnant woman who wanted a drink badly, with three children at home and a part-time husband, and Willie running ahead of her into the parking lot, oblivious of cars, oblivious of the snow.

What could he possibly do with all that?

It was alcohol that was killing the bodies and spirits of so many. It was like a quicksand they couldn't seem to get out of. He had no idea until he got there what so many tribes had to suffer. The children left with grandparents, the drunks with tuberculosis, the fetal alcohol babies born with so little chance in this world —what did he have in his professional arsenal that could possibly help them? Pill them all out? No, he couldn't do it. He was going to have to learn more.

He pulled himself up short. Wait a minute. Sure, one needed weapons to fight, and if he didn't know what to do, he'd better work like hell to find out – get consultants, talk to people with a history of working out here with success. But, first of all, they had to know that he cared, that they could trust him. He had learned that since he had been here. And he had gotten to admire the toughness of the Apache, their will to survive, their fighting spirit. They had the ability to struggle on, regardless of the conditions around them. And the outside world saw them so incorrectly, if they saw them at all. Outsiders either idolized them as the original ecologists with a special wave length to God, or they saw them as drunken Indians, unclean, lazy. They were not seen as real people by the rest of society. What a travesty.

He thought about Geronimo again. He was from an Apache tribe; after all, he was their blood, even if he was Chiricahua. In his searching for information, Tom had read that Geronimo's wife, his mother and his children had been killed by Mexican soldiers. When faced with this devastation, he walked to the site of the battle, saw his dead family, then went to the Tribal Council and joined them to take a leadership role. He joined revenge attacks and raids, especially against the Mexicans who killed his family, until he was finally captured by the Cavalry. Yet, even when captured and sent to Oklahoma, he maintained his leadership ability. But, he had also killed white children, men and women, rampaging up and down the country; he had killed other Indians; he had killed Mexicans. Tom frowned. No race has a monopoly on the good; no one race has a monopoly on the bad. The man had done harmful deeds in his lifetime; horrific deeds were done to him. He pulled himself up short. No, he was idolizing a man, and he refused to do like so many people about Indians. This man was a human being, not an idol. Not a politically correct Native American, but a man.

Rev had told Tom that Geronimo had great respect, in his later years, for the Christian faith, telling others that it offered more than the spirits of his fathers. So, Tom realized, this mixture of Christianity and Apache beliefs had existed for at least almost two centuries. It was taking years for this reconciliation of faiths to take place, for it all to sift itself out. This was what the N'dee, the Apache, had been given; this was the task that only they could complete.

He looked at his own emotional growth. He had to face it honestly. He believed that he was more mature now than when he arrived here. How could he tell? He had learned from his mistakes. He knew some things he had not known in Arlington: It wasn't his therapeutic techniques, his access to meds, his referrals to helpful resources. It was something that had changed inside of him.

Somehow, people, and even he himself, had never seemed satisfied when he offered his stock and trade. No, he now saw all of his professional knowledge as merely an adjunct to his real purpose in being here: forming relationships with respect, bonding with others, and caring about what happened to others. It was never going to mean putting them on a pedestal. One old Apache man had said to him, laughingly

"We still throw baby diapers out the truck window along with the beer cans. Don't you forget that."

In the rest of the U.S., Tom thought, we would say that all men put their pants on the way – one leg at a time.

Caring about people meant helping them to be what they wanted, to find the good in each of them, and to help it come out. There were those that thought that this kind of closeness with patients was not professional. None of these relationship actions that he mentioned were listed in the Diagnostic and Statistical Manual, but he knew now that that's what it was all about. Life was about touching another soul – don't ask him how he knew – he just did.

XXII

When he got back to the trailer that evening, his intention was to continue reading up on Apache ways. First, he grabbed a bite, but just as he was beginning to watch the news from Phoenix while eating a bowl of cereal and badly scrambled eggs, his cell phone rang. It was a familiar voice, one he couldn't quite place, until it hit him and sent a spark through him. Tentatively, the voice spoke.

"Tom, this is Ada. Remember me? How are you?" No need for a last name.

"Ada! Great! How did you find me? I'm glad I kept my old cell number. Where are you?" Somehow he thought she'd be right around the corner. Instead, she was probably back in D.C. All of a sudden, he realized he wasn't giving her a chance to talk.

"I'm at Fort Huachuca. You know, South of where you are. It's an intel center, which is right up my alley. Ed Baines told me where you were, here, in Arizona, like me! One year in an Afghan desert, and then they send me to a desert."

She laughed her old laugh. He had missed hearing it, and he didn't even know it.

She asked again, "How are you?" as if she really wanted to know. Pause in the conversation on her part, when he didn't answer right away.

"I just wanted to check in with you." Maybe she had done the wrong thing by calling him, she thought. He sounded different.

He jumped in to reply this time. "Fine. I'm learning the ropes here – different people, different ways. It's really beautiful up here. Ada, I had a lot to learn, and I think it's finally sinking in."

He had told her a year ago some of his feelings about working with wounded warriors. Now, he thought he heard a long breath escape from her after his last remarks. She knew what he had been through and she hadn't forgotten it. He felt his heart jump.

He spoke quickly. "Can we get together some time? I'd really like to see you."

"I'd love that." She paused. "In fact, I was wondering, the reason I called – well, my family is all up in Maine, and I remember that your dad just remarried – would you like to come down here for Christmas? It can't be that far, and—unless, maybe you don't—"

"I'll be there."

He jumped in quickly before she could finish her sentence. They kept talking until she had to go back on duty. They talked about where and when, how they would get together, everything but why. Somehow, it didn't matter. All that mattered was that she had called him. He felt happy and alive. He remembered that somewhere in his belongings he had a picture of her. She had given it to him just before she went to Afghanistan. There had not been a romance between them, but he felt an unspoken tie to her. There had been something about them that, at the time, he had felt would never be completed.

After they finally hung up, he went to a box in the bottom of his little closet, mostly filled with papers of value, a picture of his parents, and, at the bottom, the picture of Ada. There she was, light brown hair, no make-up, regular features. The smile widened her delicate mouth. He took the picture out and put it behind the keyboard of his computer. He had seen a guy do that with a picture of the Virgin Mary. He told Tom he didn't forget her that way.

There was a lot to do, he thought. He was like a kid waiting for Christmas. He'd get his Jeep ready, get its check-up done, even get some new underwear in Pinetop up at the Dollar Store. He really needed some underwear, anyway, he rationalized. Most of the time he had known Ada, their relationship had been strictly professional, no underwear involved. She was an intelligence officer whom he met when he needed to talk with someone about one of his patients.

Then one day he got brave and asked her to have coffee with him in the cafeteria. She said yes, and he remembered that she pushed her light brown hair back from her forehead to behind her ear. He didn't know why he remembered that. After that, they had a few dates, a few slow kisses, then, bam – she was transferred and gone. They e-mailed a couple of times, but almost by mutual consent they dropped their communication. Too many factors seemed to stand in the way.

No, that's not what happened at all, he admitted to himself. He, not she, quit writing. There was something going on in his head. It was as if he couldn't accept love. He didn't know why. How about now? Could he do now what was impossible before? He had been so absorbed with himself then, so selfish. The frosty Lou, she didn't have the capacity to hurt him; she was never going to love him. But with Ada he knew it would be different. Was he still afraid? That's what he was going to find out. Now, it all seemed possible again. Had he really changed in so short a time? Pretty hard to believe.

Stop the day dream. You've got work to do, he said to himself. The first thing he would do would be to put in his leave slips, make any needed contact visits and do reports on all his patients. Oh, yeah, he'd assign Ina and Arlene to check on patients out in the community. Roxy would help, too. Then he grinned to himself. We're just talking about a few days here, not a life time. He'd go see Rev when he got back when he had more time. Tom's research on tribal customs and mores got put on the back burner one more time.

He'd do it, he promised himself. And he was also going to get a picture of Geronimo for his trailer. He felt a connection with him, no matter what kind of person he might have been. He could do it after Christmas. He'd better look up the history of Fort Huachuca before he left, too. He was pretty sure that one of the reasons Huachuca had been built was because of Geronimo. But, there had been fighting on the border for a long time, so how did he really know?

Ina and Shirley noticed his new mood when he came to work the next morning. He was whistling a Christmas carol. They looked at each other.

"Mr. Doc, you look so happy!" said Ina. "Did you get some good news?"

He looked up, feeling embarrassed.

"In a way. An old friend called, and we had a long talk last night."

"Boy or girl?" said Shirley bravely.

"That's none of your business, Shirley," called out Arlene from within her cubicle.

Tom ignored her remark and replied to Shirley.

"Girl – a good friend. She's now stationed at Fort Huachuca."

Ina and Shirley grinned.

"A nice Christmas present." Arlene said. She had actually made a pleasant comment, but she didn't come out of her office.

"Maybe so," he responded. "Maybe so."

XXIII

The holidays were coming up fast. One more week before Christmas.
That Friday after work, Tom was finally ready for the trip down
to Huachuca. He gave his new tires their first real workout by heading down the Salt River Canyon road toward the South. He had to go
past the San Carlos Apache reservation and the copper mining town
of Globe. He headed straight into the Canyon, the second largest one
in Arizona. If this were the second largest one, he thought, the Grand
Canyon really must be something. The roads were sinuous and required
all his attention.

These roads were sinewy, like a snake, carrying him into the depths
of the Canyon toward the winding Salt River, then pushing him back up
and away from the river. It was nothing like being in the Shenandoah
Mountains he had crossed back East, where the trees hid the ground and
seemed like a protective cover. No, everything was bare down here. In a
way, it was frightening to see everything exposed, to understand that the
possibility of danger was always around the corner, whether it be from
rocks or semis who were trying to brake as they went. He saw cars down
below him, little matchbook cars. It was all open, exposed; nothing was
hidden.

After an hour of driving, the snow was beginning to melt off the top
of his Jeep, and the sun blazed. Water was running down the side of the
road, periodically bringing with it chunks of rock and pebbles. One lone
palm tree stood by the edge of the canyon, beckoning him like an allur-
ing siren. The sun, thrusting through his windshield, hit his face. It was

diffused, warm like the first beer on a summer's day. After the weather in Whiteriver, it was as if he were heading for the tropics.

After the roller coaster ride down and back up the Canyon, the landscape was changing again. Fort Huachuca, far from the Salt River Canyon, lay close to the Mexican border by about fifteen miles, established back in the 1870's to block the traditional Apache escape routes to Mexico and protect settler and travel routes. He had been right about Geronimo's connection. He had taken the trouble to look up the history of the fort before his trip.

He remembered an old soldier, a friend of his family, who had told Tom a story about the fort when he was just a kid. The man would be over a hundred now, and he was long dead, but he had told Tom how the families of the men at the fort had to leave on the train, hiding on the floor to escape bullets as they headed for Tucson. Real fighting had gone on there.

Tom looked around at the vast expanse as he drove. It was so different from the higher elevations. Not only was it warmer, but the air was drier. It looked like everyone's stereotypical post card of Arizona. There were even some Saguaro cactus plants standing erectly, sticking out of the dry landscape, seeming to wave their arms at him. The penetrating sun had the power to make him sleepy. Not a good thing on these roads. He stopped at a little roadside stand and drank down a coke with caffeine before he got back into the car.

A few hours later, he was nearing Huachuca which was ahead of him to the South. Things looked bare but felt even warmer than back in the Canyon. He began to see the signs for the post and for the town of Sierra Vista adjacent to it. He drove through Huachuca City, and turned right at the traffic light to enter the post. GPS Georgette had actually been a help to him this time. At the gate, almost instinctively, he reached for his wallet and his military I.D. It was always in his back pocket. No, of course not. He didn't have one anymore. He felt something akin to a twinge of regret, like a man who had been married, but now was divorced. There was also a regret that he and Ada didn't share this military bond anymore. Maybe it wouldn't matter to her. He hoped so.

He went through the procedures to get into the fort. As he had promised, Tom called Ada when he got to the gate. She sounded happy and said she'd wait for him in front of the Officers' Club. At least she hadn't changed her mind. At the front gate, Tom automatically saluted the guard, who checked his driver's license, inspected his Jeep, and directed him toward the O Club. He kind of liked being called 'Sir' again. He thought about Fort Apache and the similar layout patterns that had still existed there. The Cavalry had to be given a lot of credit to accomplish all they did with only horsepower as an energy source.

The Club was easy for him to find. His first impression after entering the post and heading for it was the sameness of it all; the military was always the military. Funny. He didn't mind being here. Instead of feeling trapped as he had before, he was now experiencing a kind of comfort with the sheer regularity, the order of it all.

Suddenly, there she was waiting for him in front of the building, wearing her BDUs, dusty boots and a smile that lit up her face. She hopped into his Jeep to direct him to the parking lot, kissing him on the cheek quickly. He was surprised to find that she was turning a bright red. He grinned. Here he was, all dressed up for her – at least for him – khakis, new sweat shirt and baseball cap. Wonder what she thought of him now without a uniform? And, this sweatshirt, a bad choice. He could feel the heat enclosed within.

The blush on her face had subsided. She patted his hand.

"I thought you might like a cold beer?"

"You bet! I don't drink on the reservation. It doesn't seem right."

She looked at him. He had changed. She couldn't put her finger on it. He looked older, not so much in age, just in the way he carried himself.

They went into the Officers' Club and sat at a table for two in the dark tap room. It was too early for dinner and too late for lunch. A lone server handed them two cold glasses and cold bottles of beer. It was the best beer Tom had ever tasted, he assured Ada. It could have been the heat, the hours in the car, or the feel of the frosted glass in his two hands. Or it could have been just being there with Ada. The pair stayed there for more than an hour, comparing notes, checking each other out surreptitiously. It was a safe, neutral spot for throwing out lines, for seeing if they got picked up. After he finished the beer, he found that he didn't need and didn't want a second one. Neither did she, nor did she comment on the fact that he was drinking less. But she notice, she told him later.

On Tom's part, he watched Ada as she took a sip of beer. She looked exactly the same as he remembered, only he noticed for the first time how professional, how calm she seemed. He hadn't paid much attention to her demeanor before, but for some reason it now made her more attractive to him. She seemed to have her life together, yet she wasn't controlling or self-centered.

Ada and Tom made the most of their time during the holiday week. They ate turkey with all the trimmings at the Christmas brunch, went to Christmas services on the post, in the chapel, holding hands when no one was watching. It was so normal, so natural, this fusing of their lives. Being with her seemed to be like a sort of balm that soothed his old wounds. There was a kind of regularity, a structure, about it, and she was one who made it so for him.

Love came so quickly that they wondered why it hadn't before back East. He knew she had almost a year to go out here, and he knew he had to go back to his job. Neither of them bemoaned the facts. Neither one raised concerns about what was, or even about what was to be. He found, to his surprise, that he was beginning to accept things like life and love and even death, somehow. He had the Apache world to thank for that.

Before he had to leave her, he found the courage to ask her to come up to Whiteriver, and she answered by saying that she could probably come up to see him in a month, maybe for a few days if she were lucky. They were saying their good-byes, she standing by the side of his Jeep.

"I'll try to get leave for a week. I'll let you know, but I may not be able to get as much as that" she told him.

"I can't do without you," was all he said.

Their last kiss was through the open window of the Jeep. It was a long, almost desperate one. This was the only time during his week's stay that he felt anxiety like he had felt in Arlington, a fear that things wouldn't turn out well, but the forebodings dispersed on the trip home. His old, worrying ways hadn't taken him over this time.

By the time he was back on the road and heading down the sinuous highway into the Salt River Canyon again, he was all right. He was doing his job, and she was doing hers. She said she loved him. Unbelievable! Everything would be all right this time. He hardly remembered driving back to Whiteriver. Once back there, his cell phone bill climbed to an exorbitant amount in one month. She didn't drop him; she wouldn't go on dating others, she told him. How could he be so fortunate? When he got back to the trailer and into bed, he fantasized about her coming visit until he dropped off to sleep

XXIV

The second day after his return to Whiteriver, Big Boy died. Ina told him that he died at home as Arlene had wished. Roxy had taken care of him just the way Arlene had wanted. Tom, Ina and Shirley went together to the funeral service at the Lutheran church. It was a gray day, raining slightly. At least it wasn't snowing.

The church was dark inside, old fashioned and traditional. It was the first time Tom had been there. The three of them sat together in a pew near the front of the church, one woman on either side of Tom. When he thought about it later, he wondered if they hadn't been protecting him in some way, or whether it was the opposite and he was their protection. The casket, open and small, sat in the back of the nave of the dark church. A buffalo nickel lay on each of Big Boy's eyes to keep them shut. That had been the reason for the nickels in the old days, Ina told him, but now it was just tradition.

He wasn't big at all, Tom thought. He was five years old, and a brain tumor had killed him. He remembered that Ina had told him that some people thought that the tumor was caused by Arlene's husband's drunken act of kicking her in the stomach when she was pregnant with Big Boy. Ina hadn't mentioned the witchcraft possibility, and Tom hadn't either. Maybe she didn't know what Arlene had been thinking, but he doubted it. Ina knew a lot about what others were saying and doing. Anyway, a church would not be the place to talk about witchcraft. He'd make sure to find out what she knew later.

After the service, all mourners passed the casket and went to the nearby graveyard. The closed coffin was brought out and lowered into the ground. Next to the grave, Tom saw some plastic toys, a little, wet teddy bear, a snow coat and a blanket with what looked like a Pendleton design on it. The family must have piled all of Big Boy's possessions next to the open hole, and, one by one, they were putting all of them on top of the closed coffin that had been lowered into the ground. The earth around the grave looked half-frozen and hard, but the rain at least was holding off for the moment, a respectful gesture from the skies.

Tom's first reaction to the lowering of the belongings into the ground was to think it was too bad to destroy things that others could use. Later, however, after the ceremony was over, he began to think of the act differently. Maybe it was a showing of love; maybe it was hope that Big Boy would be able to use his favorite objects in an afterlife. He didn't really know why they did it, but they must have had a good reason, rooted in the past.

Then, it came to him that he had not done either the research on the tribe that he had meant to do, nor had he talked to Rev. He hadn't even gotten the picture of Geronimo that he wanted. Ada's entrance into his life had put everything else to the back of his mind. He had not done what he promised himself to do. He told himself that he would make up for it, that he would take on the duties that went with his job, duties he had assigned to himself. No one was going to make him; it had to come from him. He wasn't going to run from what he had to do. God, I'm sick of hearing you whine, he said to himself.

This gloomy day, the funeral brought reality back to him loud and clear: This little brown boy was dead, and his mother thought he bore some responsibility for it. He needed to talk to Rev as soon as possible. He noticed that neither at the service nor at the graveside did Arlene acknowledge him in any way. None of the family spoke to him either. He rationalized this by the thought that they really didn't know him. Later, he had heard that Arlene's husband had not attended the funeral. It was said that he couldn't face being there. Ina and Shirley, however, kept with Tom at all times, one on each side of him, so he was never really alone.

As Tom stood there waiting for the appropriate moment for them to leave, Ronnie Kane suddenly appeared within Tom's eyesight, standing by Big Boy's grave as if he were an honor guard, watching over all. His eyes looked like eagle eyes, sharp and penetrating. He saw Tom and left his post, coming over to him directly. Tom had seen him in the church from afar and noticed that Ronnie seemed to be held in great respect by the mourners, almost as if he were still tribal chairman. People moved over in the pew when he stood waiting to sit down next to them. They deferred to him, letting him go first up to the casket. In church, he had not taken off his hat, but sat erect, hands folded in front of him.

Ronnie's first words to Tom were, "Good of you to come." He looked back toward the grave for a minute. "That boy deserved a full life. We say that everyone deserves a full life, unless violence or even witchcraft intervenes."

Tom nodded to be polite. He was still uneasy around Ronnie.

"Did you see that we hate death, and throw all belongings away that were touched by it? Have you analyzed that yet?"

It was as if he were continuing to lecture Tom on his people's history. Tom detected the sarcasm in Ronnie's tone, but he nodded as if he had not. Ronnie went on.

"Probably looks kind of funny to you, our putting Big Boy's things in the grave?"

Tom merely nodded again. He was not going to get into a conversation with him at this point.

"As a people, we hate death; we're afraid of it, like everybody else, but we go a step farther and believe that it's not good to keep belongings that have been touched by death. We don't want to have anything to do with people or things that can harm us."

He looked back over his shoulder toward the church. "This is not precisely a church belief, but it is for us, regardless."

Was Ronnie accusing him? Tom wondered if he knew about Arlene's seeing Tom as a conduit for evil. Probably. Everybody knew everything around here. He was really beginning to distrust this guy.

Ronnie stopped speaking. Ina and Shirley, still next to Tom, kept their eyes down. Tom still chose not to answer him. Ronnie continued.

"Death is a strange thing here, like everywhere, I guess. In a way, we think death is contagious, waiting around to get you and me. We believe that we must do certain things to keep the dead from coming back and getting us to go with them. Burying them is a way of keeping them from returning."

"I see," said Tom, noncommittally. Ronnie's lecture continued, as if he and Tom were touring the reservation.

"I guess you think it's kind of primitive that we think that some people have more power over death than others. We call that person a diyin."

Tom still said nothing. He was learning from the Apaches that he didn't have to comment. It was better to wait things out.

"Just a friendly word, my friend: Watch for this up at the hospital and other places. You never know who has that power over life and death. And, you don't want to get mixed up with it."

Ronnie slipped away before Tom could make another pretense of listening. It was if he had faded into the gray atmosphere around them. After he disappeared, Ina and Shirley came out from under their subservient looks, finally raising their eyes up toward Tom's face. Not here, Tom said to himself, but at the next opportunity he was going to confront Ronnie, make him say what he had in mind. He was getting sick and tired of this cat and mouse game and fed up with people around here who hinted at something awful, yet never came up with the proof.

His boots felt damp; he couldn't think of any reason to stay longer. Arlene was nowhere to be seen at the moment. The warmth and protection of the car sounded good to him.

XXV

It was really getting cold, standing outside here in the graveyard, and Tom was just about to tell Ina and Shirley that they'd better be going and to get into the car. He had had it up to his neck with Ronnie's lectures, and he was pulling up the collar of his coat when, looking over his shoulder, he saw Bessie Baha standing near the grave site. He hadn't noticed her in the church. She was plumper than he remembered, still wearing her old-fashioned, red camp dress with the white embroidery around the hem. Maybe the only one she had, he thought. A dark blue shawl covered up the top half of her body. Long wisps of feathers hung from her earrings, worn perhaps to mark this special occasion. Though Ina had told him earlier that Bessie was of the same clan as Arlene, she stood alone, behind the others. The rest of Big Boy's family had moved toward the edge of the cemetery; only two fat funeral directors were standing by the grave, watching as a worker put the cold dirt back where it came from.

Like Ronnie, Bessie seemed to be interested in Tom. She turned and looked at him, and walked slowly toward him and the two women, saying in a low voice,

"Mr. Doc." She smiled at him as if she were glad to see him. Her teeth were few and far between.

"Thought you'd be here. Bad business, this."

"How are you, Bessie?" said Tom. He noticed that Ina and Shirley were no longer beside him anymore, but were walking quickly away toward his Jeep. It was as if they were afraid of her. Funny. Their fears seemed only to give him more courage. He faced Bessie directly.

"Busy with them grandchildren. If you ever need to buy another basket or a cradle board or maybe some pretty earrings for your girl-friend, I'd sure like to help you out."

Tom was surprised at how fast the Indian smoke signals appeared to be communicating in carrying information about him throughout the tribe. Somehow, she already knew about his relationship with Ada

"Maybe some time. Are you related to Big Boy?"

"We're all connected. But this family kind of moves away from me when they can."

She looked around. "We're still the same blood, anyway. Nobody can change that but the Creator."

It was getting damper by the minute. The clouds had covered up the sun, and a brisk wind was rolling around the cemetery. Bessie's long black hair broke away from the beaded barrette holding it back and it flew loose in a circle. She didn't seem to notice. She reached into one of the deep pockets of her dress.

"Thinking you was going to be here, I made a little card to give you to thank you for your business. Every little bit sure helps." She brought forth an envelope and gave it to Tom. "Open it later. Not a good time right now."

"Thanks, Bessie. I'll do that." He put the envelope in his coat pocket and was preparing to move toward the Jeep, wondering if Ina and Shirley had not wanted to be around Bessie, as he surmised, or if they had just gotten cold and left for the car.

Bessie stopped him.

"Mr. Doc, you and me, I told you once, have some things in common."

He remembered what she had said before, but he listened.

"It's our words. They've got power in them. It's a burden to carry. I just want to say, be careful, like when you're talking to Ronnie Kane. He might try to steer you the old way."

Tom hadn't expected to hear condemnation of Ronnie from her, since they seemed to friends the day of his visit to her house. She herself had been talked about badly in the community. He was surprised that she would do the same thing to Ronnie. Maybe she disliked Ronnie as much as he was beginning to himself, but she covered it up to keep on his good side.

Bessie seemed ready to say more, but she turned her head to see Arlene coming up behind them. As if she didn't want to have anything to do with Arlene, Bessie picked up her skirts and went off without saying goodbye to Tom. Arlene, a few minutes ago, had been standing on the edge of the cemetery with her family. Then, she had begun to walk back toward the grave, her head down, ignoring Tom as he talked to Bessie. After Bessie's retreat, he stood alone for a minute, watching her, then he turned toward the Jeep where Ina and Shirley were waiting. He decided to wait to give his condolences to Arlene until she returned to work. He was not going to intrude on her private moment at the graveside of her son.

He moved toward the car. As he was unlocking the doors of the jeep for Ina and Shirley, Ina said in a low voice,

"What did she say to you?"

She was visibly upset. Her eyes were bright, her lips moving. He was beginning to see that there was more going on with Ina than the cheerful, funny woman he knew.

"You mean Bessie? She was warning me against Ronnie Kane. Funny thing to do at a funeral," he puzzled. He opened the Jeep doors for the two women, and they climbed in quickly.

"And," he added when he got inside," she gave me some kind of note to thank me for buying the burden basket I got from her when I first met her."

He pulled the note out of his pocket, opening the envelope. It was a card, probably meant for a child, with Winnie the Pooh figures on it —Eeyore, Pooh, Piglet, Christopher Robin and Owl. Inside it said Happy Birthday, but Bessie had crossed out the greeting and had written instead: "To Mr. Doc. Take care of yourself. Truly, Bessie."

He showed it to Ina who was sitting in the front seat next to him. She looked at the drawings, read the message and pushed the card toward Shirley in the back seat. Shirley read it quickly. They looked at each other.

"You tell him, Ina, tell him," said Shirley. She made a motion of trying to cover her head with her shawl, as if trying to hide herself.

"Tell me what?" he said. Ina pushed the button to make sure her window was rolled all the way up before she spoke. She turned back toward Tom, letting out a deep breath.

"O.K. We should have told you this before, but nobody talks much to you white guys about it. Everybody here knows, everybody – that Bessie is a -- witch. She can put a spell on anybody, family, anybody she wants to. A lot of us have seen things she has done before." She turned to Tom. "Please. Let's get out of here, go back to the hospital. It's not good to talk about these things, just causes more trouble, especially here."

"But, Ina, what does she do? I need to know." He wasn't going until he got an answer.

He could barely hear her response.

"People get sick, like maybe Big Boy. She can use someone as a go-between to get through to the one she wants to harm. And, you're not going to believe this, but there are some that think that Arlene is walking in her footsteps, trying to get some of Bessie's power – especially after Big Boy got sick. It's like a fight between these two for power."

She made a choking sound. "See, I've got kids, Shirley's got kids. We don't want to take chances. We try to be real careful around Arlene, let her do what she wants in the office."

Tom suddenly understood the tensions running rampant in the office.

"But Arlene claims she's close to Rev, and that she's a good church member," he answered.

"So do a lot of people," said Ina, grimly.

There wasn't much he could say right now, in this place. Tom drove off, keeping his eyes on the people walking away from the grave and onto the road. What else was going on that he wasn't aware of? All of this had triggered a kind of anger in him. He wondered how many people here were afraid for themselves and their families, yet having to live with that fear from day to day.

Ina spoke up, more courageously as they moved away from the graveyard.

"Go on, Shirley, you tell him the rest."

Shirley said in a small voice, "Did you notice that Bessie wasn't in the church? They say she's afraid of Rev. He's the one person she doesn't want to be around."

"And look," Ina added. She pointed at the figures in the greeting card that Tom had put on the car seat.

"You saw it, Shirley. She gave him a card with an owl on it. Probably thought he would keep it, because it was a gift."

She took her finger away from the card quickly. It lay where Tom had put it.

Shirley almost moaned. "Throw it away! Rip it up, Mr. Doc!"

"What's wrong, Shirley? What is it?" Tom was beginning to feel as if he were in a soap opera. He was tired of all this.

"Listen, tell me everything, and I mean now!" He had never raised his voice to them before.

Both women answered in chorus: "Death. An owl around someone means death."

Ina said, "She wants you dead, Mr. Doc. She thinks you're powerful. She wants you away from here one way or the other."

The women seemed close to tears. He had never seen either one of them like this before.

"Shirley, you have to tell him everything,"

Ina's eyes burned into Shirley, who looked as if she had been forced to talk.

"I think she's put a spell on my husband, something real mean and evil – I think she's done it to get to me – she thinks the tribal council gave me the house that she should have had. If she has made my husband act so bad, what else will she do?"

"Is this all? You've told me everything you feel about Bessie?"

"Yes, yes," they both answered.

"O.K., because it looks like sooner or later she and I will have to have it out. If I'm going to work here, and I care, she is going to have to lose some of her hold over the whole damn reservation!"

Ina worked up her courage again. She had one more thing to tell Mr. Doc, and she wasn't afraid of him, wasn't afraid of him at all. He was the one who needed protection right now; there was no one to give it to him, she found herself thinking. Only she and Shirley could help him.

"Mr. Doc, listen. Watch out for Ronnie, too. Nobody knows what he's up to, what he really wants. Just keep your eyes open."

He didn't answer. Nobody said any more for the duration of the drive. This damned place was getting to be like a battleground, only nobody ever knew who the enemy was. Were they telling him all they knew about Ronnie Kane? Maybe Roxy was the person who could tell him more about the man.

XXVI

The whole day had been exhausting for all three of them. The funeral service, the burial, Ronnie, Bessie, Arlene, and then Shirley and Ina's revelations. Tom decided to drop them off at their homes instead of going back to work. The work day was almost over anyway.

Shirley looked relieved, but, as she told Tom later, she had been worried at the same time. Maybe her husband would be angry if he saw her dropped off by Tom. She hadn't wanted Tom to know how scared she really was of what her husband might do. Even if Tom had known this, he was at the point where he didn't care. He wasn't going to hide from anything around here.

His first stop was at Shirley's, another HUD-built house that Bessie apparently had coveted. A wisp of wood smoke was coming out of the chimney as Tom helped Shirley out. She ran for the front door, saying nothing, not looking back. Tom was already turning around when Shirley scooted into the front door and disappeared.

By the time he drove off, he was occupied with examining his own performance as head of the Mental Health Department. He knew that, like in the Army, the unit depends on its individuals. He was going to have to work on seeing that his staff gained more confidence. Arlene and Ina were right – he would see that all three women got more training. And, most importantly, he was going to have to find a way to destroy Arlene's control over Ina and Shirley. As far as what Ina and Shirley had told him about Bessie, it had all seemed absurd to him. And, that idea of Arlene and Bessie fighting over control – that seemed like a product of their imagination.

Ina lived closer to Tom's trailer. When she got out of the car, she thanked him, but made sure that Bessie's card was left on the front seat. If she had been braver, she said to Shirley later, she would have taken the card with her and burned it. She didn't want to see Mr. Doc hurt. He had been a pretty good boss so far.

That night, Arlene and her family were exhausted. There had been a wake, food to prepare, Big Boy's room to clean out, and the other kids to take care of. Arlene was saying little to the rest of the family, but inside herself she was wondering where her husband had taken off to and if he would ever come back.

He'll probably come back, she said to herself. He's got nowhere else to go. He'll come back to me. She carefully closed the door to the room where Big Boy had slept, to make sure that he wouldn't be able to get back in it. She went to bed and slept without dreaming.

XXVII

Tom went home, and this time he didn't get on the phone to Ada. Instead, he sat at his computer. He googled White Mountain Apache, again finding the old information that he had seen before, but he read it seriously this time, looking for clues to help his understanding, comparing the descriptions of witchcraft, myths, religion, culture, even comparing life in the traditional part of the reservation, Cibecue, to what he was hearing about today.

It had really been an exhausting day. In another hour, he sat back in his chair, his back aching. What did he know? He wasn't sure if the old ways were still in existence, and he couldn't prove it anyway. But he did know for a fact that some people believed in spells and witchcraft. So, let's start with that, he said to himself. That's fact numero uno. What else did he know for a fact? An owl is a sign of impending death. That's number two. And people believe that an innocent person can be an unwitting carrier of a spell, for fact number three. He ran his fingers through his short hair. The fact that some people held these beliefs was certainly true, but the reality of those beliefs, that was something else.

Then, there was what he thought was the most dangerous part of all for the people: Great harm, what Rev called evil, was perceived by many to run through the community, and fear of these evils that were controlled by witches had caused people to possibly become sick, even die. They had to live under the specter of this fear all the time. If all that were true, he thought, then it was all the more likely that people who were considered good Christians did not want Rev to know what they were going through. They had been walking in two worlds, struggling to keep each world from knowing about the other one's existence

All of these undercurrents now made sense to him, in terms of what Sheena, George, Bessie, Arlene and even Ronnie were saying to him. But why get him involved in all this, anyway? Could it be that they all saw him as someone who could stand in opposition to witchcraft? Why would they think that an Anglo, a stranger, could do that? George and Bessie had both told him that he used good words, as they said. Maybe that's what they were looking for in him. Or did some of them see him as an opponent to their way of life? It was all sort of ironic. He was what people called a fair weather Christian; he only thought about it when the world looked good, and as for his so-called 'good words,' he wasn't sure what all that meant. That was another thing he couldn't understand. Why was he seen as someone who could stand up against the enemy?

Obviously, Rev was a proven fighter, but maybe they thought that Tom could fight, too. Maybe that was it. A fighter. He who had arrived here thinking of himself as a coward. This was all too crazy. Was he really starting to believe it himself? Hell! He should have done something about all this a long time ago, at least gone to see Rev again to get him to offer more explanations. At the rate things were going, Somebody was going to get hurt, either intentionally, or someone might do himself harm listening to these potentially dangerous messages. He wasn't afraid for himself, but there were a lot of others who were more vulnerable than he was.

He had been – and was – so besotted by Ada that he had not been paying attention to what was going on around him, but that was all right, he assured himself. He could love her and fight this mess at the same time. He had to. She would want him to. He was sure of that by now. Funny. His love for her seemed a lot more than romance, more than the kind of romantic feelings he had known so far. This was more solid. She gave him the kind of love that shored him up, made him stronger.

He needed to talk with her now. He reached for his cell phone and tried to call her, but got her answering machine that said she was on duty. He found himself needing her more and more, to sound out his ideas to her, to hear what she would say. He left a short message. He knew she'd call when she could. He went back to the computer, this time reading about Geronimo, trying to figure out how he came to be so strong.

He stared at the computer image of the man that popped up. His skin had the deep lines of someone who had lived in the sunlight, yet his eyes had a lightness about them. The sepia tone of the picture made his skin look bronze; it was obviously a posed picture taken by someone who did his best to make the Chief look like a chief. Here was a man who began with experiencing the murder of his family, his constant warfare and raids, yet ended up in parades and rodeos. Did he ever feel the loss of dignity? His last days were spent in exile from his people. He must have experienced the ambivalency of the two parts of his life. What did he really feel in the end? He printed the picture and turned off the computer.

Just as he was about to turn in for the night, Ada called back, from a world where witchcraft was not allowed. He found himself missing the Army.

"Tommy, sorry. I was on duty."

"No matter. I just wanted to hear your voice."

She sounded pleased. He told her about the funeral. He asked her what she thought about it and told her his feelings about the undercurrents of which he was learning. It was something so out of her element, she said, but she would try to give him a response anyway.

"It's definitely something I've never run up against, but is it really as weird as it sounds, Tom? Are you sure all of this is going on?"

He told her that he was pretty sure, at least he knew that this kind of thing had been going on for centuries, in one form or another. Nobody, however, wanted to tell him the whole story.

"Well, except for Ina and Shirley," he said. "I'm pretty sure they are leveling with me, but I don't know how much of what they are telling me is reliable."

"I've never experienced anything like what you are describing," she repeated. They told us about cultural issues like this in the Mid-East, though. You know I am experienced with covert action, and it's crazy, but it sounds similar – undercurrents all over the place. They tell us that when we come across cultural issues we don't understand, we have to step back and look at it objectively. For example, we need to know if there is some other more logical reason why all this is happening."

"I see what you're saying. It's like some kind of mind game being played by someone you don't know. I'm going to really work hard on keeping my own focus, my own point of view."

They changed the subject after Tom had talked it all out of his system. They discussed her plans to come up, now only a few weeks away. He had driven up to Sunrise, the ski lodge on the reservation, that was not far from Pinetop, to check it out. There was plenty of snow on the ground up there, and they could rent skis, even stay in a little lodge near the big one. He was surprised to find when he looked it up on the computer, that the elevation was almost 11,000 feet up there. It was like another world. The nearby lake was silver, the trees clearly defined against the patches of snow, but the most amazing thing to Tom was the scarcity of people. It was like being in another land, removed from the world of today.

They only had a few days, so there wasn't time to go far. Maybe the ski lodge would be perfect. Sooner or later though, people in Whiteriver were going to have to meet her. He wasn't quite ready for his whole life to be put in front of them yet. She said it would be heaven to get away from the desert for a while. He hoped she meant getting away with him, but he didn't say so.

Every time they talked, he found himself separating from the events of the day, and planning for the future. They'd go away for a couple of days, somewhere quiet, with no godforsaken owls, he said. What the hell, with the moccasin telegraph around here, everybody probably already knew what their plans were; the whole reservation probably already knew what room had been reserved for them.

This weekend he would go back up to Sunrise just for the heck of it, maybe even up to Pinetop to scout out a good restaurant. There were still some Christmas decorations up that made the whole area, with its wooden houses, look like a scene out of Alpine Germany. Ada would like that after her stay in the Sonoran Desert.

He was happiest when he was thinking of ways to please her. One little restaurant they might go to claimed to have bratwurst and potato pancakes. She'd like that, too. Did she ski? She had been stationed in Germany. It didn't matter. Nothing mattered as long as he could be with her.

XXVIII

Arlene was still on her week's leave after Big Boy's funeral when Tom decided that he needed to make the rounds of the patients he needed to see in the hospital. He was surprised to find that George's name was on the roster of newly arrived patients that morning. Tom looked at his chart and saw that there were a lot of medical issues listed, including diabetes, recovering ETOH alcohol abuse, brain surgery, depression. He couldn't tell among all of these medical problems which one was the presenting diagnosis that brought him into the hospital. It could have been any one of them, Tom thought. All he could tell was that the vital signs were not good, his affect slow and non-responding.

Tom was beginning the walk over to the men's ward, when Ina ran up behind him.

"Mr. Doc, they want to see you over in the dental clinic?"

She had a way of asking, not telling him things. There was a lilting kind of politeness about it that he liked.

"Me?"

"They've got a mother and a two-year old in there they want you to see. Mr. Doc, I would go, but I don't – you know," Ina was stumbling with her words. Tom picked up on what he thought that she meant.

"You will, Ina, I promise. We'll get you that education you want."

She looked happy but embarrassed. She added, "Thanks. But also, the mother is my cousin."

"That's all right. You'll do fine," replied Tom. "Could you see her after I do? Do you mind?"

"No, I don't mind. Just tell me what to do."

Tom walked on, entered the clinic and was taken into the room that held the dental equipment, a chair and a crying child. Don Shenck, the dentist, was standing next to the little boy, and a woman who appeared to be his mother was sitting slumped in a nearby chair. Don had picked the right profession; he was good at what he did, but his manner with patients left something to be desired.

Tom looked at the boy, then at Don.

"What's going on?"

The woman, who appeared to be drunk, thought he was asking her. She answered by mumbling,

"Nothing, nothing. Just want to leave here."

Don took Tom by the arm and walked him into the adjoining room.

"Listen, this kid's eight front teeth, uppers and lowers, are all eaten down in a circular pattern. These are baby teeth, but it's going to harm the permanent teeth coming in."

"What caused it?"

"Not uncommon. They give the kids liquid kool-aid in the bottle at night, and after a while it rots just about anything."

"What can I do?"

Don looked frustrated. "Social Services won't do anything – they say they'd have to take the kid away from the mother, and they don't advise it in a case like this. Can't you do something, diagnose the mom – do some kind of therapy with her?"

This was a new one. This was something that Ina could have done well if she had been given the training. She would understand how to work with a drunk mother and a child in need, without taking the boy away to a strange place. He answered Don Schenk.

"Let me speak with her. Maybe she'll let me get her into our group for alcohol addiction. That's got to be dealt with before she learns how to care for the child."

Don looked angry.

"Forget it. I'll deal with it myself. Sorry to bother you." He was motioning to Tom to leave.

"That child should be taken to Social Services now!"

"Just a minute," Tom replied. He went over to the woman and knelt down in front of her. Her breath was powerful.

"What's your name?"

"Myra — Maldonada — I ain't done nothin'. I want to go home."

"Myra, do you know Ina here at the hospital?"

"Maybe."

"I'd like to ask her to take you and the boy home. Would that be all right?"

She nodded slowly, as if trying to comprehend what he was saying.

"Good. She'll come in here and pick you up. Could you promise me one thing?"

"What?"

"Will you come back when you're feeling better and talk with Ina? We want to see what we can do to help you."

She said yes, but Tom knew it wouldn't mean much in the morning. But Ina would be able to approach her when she was sober, probably better than he could.

He helped her into the outer office. The mother was able to hold onto the hand of the boy who had now stopped crying. Making a quick call to Ina, he waited until she came to the dental department, talked to her briefly, and left for the ward. Don grudgingly assented to it all. That was all Tom could do right now, but he was going to do all he could to help her get off the beer. He might be able to save some lives down the road, not just hers but her family's lives as well.

Ina could do this. She had the right personality for it. He would push that training through ASAP. He had already looked at the spring catalogue of the community college in Whiteriver. A class was forming for helping professionals next semester. It wouldn't be the perfect answer, but it would give her confidence. Don Schenk might not have liked his decision, but it was more under Tom's authority than his. Come to think of it, he used to work with another guy named Don, and he hadn't thought much of him, either.

XXIX

After Tom left Myra Maldonada and her son, he went down the hall-way to the right and entered the ward, recognizing George from afar almost immediately. The curtains around his bed were partly open, and one of his hands was dangling limply from the bed. Tom had a momentary fear that he was dead, until he lightly touched George's arm, and it moved slightly.

"George, it's Tom. Remember me?"

"Mr. Doc?" A spark of interest came into his eyes. Tom shook his limp hand, holding it for a minute.

"George, what's happened? You seemed to be doing O.K. when Roxy and I came to see you."

George motioned to Tom to sit down in the sole chair. He didn't lift his head off the pillow. He answered Tom slowly.

"Maybe it's my sugar, maybe this old, mangy head is quitting on me. Don't have no energy. Can you pull that curtain closed, Mr. Doc? Too many eyes here." Tom did as he was told.

George opened the palm of his hand in a weak gesture, as if to welcome him. His head rose for a few seconds; then he lay back on the pillow, speaking in a low voice.

"You bring that chair close. I got to talk to you."

Tom obeyed him. The gray metal chair made a scraping sound of protest as Tom pulled it toward George's bed side. George turned his head toward Tom, speaking in a low voice.

"I knew from the first you was O.K. I know about people." His eyes were cloudy, but he seemed to look directly at Tom.

"I can see it in your eyes – that wound of yours."

Tom didn't protest anymore. He knew that George was right. They had a bond.

"Kinda healed over. That's good. Listen, I ain't got much time left. I'm a stranger in a strange land, kicked out by my own people. They's one here that thinks that strangers are evil, even if our tribes are not enemies. You know us Hopis and these Apaches, we're different people. We ain't fond of each other, but we know we're all part of the land." He was struggling to speak.

"But, you seen Kinishbah, yes?" Tom said yes.

"That's my people who built that, before these Apaches got here. So, see, I do have some place here."

Tom nodded as if he knew, but he hadn't really been aware of what George was telling him until now. George's ancestors might very well have built Kinishbah. He wanted George to keep talking anyway, about anything.

"These docs here they know some things, and they don't know others. I been cursed, but I accept it now."

Now Tom was alarmed. He saw that George's hands were shaking slightly.

"What can I do, George?" George slipped further and further into the pillow. His voice was fainter when he spoke this time..

"Two things. Reach into that drawer and take the kachina, Found Face, the one I was making the other night when you was there. I want you to have it. It won't do me no good anymore, and I want it in good hands." He was losing strength, but he whispered,

"And promise that they'll take me back to Hopi, to my people. Promise me. No burial here." Tom patted George's arm.

"I promise," he said immediately. It wasn't the time to protest with him.

"See, I got to be with my people, even if they was against me. They can't kick me out when I'm buried. Too many spirits around that would get them."

"George, who did it? Who cursed you? Tell me so I can help. Help me fight for you."

"Too late. I ain't — I don't want to say. There's them that say I'd be putting you in trouble if I did that. I've caused enough bad in my life. Don't want to do that anymore."

"Listen to me, George. I don't want to see you die because you think someone has the power to kill you. They don't have that power. We're going to fight against that."

"You got the power. I ain't got no more."

Suddenly George coughed, a paroxysm of choking sounds that set off the machines beside the bed. He tried to sit up. Speckles of blood appeared on the sheets from the explosion of his coughs. Tom got up from the chair, quickly opened the curtain around the bed and began to go the nurses' station for help, just as two nurses came running, moving past him to the bed. They didn't need him around now, and George didn't either. Tom saw the convulsive movements that were coming from George's arms and legs, but he couldn't make himself leave. He stood there, watching.

On the bedside table, looking dusty and crumpled, lay George's old cap. Without thinking, Tom grabbed it, and while the nurses were occupied with George, Tom opened the drawer of the bedside table and took out the kachina. He covered it with the cap as he moved away from the bedside, putting it in his pocket. He found himself almost running back to his office, as if he had stolen something.

If he kept the cap and the kachina, maybe George would be safe. On the way back to his office, however, he felt almost ashamed. He slowed down. Here he was acting on superstition just like those he was trying to help. Nevertheless, when he got back to his office, he put the cap, almost proudly, on his desk. He hid the kachina in his desk drawer. It would go home with him and sit near his bedside. These two things are just reminders, he said to himself, of the battle I have to fight.

He was on his way back to his office when it hit him what George had actually said. Someone had scared him into believing he was going to die, and he was acquiescing to their commands. Someone put the idea into his head. If anything happened to him, Tom thought angrily, could they be held responsible ? Could they be arrested for that?

XXX

After Tom went back to the office and put up the cap and the kachina, he told Ina and Shirley about George. Ina had just come back from taking Myra and her son home. The women said very little, except to express their sympathy about George. Since the funeral they had been acting almost motherly towards him. Shirley called the nurses' station a few minutes later, at Tom's request. The head nurse finally answered and she reported that George was calmer now, but it wouldn't be good for him to have visitors. When Shirley told him this, Tom felt guilty, as if somehow he had been the cause of it all. He made himself shake off the feeling. It wasn't a helpful way to react.

He and Ina were discussing her conversation with Myra Maldonado when Shirley interrupted.

"Oh, Mr. Doc, I forgot," said Shirley. "While you were gone, Sheena came in to see you.

Said she got out of the car and into the wheelchair by herself. She's gone to see Roxy, and she'll try you again after lunch. Her mother drove her over here."

"Good," Said Tom. "I'd like to talk with her as soon as I can."

Things had calmed down in the office at last, probably because Arlene was still out on leave. Ina was trying to begin to write a report about Myra with her limited English skills, and Tom was answering her questions about what verbs to use. He had the idea of making a form they could use for the reports in order to make it easier. He'd work on that soon. Shirley was filing papers into the gray metal cabinet.

After helping Ina, Tom, true to his word, started working on putting in requests for training for all three women, training that matched their abilities. He wanted to see them move forward, even get more formal education. He was concentrating on filling in the necessary forms, but every time he looked up from his papers, Tom noticed that Shirley was looking over her shoulder at Ina and Tom, as if she wanted to say something.

Finally lunchtime came, and Ina went home to her family. Shirley found the chance she was looking for.

"Mr. Doc, can you spare a few minutes?"

"Sure, Shirley."

By the looks of her, he had a feeling it was something personal, not office related. He motioned to her to come into his office, closing the door. She laughed nervously.

"My husband, if he saw us in here, would get mad at me." Tom looked steadily at her.

"And he'd be wrong."

She answered quickly, embarrassed. "Oh, sure, but you know what I told you about somebody putting a spell on him, to get even with me?"

"Here we go again," thought Tom. He was getting tired of all this. He thought about telling her that this witchcraft was nonsense, but he held his tongue. He wanted her to be open with him; he wanted all the information he could get.

Before he could respond, Shirley suddenly threw off the shawl she always wore. What Tom saw horrified him. There were bruises of all colors on her arms, yellow, purple, even black. Where her sleeveless sweater ended and her neck began, just at the line between cloth and skin, he could see two small round scabs.

She began to shake. "I have to tell someone. He'll kill me if he knows I talked to anyone. My kids, I have to stay alive for my kids!"

He could do nothing but hand her a tissue. He had to control himself.

"Why haven't you told anyone before?"

"He said if I did, he'd do worse. He said he'd kill me and take the kids. Mr. Doc, after you dropped me off from Big Boy's funeral, he accused me of being with you. That's when he burned me up here with his cigarette."

That explained the two scabs. Tom stood up abruptly, face flushed. An adrenalin rush of anger over what Shirley's husband had done pulsated throughout his body. He didn't even know the guy's name, and he didn't give a damn if his actions were caused by drinking or not. He didn't care if he needed a job; he didn't care about anything. All he wanted to do was to get even.

Let that guy pick on me if he wants to fight, not his wife and kids. For some reason, the words 'heart and mind and sinew' kept pounding in his head. He couldn't remember where the words came from. All he knew was that was how he was going to fight from now on, with heart, mind and sinew. He stood up.

"Come with me now, Shirley. We're going down to the tribal court. Somebody has to do something about this, and you and I will do it."

"But, I've got nowhere to hide, me and my kids. My relatives would be too afraid to take me in. They've got more than they can handle, anyway."

Tom had a sudden thought. "Let me call Roxy. I'm sure she'll let you and the kids stay with her until we get this straightened out. Come on. Let's get down to the court right now."

She stood up erectly, put her shawl back on her shoulders, and nodded affirmatively. She didn't look so submissive now. There was a spark in her brown eyes.

"O.K., I will – but I got to tell you one more thing." She looked angry this time.

"He's started trying to get in bed with my six year old." Tears rolled down her cheeks. Tom could have beaten the guy with his bare hands.

He opened the door of his office, grabbed his coat on the rack and ushered her to his car. He wasn't supposed to leave the office empty, but in this case he didn't care one damn.

Within an hour it was done, paperwork and all. There was a court protection order issued, and Roxy was waiting to pick up Shirley and the kids and take them up to Pinetop. Shirley went back to the office to grab her coat and wait for Roxy who already had the kids. Tom said to himself, "At least this is one so-called spell we've gotten the best of!"

"You'll be O.K. if I leave for home?" Tom said to her.

"Yes. My husband's not around now. Maybe he's even gone out of town. That's what some people are telling me. He'll find out soon, even if he's out of town, but it'll be too late by then. News spreads fast, but not as fast as we have been doing things today. Sure, I'll be all right, and thanks, thanks for making me do it."

Tom handed her a scrap of paper with his cell phone number on it and asked her to let him know what was happening. She thanked him and folded the paper carefully, putting it into her pocket.

She frowned. "Looks like I'll need to take a couple of days off. That all right with you?"

"Of course," he replied. "Just stay away for a few days until everything settles down."

"And the kids, too. I'll tell their teacher. But not where we're going. Word travels fast."

"You bet it does."

She put on her coat and went out the side door.

XXXI

Tom went home for dinner and wolfed down four kosher hot dogs with sauerkraut that had been placed on two buns. He had zapped the dogs, sauerkraut and buns in the microwave. They were moist and warm. He ate greedily. In about fifteen minutes, he found himself calming down. At least Shirley and the kids were in safe hands. He sat back in his only comfortable chair and let the food take effect. Stretching his feet out in front of him, he closed his eyes and stayed still.

But, in his mind, he was ferreting out prospects as to who could be playing the part of the witch. Ina and Shirley had said that Bessie was the witch, but there could be more than one person playing these tricks. The question was not who the witch was, but who had gone to such lengths as to try to kill George. They weren't sure, Ina and Shirley told him. They said that Bessie, Ronnie, and even Arlene in her own perverse way might be practicing witchcraft. So, he was left with no answer, as usual. This was ridiculous. Even Sheena could be doing it, for all he knew.

To his way of thinking, the truth was simple: Big Boy died of a brain tumor, George had drunk himself into a stupor, Sheena caused her own troubles — even that second-hand card from Bessie didn't mean anything. Maybe that's all there was to it. Except for what was happening to George. There was something going on in his mind that was influencing his illnesses. He was sure of it.

Wait a minute. Even Roxy said she thought she knew who was doing it. Maybe everybody knew and they just wouldn't tell him. It had been part of their lives for a very long time. After all, he was an outsider. How could he be trusted? What would he do with the information? Even if he knew, the reality was that he couldn't go to anyone, to the police, even to Rev, and tell them to do something. There wasn't a law against witchcraft, was there? Well, there had been in Salem, Massachusetts, and it hadn't turned out for the best.

He wasn't raised to believe this. He wasn't much of a church -goer, but he was a believer, and he knew that there were numerous warnings in the Bible about being wary of soothsayers and false prophets. His mother had told him about that once when he, along with a bunch of high school friends, had gone to a psychic. He hadn't known if she were really serious or not at the time, but everything in his background, his culture, told him that this was all nonsense. And that's what he'd go with. Cultural relativism – well, it could just go and screw itself. All beliefs just may not be equal, after all.

Someone out there was coming close to committing murder, if they hadn't already done so. The intent to murder doesn't have to be a physical act; nobody has to shoot or stab someone. All they need to do is control minds. There's no law that can get them, can it? How many people can be hurt without anybody going to jail for it? How can the proof of the intent to murder by mind control be found and used in court as evidence?

Only Ina and Shirley had been brave enough to identify Bessie as a witch, but nobody else had said anything. It could be that there were others who practiced the black arts, maybe a man or a woman. It could be Bessie or it could be somebody he didn't know, as well as somebody he suspected at the moment. How many damn people around here were playing the witch game? It could be Sheena's old boyfriend, no, probably not. It was more likely someone older, with a more powerful position in the community – it could even be Roxy, God forbid. What if he had turned Shirley over to her own enemy? Stop it! Get yourself together! No wonder people seemed to think that he, Tom, had been the conduit for evil since he had been here. He had been opening himself up to evil, letting it come in, letting harmful thoughts run through his body, sapping his own strength. He had been bewitching his own self in Arlington, tearing himself down.

"Paranoia is everywhere around here, even in me."

Here he was – the jerk who ran away because he couldn't face things. Because he couldn't help them, he ran. It was like going from the frying pan to the fire, he thought ruefully. Here he was, fighting another battle, but this time the battle was with the minds of others, maybe a whole coven of witches. He hoped he was up to it this time. Whoever was doing it didn't use a physical weapon. So, how can they ever be proved guilty?

He got up from his comfortable chair and went back to the computer oracle, searching for explanations, of what he wasn't sure. He read more and more on Wikipedia about Geronimo. There was a whole paragraph about his religion that fascinated him. It was taken from his 1905 auto-biography. It was about Apache religious views:

"…We had no idea of our relations and surroundings in after life… We hoped that in the future life, family and tribal relations would be resumed. In a way we believed this, but we did not know it."

That sounded vague but not vindictive, nothing in it about getting back at others. So far, Tom hadn't found any evidence in Geronimo's writings of witchcraft, or trying to avenge another person within the tribe. Nothing he said about daily life mentioned witchcraft. Then, again, maybe he wouldn't want to put something in writing like that that would be read primarily by Anglos. Tom read on.

"In his later years, Geronimo embraced Christianity:….'I have heard the teachings of the white man's religion, and in many aspects believe it to be better than the religion of my fathers…I believe that the church has helped me much during the short time I have been a member…I have advised all of my people who are not Christians to study that religion because it seems to me to be the best religion in enabling one to live right'….To the end of his life he seemed to harbor ambivalent feelings, telling Christian missionaries that he wanted to start all over, while at the same time telling his tribesmen that he held to the old Apache religion."

He was not surprised at Geronimo's words, especially the last part. He printed out all the pages, one of which included what looked like the same picture he had printed before, the sepia-colored picture of Geronimo in profile, with harsh lines covering his face. After he printed it. he cut it out, taping it to the top of the desk next to his computer and by the side of the first picture he had printed.

Geronimo had incorporated two ways of spiritual life into one, and his descendants, the Apaches, seemed to have done the same. But, at this moment, the older way appeared to be winning with the people. Wait a minute. He had no proof of that. The involvement of several people around him, and their belief in witchcraft as well, didn't mean that the whole community was like that. There might be many on the other side who were opposed to the old ways but afraid to face it directly. Hmmm, he thought. That sounded a lot like his own position.

No, not true anymore. He wasn't afraid anymore. He didn't even know why; he just knew.

XXXII

When he got back to the office the next day, Sheena was wheeling herself in the side door. She saw him and waved, pushing her chair toward him.

"Mr. Doc, look. I'm doing this myself. Nobody helped me! This is the farthest I've ever pushed myself."

Her eyes were more beautiful than ever. She looked around the office, seeing only Ina in her cubicle. Ina smiled back.

"Can I get this chair into your office, Mr. Doc?"

He helped her and closed the door. It was a tight squeeze, but they made it. Sheena's demeanor suddenly changed as soon as the door was closed.

She let out a sigh, losing some of her vivacity. She changed abruptly from the happy person who was wheeling around on her own power to a somber woman. She wanted to talk.

"You said I was to come, didn't you?"

"Of course, Sheena. I meant it."

"Well, it seems like everything I touch turns out bad. First, my boyfriend, then me, and now my sister's baby." Tom looked questioningly.

"My sister and her husband just lost their new baby, a beautiful little girl. She was named for me, to take my place in a way." She put her hands on the wheels of the chair. "Because I'm never going to be much good now. And now baby Sheena is gone."

"Sheena, I'm sorry." She pulled herself together quickly. No tears. No more signs of emotion. Tom thought of all the years Apaches had to steel themselves against enemies and hardships, and he suddenly understood why the mother he saw when he first arrived there let her toddler struggle to keep up with her, toughening him for the future.

"This is why I wanted to see you. The wake for the baby is tomorrow night at our house. We're building a big ramada outside with a fire. There'll be a lot of us. It's cold, but the fire outside will keep everybody warm. Our family is providing the food, and there's always beer even if we don't ask for it. That's just the way it is."

She looked down, almost ashamed, but she wanted to prepare him.

"Mr. Doc, please come. I need you. We need you. I don't know how I can hold up."

She was tensing the muscles of her arms and shoulders.

"And with you and Roxy there, nobody is going to hurt us."

"I'll be there, Sheena, as long as you understand one thing – I've got no special magic. I don't believe in the powers you are talking about. You've got to get out from under these beliefs, or they'll control you."

She nodded, seemed satisfied, but he wasn't sure she had really heard him about getting from under these beliefs of hers. Her main concern was to get him to be there, to protect her from these very powers he was trying to get her away from.

"That's why we want you to come, because this bad stuff doesn't control you."

He didn't know why, but he was uncomfortable about going, even though he had accepted so readily. This would be his second funeral, and they must trust him to invite him. That was a good thing. Well, maybe Arlene hadn't wanted him at Big Boy's funeral, but he knew for sure that Sheena did want him at this wake, even it were for the wrong reasons. He couldn't perform miracles, even for them. He was a stranger, really, just like George.

After she left the office, he made some notes, locking them in his cabinet. He hated not having a window to see what was going on outside. He walked over to the side entrance to look out the door. Early as it was, the day seemed to be getting darker. He thought of how cold it would be tonight under the ramada, its dry branches of little help this time of year. Winter provided no letup for the poor, the weary, the sad.

As he walked back to his office, Ina ran over to answer Shirley's phone, which was on its third ring. His thoughts were interrupted as he listened to her. She spoke, briefly, put the phone down and almost tiptoed over to him.

"That was the nurses' station. George died a few minutes ago. They asked if you'd come by."

Tom's heart sank.

He slung his long legs forward and walked briskly down the hall. It wasn't a long walk, but he had to cut through the waiting room crowded with crying babies, clumps of mud on the floor from the boots of people who had travelled by foot to get there, and old ladies covered in shawls who looked glad just to have a seat. Around them was always a slight smell of smoke, of campfires, lingering on their clothes. These babies here got born and serve their time and died too soon. There was always alcohol, the enemy, waiting to get some of them, waiting to attack them in their homes, waiting to destroy them in a way that none of their other enemies had ever been able to do. But, this day, at this moment, he walked past them all, not even acknowledging them with a greeting. He walked until he came to the men's ward and over to the curtained-off area where George had lain when he saw him last.

There lay George, still in his hospital bed and gown. His eyes hadn't been closed yet; the scar on his head was still visible, his bony hands clinched. But, he had gone to another place. He wasn't afraid anymore. Nothing had the power to hurt him. If only Tom could read the answers to his questions in George's dead eyes. But it was no use. The nurse appeared from the other side of the curtain, walked quietly over and closed George's eyelids as if she had done it a hundred times before for others. Then, she spoke to Tom, saying in a low voice,

"The last few minutes he was speaking Hopi. I understood some of it. He called your name. We couldn't get to you sooner. I'm sorry."

Tom said, "He's not a foreigner anymore." He put his head down for a few seconds before he spoke again.

"Rev's away. Can we get the minister down at East Fork to come? I think he would like to have some kind of ceremony. Just to say some words over him before they take him away."

She said yes. It was as if she acknowledged Tom as a relative of George.

"And, he wants to be buried somewhere near his people. I'll see what I can arrange up there. I'll have to find out more about it, where to put him. Maybe he's got some relatives. This trip's on me. I'll foot the bill. Please tell the funeral people to come talk with me. Do you know what he wanted with me?"

"It wasn't clear to me. It was like he was asking you to help him. I couldn't make it all out."

She paused. "You did everything you could."

"Probably not," he couldn't help saying.

He thanked her, silently asking God to bless George's soul and walked out. It had seemed useless to ask the cause of death. It was fear. It was murder, and the one who did it couldn't be arrested. They were still free to harm others.

George's death in an awful way made Tom stronger. It hardened him. When he got back to his office, he took George's cap out of the drawer where he had kept it. He was going to take it home and wash it. He had already taken the kachina home and put it next to his bed. Wonder what will happen to his shack. It was no HUD house. Nobody would want it.

But, when he drove by it some weeks later, smoke was coming out of the chimney and an old bicycle was parked by the closed door. There was a pile of what looked like trash next to the shack, and on top of the pile lay bits and pieces of wool and feathers. Guess that whoever moved in didn't think those pieces would burn well in the fire, Tom said to himself.

XXXIII

The wake for baby Sheena was in full swing when Tom got there. This was his second experience with death in the last few weeks, and his second memorial for a child, but he still hadn't gotten used to it. The little casket was propped up by two saw horses and sat by the side of the house, as well protected under the ramada as it could be. Male relatives were banding together in the corner of the yard by the fence, talking, drinking and rubbing their hands against the cold. The women were cooking in the kitchen and bringing dishes of stew and fry bread outside to a big wooden table. As far as Tom could tell, almost everyone there seemed to have some relationship to each other, except for him. On one hand, he felt honored to be invited, and on the other, out of place. He had never met the parents of the dead baby before. Sheena was his only connection to the group.

He was still reeling from another death – that of George. There was no one here he could tell about it, no one who would be sorry. There would be no wake for George Dewakuku. By now, his body would be lying up in the mortuary in Pinetop in a pine box paid for by Tom; it was waiting for Tom to complete the instructions as to where the body would have its final resting place. The minister from East Fork had not been able to come up to the hospital; he was recovering from a heart attack, he told Tom, apologetically.

Tom had called up to Polaca and Second Mesa several times, both towns being in the land of the Hopis, but nobody was able to help him. They kept referring him to others who might be related to George, but who had no telephones. There were no clear directions about where they lived, either. He had not been able to find anyone in George's clan to say the words that would carry him into the afterlife.

He hated to add one more thing to Rev's plate now that he was back home, but tomorrow he would ask him to go up to Pinetop with him and say a prayer over George's remains. It might not be a prayer in the Hopi tradition, but it needed to be done. He didn't feel right in asking Rev to go all the way up North to some Hopi land with him, but he knew Rev wouldn't mind going up to Pinetop. That would be better than his asking the sick minister out at East Fork, who hadn't known George at all. At least, Rev knew him.

His thoughts about George ended as he looked around for familiar faces at the wake tonight. He spotted a couple of men standing around in the back who had been referred to him for alcohol abuse. They studiously avoided eye contact with him, holding their beers behind their backs. The mother of little Sheena was standing, almost on guard, by the casket. She acknowledged Tom with a nod. Tom went up to her and gave her his condolences. He had greeted Sheena and her mother earlier when he came through the kitchen where they were talking with Roxy.

As he continued looking around at the crowd of people, he found that there was someone else here that he knew. There was Bessie, the ever-present Bessie at funerals and wakes. He should have expected that she would be there. He was going to have a talk with her, but this was not the time nor the place to do it. Roxy had once told him that Bessie made it her business to attend all kinds of events, partly for the food she could take home to her grandchildren, and because she relished being in places where she was both respected and feared. She was from a big clan and related to many. Tonight, she seemed to deliberately fail to acknowledge Tom as she had gone out of her way to do at Big Boy's funeral. He knew she had seen him, but she turned her back and began to talk with two older ladies sitting near her. That was a relief. He wanted to deal with her on his own territory, in the office.

Tom had been right about the weather. It was bitterly cold; the air had a sharpness about it. It had been his plan to make this a courtesy call, then to leave, but Sheena wheeled over to the open door of the kitchen and motioned to him. He saw her look past him warily. She had been drinking. He could tell by her dilated pupils, as well as the open beer can he could see that she had put between her body and the arm of the wheel chair. She looked as if she were at a party rather than a wake.

She said excitedly to him, "I've got to tell you something! I'm better, Mr. Doc. I know you won't believe it, but I've had some feeling in my right big toe. Roxy thinks I'm better, too."

Tom thought it was the drink talking, but she pointed to her right foot shod in sandals. "Look." Her right toe did seem to move slightly.

"Roxy told me to come up to the hospital tomorrow."

Tom replied," Sheena, that's great. But you won't know anything for sure until you get it checked out, probably at Phoenix Indian Medical Center." He wasn't going to encourage her euphoria.

She smiled anyway. She wasn't going to give up her hopes that easily, she told him, whether he believed it or not. Tom guessed that she was covering up her despair. Boldly, she pulled out the can of beer from next to her body. She took a long drink from it and tossed the empty aluminum container into a trash can at the door, almost as if she were daring him to do something.

She gurgled with laughter and spoke in a loud voice to the people outside. "Listen to this, everyone! I'm going to take up my bed and walk! What you do think of that?"

Nobody responded. She went on. "Rev would be pleased with me! I'm going to be saved!"

Her emotions, however, were riding for a fall. Tom had seen this before with others. Suddenly, she slumped back into her chair and whimpered. Nobody moved. She was left alone. She pulled a second beer can, now warm, out from between her body and the arm of the wheel chair. Holding it to her lips, she gurgled down the whole can, throwing it this time with a strong thrust into the bushes in the yard. Tom knew it was useless to speak with her while she was drinking.

The wake was getting louder in the background. Voices rose in laughter and anger and wails as the night progressed. Tom was wary; he wanted to go. After this fever pitch, anything might happen. He was right. Suddenly, the father of the baby broke loose out of the group of men, wailing, and staggered up to the casket of baby Sheena. He began to wail in a way Tom had never heard from any human being. It was a cry of despair learned from generation to generation. His voice rose to a yell.

"I saw her move!"

He went toward the baby before his wife could stop him. He picked up Baby Sheena in her long dress and beads and cradled her in his arms, walking her around, showing her to all. The crowd was working up to a fever pitch.

"It's a cure! A miracle!"

An old lady yelled out in English, and the others followed, speaking in Apache.

Suddenly, there was Bessie, prominent in the midst of it all. She had gotten up quickly from her chair in spite of her weight and moved toward the father. With a fierce motion of her arm, she pointed at the father and said,

"Billy, put the baby back now."

He stopped, suddenly sober. The crowd quieted, stumbling, moving back toward the fence.

"Put her back to rest. That's the way it's supposed to be. She's gone. Our Creator speaks to me. Put her down now, or something will happen."

There was dead silence as Billy obeyed. He put the baby's body back in the casket and stepped back with his head down. People had begun to sober up rapidly now and fade away, escaping into the kitchen and out the front door. Some sat in the living room; some remained wordlessly on the benches outside. It was over. Tom wanted out of there.

Bessie stood still a minute, watching the mourners leave one by one. Sheena had disappeared, nowhere to be seen. Only the old people, maybe the brave ones, remained. Bessie deliberately walked over to Tom, while everybody remaining, now silent, watched her. It was as if she were a chief of old. She held her head high as she stood in front of Tom. No longer was she the poor grandmother foraging for her grandchildren.

"You don't know me, Mr. Doc. I walk with the Creator. I can command others. They listen. I decide what is needed. They think I cast spells, but they harm themselves, not me. I have the power here inside me, and those who come to you for help will find that out."

She turned without waiting for him to reply, walked into the kitchen and out the front door, holding a bag of food in her hands that she had picked up from the kitchen table. She disappeared into the night.

Sheena remained in the kitchen, hidden behind her mother, watching until Bessie could no longer be seen. She was as sober now as everyone else. After the front door closed behind Bessie, Sheena started to moan.

"See! It is her! She decides who lives and dies. She'll keep me from getting better. Aiyee!" Her yell was long and piercing.

"She's going to keep me from being cured!"

Her mother had tears running down her cheeks, but tried to comfort her daughter, speaking in Apache. There was nothing more to do or say. Tom left. He was not going to dispute with Sheena at this time.

XXXIV

It took Tom a long time to stop going over what happened at the wake. He found himself thinking about it at odd moments. Questions but no answers. Always the same. Things happening he couldn't understand. Would there never be an end to it? What happened to his grand resolve to confront Bessie? When she left the wake that night, she had definitely asserted control over all, including him.

The day after the wake, Tom galvanized himself to take some future actions. He did two things: First he made a call to Rev to ask him to go up to the Pinetop mortuary with him. And, second, he was going to Bessie's house to confront her after his trip to Pinetop.

Rev said yes, he would go to Pinetop. Tom picked him up in the Jeep, and they made the trip in record time.

"Whoa, Son! George isn't going anywhere. You're acting like a wild cat going after prey."

"Sorry, Sir," said Tom. He slowed down. "There are things I promised myself to get done. Guess I'm over-doing it."

"I see. Can I ask you what has given you all this sudden resolve? You don't seem to be asking questions anymore. It's as if you've made up your mind about some things."

"That's true." He told Rev about the way George died, his suspicions that a spell had been put upon him.

"That was the breaking point with me. I want to find out who did this – clear up this mess."

He told him about Shirley, Arlene, Bessie, even Sheena. It took the whole half-hour they were in the car. Rev let him go on, not interrupting.

Finally, Rev said, "So, what are you going to do about it?"

"I am going to Bessie's, bring her out of that house to my office. We're going to have it out."

"My boy, I've got to say one thing: you are a heck of a lot like me when I was young. I thought if I confronted everything that was wrong, it would all be solved. Well, I've got a surprise for you: It won't be solved."

"But I thought," said Tom.

"Listen, go on, confront her, but be advised that it won't end there. After you have it out with her, come on over to the parsonage and talk to me. Maybe we can figure out something to do together. Will you do that?"

"I'd like that. I'd like your support."

"O.K. Let's do it."

By the time they got to the mortuary, Tom had talked it all out. He parked facing a two story building with a front porch, and they got out. They spoke to the receptionist, and they were ushered into a big room full of coffins and caskets by a man in a black suit. Some of the boxes were big; some were small. Some were bronze; some caskets were puffy white on the inside. They were empty; they were for sale. Going through the sales room, the very fat mortician in the black suit took them into a smaller room, cold and dark. He looked like one of the men at Big Boy's funeral. He stood there on duty while Tom and Rev were shown a plain pine coffin. The lid was closed.

"Do you gentlemen want it opened? We did the best job we could, but it's been some time now, and I'm afraid......"

"No," said Tom quickly. "We just want to say a few prayers."

The mortician backed out, leaving them alone with the coffin.

Rev had obviously been through all this before. He put on a simple white stole that he had in his pocket, and began to pray aloud. Tom didn't know what the words were from, probably something Lutheran, but he felt a kind of calmness come over him. When it was over, he felt at peace and hoped that George was at peace also. He reached over and patted the coffin. They left in silence.

On the way out, Tom spoke with the funeral director who asked in a low voice about where George's body was to be buried. By now, Tom had given up on finding George's clan or relatives. The funeral director looked relieved. He said that he was only too glad to help. He had contacts up North near Tuba City who could help them. He'd call Tom the minute they could find possible arrangements, to get Tom's consent.

"Do you have a preference about when the body should be moved, Sir?"

"No, as long as it happens soon," answered Tom. If he were going up North for the burial, he would need to be away from the office at least a day. Better do it right away.

The two men went back down to Whiteriver slower than they had come up. It was the dead of winter, but strangely enough there had been no new snow for a few weeks, just dry cold and sometimes an icy rain. The old snow lay covering the ground, but it looked used and dirty now. Everybody in Pinetop was talking about the lack of snow, about what it would mean for the farmers who had enough hard times anyway. Even in Phoenix, people said, they were worried about the lack of snow in the mountains, for it would mean less water for them in the summer. That was what the Anglos were talking about, but the Apaches wondered if they were going to have a dry summer season that would burn up all the timber when the lightning came with the summer storms. It wasn't helping business at the ski lodge, either.

Tom felt relaxed on the way back. He and Rev had done their duty. They were now free to talk about other things. Rev spoke, moving his hand toward the right window of the car in an expansive way, toward the downward slope and the hills beyond. There were large patches of untouched snow primarily in the shady places.

"Sure hope this doesn't mean big forest fires this summer. A lot of good timber means good profit for our logging business. Well, at least there's one good thing about the forest fires: The men get hired by the Bureau of Indian Affairs to fight the fires in places all over the West. They get good pay, and I hear that spouse abuse drops by a lot. Thank God for that. About this weather, though, we had some pretty good storms weeks ago, but nothing seems to be coming now."

He looked out the passenger side of the window.

"Well, speak of the devil! Tom, look over on that hill."

About a hundred yards from the road, there was a puff of smoke and a searing fire that suddenly rose from the soil to the top of the pine trees. It happened so fast that the whole area in a hundred-foot circle was up in flames.

"Lord, this isn't supposed to happen this time of year! We better get back down and call the BIA right away."

Tom agreed and they sped down the hill even faster than they went up, in a hurry to reach a telephone. For some dumb reason, Tom had forgotten to charge his, and Rev wouldn't have known what to do with a cell phone if he had one in his hand.

They found out within a few hours that the fire had been put out quickly before it had time to spread. The BIA said that fires like this were usually caused by spontaneous combustion, but that would hardly be likely this time of year. They were exploring the possibility that someone had started it. There had been a couple of suspicious conflagrations within the last month.

"If someone was crazy enough to start it, it wouldn't have done much harm, anyway, in the winter," Rev told him later. Well, we've got bigger things to worry about than that. Maybe it was God's way of saying hello to George."

Tom looked at him. He wasn't kidding.

Tom dropped Rev off at his house and headed back to the office. It was past the end of the work day, and Shirley and Ina should have been gone over an hour by now. Shirley had only been back from her stay in Pinetop a few days. Tom wanted to make sure he had turned off his computer and put away some records he had left out on his desk.

Walking in the side door, he flipped on the light switch next to his department, went to his office to power down the computer, and grabbed the files on his desk. He walked toward the gray government file located near Shirley's desk and opened the top file drawer. He stopped, surprised. It was empty. There was nothing in the drawer.

Hurriedly, he opened the other two drawers below it. Nothing. All the files were gone. He went into Ina's office and then Arlene's office, hoping that someone had decided to take them all out for some reason. Nothing. He searched through Shirley's desk drawers. Nothing.

Somebody had taken all of their files on purpose. There was no other explanation.

He picked up the phone and called Shirley, next Ina; Arlene was still on leave. Neither woman had any idea what happened to the files. They were as shocked as he was.

He could do nothing more tonight. Somebody had done it on purpose. What the hell.

They would have to start all over. First, he would report it to Ben Altaha, and then they would have to get locking, really locking file cabinets. Everyone would have to make sure that their passwords were changed to their computer files, to make sure no one was after those as well.

Always questions, always why and who. Was someone trying to destroy the records for the secrets in them, or were they trying to harm him?

XXXV

Yesterday was a heck of a day, but he was determined to put it behind him, at least for the time being. He was going to do what he told Rev he would do before anything else. The sun was out in full array when Tom drove down to Bessie's. He had refused Roxy's offer for help; he wanted to do this on his own. As he drove up to the ramshackle house, he saw a long clothes line stretching from the house to the fence bordering the house. Clothes of all colors were moving with the wind. They looked like semaphores to Tom, oranges, whites, even variegated colors. Maybe Bessie was sending out signals to the Creator.

He stopped the car in front of the house. Without hesitation, he walked up to the front door and knocked firmly. He couldn't hear sounds of any children in the background. He had to wait no longer than a few seconds before she opened the door. Bessie came outside, closing the door behind her. There was no invitation to come in. She stood in front of him, arms folded, as if waiting for him to explain his presence.

"Bessie, I need to talk with you. Some things are happening around here which directly affect my patients. I come to you since you seem to have set yourself up as a power figure."

He never liked to use the word 'patients', but in this case he used it as if the people who came to see him belonged to him, not her.

She said nothing. He went on. He was going to finish this up.

"People whom I know and I want to help are hurting, some dying, because of what they think is a spell put upon them. Since you seemed to infer that you have the power to do that when you spoke to me at the baby's wake, I need to tell you something."

Still no response.

"I am asking you to clear all this up, to admit to these hurt ones that you do not intend to do any more harm to them, nor do you have the power to do so. In order to do that, I will set up a time and place for us to get together, you, me and my patients. I'd like to do that up at the hospital sometime next week. I'll send a message out to you to confirm the plans. Roxy will be coming this way, and she'll bring you the information."

Bessie finally unclenched her arms. Holding them rigidly at her sides, she replied slowly,

"You don't seem to understand. How did you get through all that schooling you got? You and nobody else tells me what to do. I don't go and come when you command it. You may get away with that Anglo attitude with the others around here, but not me. I do what I do when I choose to do it, and that goes for what I do to other people around here as well. I'll be here long after you are gone, and the reason why is because I am stronger than you; I'll outlast you."

She turned away from him, shaking her skirts as if to rid herself of an insect, and saying over her shoulder,

"So, go on back to the hospital with your books and hope that nothing worse happens to you than you have already experienced."

He noticed that her English was much better today than when she had been asking for his business. He heard the threat and her refusal; he had to answer her.

"You have made yourself clear; now I make myself clear. If any more criminal acts occur to my patients, I will inform the police."

"Police!" She spat on the floor of the porch. "They are as weak as you are. And don't bother telling me you'll tattle to Rev about me. He has known me for a long time, and I'll win over him and his kind any day. Do you really think anybody can pin blame on me based on the stupid superstitions of my people? You'd be the laughing stock of the town."

She opened the door to go in, saying, with a half-grin, "Better watch your step as you leave. There are plenty of snakes around here."

There was nothing he could do but leave, so he got out of there. He didn't know whether he felt better or worse. In one way he had lost, but in another, at least, he had faced her directly. She let him know that she was not through exercising her power. He'd have to be ready for what she might do next. He needed to get hold of the people he was trying to help, and do it quickly. He thought about Rev's idea that he and Tom join forces to fight against witchcraft. Maybe that needed to be explored as well.

He almost felt his Jeep groan as it started up and retraced its track back to the hospital. That's the way he himself was feeling right now. He could picture her in the hospital destroying their files. Wonder if she had a big bonfire last night.

XXXVI

Today was the day for their weekly staff meeting. They spent most of the time talking about the stolen files. Arlene was back, expressing surprise at what had happened. She said it was her guess that some of the undesirables who came into the office had done it. She was somewhat mollified when she found that Tom had put in for a week of training for her in Phoenix. She showed no signs of sadness over her son.

He had also put Ina in for a class at the local community college focusing on basic English composition and grammar and another one on providing assistance to alcoholics. Third, Shirley was going to learn record and time keeping, but that would wait until the court case with her husband was finished.

They didn't really have a conference room where they could meet as a group, so the three women were accustomed to group their chairs around the outside of Tom's office, which was a bigger space than in front of theirs. They had gotten used to the staff meetings; they all learned a lot about the needs of the community in the process. The sharing had become something Ina and Shirley looked forward to.

Their department at present was able to count fifty-seven patients on their rolls, or at least fifty-seven that had been self-referred or sent by the hospital. Fortunately, Tom had, weeks earlier, summarized patients' records in his computer. Some patients were hard to track down, and a few others refused their services. It was their job today to have a brief discussion on the status of each one and determine what needed to be done next. One of the problems was how to cover the farthest edges of the reservation. Cibecue had a clinic of its own, but there was still a vast area of terrain out there, and most people had no transportation. It was hard to discuss these personal issues when there was no privacy, since people did occasionally wander through the department from the side door access. It was evident after the robbery that they needed a more private office space. Tom would ask Ben about it.

Tom went into his office and sat at his desk before Ina, Arlene and Shirley pulled up their chairs just outside his door. Not perfect, but it had to do. Tom had his notes in his hand, his elbow on the desk. He was just about to bring up case number one, when Shirley suddenly got up, ran to her desk and grabbed the big dictionary sitting on it. He thought she must be really improving to want to find out the spelling of a word, but before he could say anything, she ran into his office and threw the dictionary on Tom's desk with a slam.

"What's going on?" said Tom, startled. The other women sat, looking.

Shirley picked up the dictionary. A huge, hairy spider lay flattened, it legs spread out in all directions. Tom couldn't help but start. Arlene ran for paper towels, and Ina was laughing nervously.

"A tarantula, Mr. Doc," said Shirley, her voice calm. "I've seen them before. You must have brought it in on something."

Tom was now standing up, shaking off his trousers, stamping his feet. The thought of more of these creatures on him gave him a shudder.

"But, it's so big – how could I have done that without seeing it?"

"If you're thinking I did it, I didn't!" Arlene, papers in hand, seemed upset for the first time.

"Arlene, nobody has accused you of anything," said Tom.

All of a sudden a new voice was heard, and a man's laughter broke out. It was Ronnie Kane, coming in from the side door.

"You sure do have a love for all the Creator's critters, don't you, Mr. Doc? Did you tell these girls how that little old reptile at Knishbah scared you, too? For a warrior, you sure do scare easy!"

He kept laughing, moving off toward the main part of the hospital.

"Don't let him get at you, Mr. Doc," said Ina. A lot of men around here have that kind of humor. It's just their way."

"Yeah," said Shirley, "but these spiders can really give you a danger-ous bite."

He tried to give her a half-smile. It was just another episode, another part of living here.

Or was it?

"Shirley, thanks! You are one brave woman."

She smiled, blushing.

"Now," said Tom, "let's get back to business. Looks like I'm going to have to say something to Ronnie Kane before long," he thought to himself.

He wondered to himself how a thing like that big spider could creep in here without being seen. Odd how his encounters with snakes and insects seemed to happen when Ronnie was nearby. It just didn't seem possible that he had inadvertently brought something as large as a taran-tula in the office hidden in his clothes without noticing it.

XXXVII

Ada couldn't get more than three days off, she told him, regret-fully. Including the time it took for her to drive up and back to Whiteriver, they would be lucky to have a couple of days together, at most. Something had come up at work at the last minute. He assured her it was all right. At least they would be able to see each other. Tom told Ada to meet him Friday evening after his work day, leave her car in the hospital parking lot, and they would head for the ski lodge in his car and come back down to Whiteriver by Sunday, so she could get on the road to Huachuca in time to get some sleep before work on Monday morning. It was a crazy schedule, he told her, but it would work.

"I have to warn you. I can't ski," she said.

"Good," said Tom. "We can sit by the fire instead." He paused. "Just to be with you is all I want."

She laughed.

"Me, too. Great minds think alike. I'll call you when I get on the reservation."

Tom worked all day Friday, completing paperwork, seeing people as if he were going to be out of the office, as he had originally planned. When Ina and Shirley found out he was meeting his girlfriend, they teased him, asking him why he hadn't chosen a nice Apache girl instead. Even Arlene smiled a little. Since he wouldn't be taking time off from the office, he wouldn't have to put her in charge now, which was a relief. She had the seniority, but he had dreaded taking that action. Fortunately, she hadn't known about his original plans, or she probably would have been upset.

It had been a cloudy day. He hoped it would snow when they got up to the lodge, but he also hoped that it would hold off until they got up there. That would be perfect. Everyone around here was still hoping for more precipitation. He had a sudden thought. Maybe he had better go out to his Jeep parked on the lot to make sure he had not forgotten something. He had packed everything he would need for the weekend into the back seat of his car that morning. What about that extra sweater he might need? It was pretty cold up at the lodge. Maybe he'd better go up to the trailer and bring it down to the car. He wasn't exactly sure what time Ada would be arriving. He wanted to, but he was not going to call her every ten minutes while she was on the road.

As Tom left through the side door of the hospital, there was a smell of smoke in the air. Funny, but he had kind of gotten used to it – that ever-present wood smell. But wait a minute. This was different; it was stronger, somewhere close by. He looked up the hill behind the hospital. In front of his trailer, something was definitely different. A big pile of wood or trash or something was sitting in front of the entrance of the trailer. It had not been there when he had left this morning. The smell was coming from that direction.

He saw a figure standing next to the pile, that now, upon a closer look, appeared to be a pile of wood. He almost jumped back when fire burst through from the wood. It lit up the sky. Tom automatically let out a loud yell, like a war cry. It was his trailer that sat about three feet from the fire.

"Hey, you! What the hell are you doing?" He found himself yelling at the top of his lungs.

The figure looked in Tom's direction, then he ran, after throwing something into the fire. Tom could only see the person's brown coat and hood as he ran up the hill and disappeared into the brush behind the trailers. As quickly as he could, Tom reached into his car and grabbed a blanket that had been covering the items in the back seat. He ran toward the trailer and the fire. By now, what was a huge bonfire was dangerously close to eating at the wooden steps, the entrance to his home. It was not a small brush fire; it had to be fueled by something.

His yell must have been heard in the hospital. First Ina, then Shirley and even Arlene appeared, followed by two patients. They all stood in the parking lot watching. Shirley turned and ran back in, leaving Arlene and Ina. Ina ran up toward the trailer. She had also seen the figure as he ran away; she was running toward the back of the trailer.

Tom reached the fire and began beating at it with the blanket, trying to smother it, but it roared up even more when fed by the extra oxygen he was advertently creating. It was eating at the bottom step of the wooden stairs leading to his door and going toward the wooden platform that served as the entrance to the trailer. Tom stamped at the fire with his feet, throwing the blanket over the highest flames, until his hands couldn't take it anymore.

By now people were coming toward the fire from all sides. Tom had been forced to step back. Dalton, the young hospital sexton, appeared out of nowhere, running with two buckets of water. He dumped them directly on the fire. It hissed, fell back, keeping the porch from going up in flames for the time being. The steps and the bonfire composed of what looked like sticks to Tom were still billowing out smoke and flames. Tom had a sudden fear that the propane tanks would explode and set off the whole trailer.

It was all happening at once. Time seemed to be rushing. It was as if this fire would consume everything he owned in a few minute's time. Suddenly, two tribal policemen drove up, jumping out with fire extinguishers in hand. The fire diminished under their control. Ina and Arlene ran up to Tom. There was fright in Arlene's eyes as she saw Tom holding out his burned hands. He had just begun to feel the pain.

"I'm sorry! I'm sorry! Oh, I wish this had never happened." The old, stoic Arlene had disappeared. She was crying as she looked at Tom's hands. "It's all my fault! Everything is my fault."

She turned and ran back toward the hospital. In a minute, Roxy appeared, medicine kit in hand. She began to treat Tom's hands. He didn't protest. Finally, his hands bandaged in the best way Roxy could, Tom sat in the passenger side of the police car to tell Sergeant Waylon Pinal what had happened while the other policeman picked up what looked like a charred can from the remains of the fire and brought it to his boss. Adrenalin spent, Tom realized how tired he was and how much his hands hurt. Waylon Pinal smelled the can.

"It's gasoline," he said, speaking to his deputy. Then he turned to Tom. "Sir, did you see who did it?"

Tom spoke slowly. "Not really. I saw someone dumping something out of a can onto the fire that was already shooting out large flames. They must have made that pile of brush before I came out. I could smell the smoke from the fire as I left the hospital. It might have been a man, maybe a boy. He was moving pretty quickly after I yelled at him. All I could tell was that he had on some sort of brown coat with a hood."

"Do you know anyone who would want to hurt you or get even with you?"

Tom was silent for a few seconds. "Not really." He paused. "I'll have to think about that." It was more complicated than he could answer simply.

Ina came up to Waylon Pinal's side of the car. He was related to her.

"I might know who did it," Ina said to him. Waylon looked at her.

"I saw him, too, not the face or anything, but I think he's got a limp in his right leg. That boy, Michael Gloshay, he lives next to me. They say he's a drug user – that's all I know."

Sgt. Pinal wrote a few notes in his small notebook; he spoke a few more minutes to Tom.

"O.K., Sir. We'll let you know if we find out anything." He added, "And, if you can think of anyone who might want to hurt you, let me know."

"What if I told him a witch was after me?" Tom thought wryly. Instead, he answered,

"I'll do that," Tom answered.

The two policemen drove off in their Cherokee Jeep, the charred empty can in the back of their car. Dalton, the custodian at the hospital, remained at the site of the fire, stomping on the charred wood, dowsing the broken steps and the charred remains of the fire with more water. He had put a ladder from the hospital up to the trailer door, gone inside with a set of hospital keys, and filled up buckets of water from Tom's sink to take back outside.

By this time, Ben Altaha had arrived and assured Tom they would get to work on a new set of steps and porch tomorrow. He would get Dalton to remove the remnants of the fire as well. Roxy, still standing next to Tom, saw how exhausted he was, and said,

"Come on with me back to the hospital, Tom. There's a cot in our community health office. You need to lie down while I check your hands again and rebandage them. I didn't do such a hot job out here."

Tom started to protest, but he followed her. He had wanted to be sure he was around when Ada drove up. As he left with Roxy, only Shirley, Ina, Dalton and a few onlookers remained. Everyone else left when the excitement had died down.

As luck would have it, Ada drove up only a few minutes after Tom had agreed to go with Roxy. It wasn't the worst time she could have arrived, but it wasn't the best. Getting no response from Tom's cell phone, she had called the hospital and gotten directions from Carla who told her what had happened.

Ada pulled into the parking lot and jumped out of her little VW. Seeing Tom's bandaged hands, she ran over to him as Roxy was helping him toward the side door. She had seen the smoke next to the trailer.

"Tom, Tom, are you all right?" She was afraid to hug him.

"Ada! Yes, just my hands – it's O.K., really."

Roxy took charge. "Tell you what. Let's get your bandages fixed, give you some meds, then I'll bring you back to this lovely lady – could we meet in the Mental Health Department?"

Tom wanted to hug Ada, but instead, he said, "Ada, this is Ina, and here's Shirley. They'll show you where to go. I'm sorry, Honey, really sorry!"

"What on earth do you have to be sorry for? Just do what you have to do. We'll have all the time in the world later."

She turned, looking at the two women.

"Come on, ladies. Show me where to go and for goodness sake tell me what's been going on."

Her nose had already turned pink from the cold, but her new boots lined with wool were keeping her warm. They were a source of admiration for both Shirley and Ina, and so was she, as they watched her kiss Tom in front of everybody.

"I love you," she said, as Roxy took Tom off.

Ina and Shirley watched as Tom said, "Me, too."

Ada, Ina and Shirley went in the side door to the mental health department. Arlene was there, sitting in a chair, wiping her eyes. The two women introduced her to Ada. Arlene looked vulnerable, ready to cry again, but she spoke directly to Ada.

"I'm so sorry. I feel like I've caused this."

"How?" asked Ada, surprised.

Her presence had a calming effect on Arlene; Ada's voice was low and quiet. Arlene seemed impelled to speak, not minding the presence of Ina and Shirley, for once.

She spoke in a flow of rapid-fire words, all about her boy's illness and death, her early-on distrust of Tom, her searching for someone to blame it all on. Ada understood some of it, but not all.

She asked Arlene," Why do you think this fire has anything to do with something you have done?"

Arlene looked at Shirley, then Ina.

"It's like I opened up the way for bad things to happen to Mr. Doc – we call him that – like I caused it, maybe caused someone to do it to him. You might not believe it, but it can happen." She was ready to argue the point.

Ina interrupted. "No, Arlene. I saw the guy. I'm pretty sure who he is. He has nothing to do with you. He's brought trouble to a lot of people."

She stopped speaking for a second, then said in a low voice, looking at Arlene,

"And, if you're thinking about the one who has power around here, I didn't see her around here at all."

But Arlene went on. "No, that's not what I meant. Somebody out there was using him – the one that started the fire -- to get to Mr. Doc."

The women looked as if they didn't understand.

"I'll talk about it later. This is not the time." She said no more.

After a few minutes, Arlene seemed to calm down somewhat. Whatever she knew, she was keeping to herself. Shirley went to Carla's office and brought back four cups of weak coffee in Styrofoam cups. The four women kept talking, about Tom's burnt hands, Shirley's husband, even Ina's upcoming training. All except for Arlene, the three women were relating in a way to Ada that they didn't with Tom. They seemed to understand each other immediately. By the time Roxy brought Tom back to them, laughter could be heard from all of them, even a small peep from Arlene.

What the heck is this, a hen party?" Tom was trying to laugh. Ada finally got to hug him.

"No, Darling. But you've got a terrific bunch of women in this office. They could win a war singlehandedly if they put their minds to it!"

Tom made an effort to smile, but he was in real pain.

"What should we do now, Ada? It looks like my trailer won't be a good place to go back to right now. Anyway, I'm all packed up in the Jeep." He looked down at his hands. "You'd have to do the driving. We could come back tomorrow. Roxy wants to look at my hands again."

Ina and Shirley were all ears.

"Then let's go. Just as long as I'm with you, it doesn't matter where it is."

The two women looked at each other and smiled. Arlene had left to go home.

After Tom and Ada left, Ina said to Shirely, "She's cute. Do you think they are serious?"

"Of course," said Shirley. "But who can you trust, nowadays?"

"No, you're wrong. Look at me. I'm happy with my old man."

"You wouldn't be if Bessie had gotten hold of him!" They both nodded at each othe

XXXVIII

They packed Ada's gear into the Jeep, locked up her car, and got in his car, Ada driving. They began the drive up to the ski lodge as they had planned before the fire. Ada drove Tom's Jeep expertly. His hands hurt, but the burns were first degree, Roxy said, and they should heal in time without special care. But, his plans for the weekend had gone out the window. Ada consoled him, saying that none of that really mattered at all. She hadn't come to go skiing, she reminded him. Finally, he sat back in the seat and relaxed. Roxy's medication was doing the trick; the pain was less.

It was dark when they arrived at Sunrise. They had not been able to start their trip up the hill earlier, as he had originally planned. This part of the reservation was at the highest elevation, and the topography was a radical change from Whiteriver. Even in the darkness they could pick out lakes, pine and aspen trees and large expanses of snow. The population seemed to be sparse, the night cold. No cars were on the road. Above them was a silver-yellow full moon that seemed to be made for the topography and this night. The temperature was dropping rapidly. Ada wasn't used to the cold. She shivered slightly. He couldn't even put his arms around her, Tom thought ruefully.

Finally, they reached the wood-framed building of the ski lodge. It stood ahead of them, its lights the only illumination for miles around. Ada stopped the car at a spot closest to the main entrance. Tom realized how much his hands had been injured when he found himself incapable of helping Ada pick up the bags. She had refused his offer anyway. He was frustrated. He had wanted so much for the weekend to be perfect.

But, when they got out of the car and they looked up into the sky, the picture was magical. They stood there, dumbstruck, by the light show of comets, meteors, and diamond-clear stars jutting toward them out of the blackness. Any earlier cloudiness of the day had disappeared, revealing a vastness Tom couldn't begin to comprehend. It was as if they were witnessing a special display made for themselves only. They were creatures in a universe that had been lit up for them and nobody else. And, it was quiet, too. Something was faintly crunching the snow behind them, and some dried leaves were scraping against a tree, nothing else. Tom turned his body around carefully to look for the source of the crunching. He couldn't see anything. He turned back to face Ada.

He tried, and was surprised to find that he was able to put his arm around Ada, their outward breaths steamy and dissipating into the dry night air. As long as he didn't touch her with his hands, it was okay. They stood there for a minute, not speaking; she put her head on his shoulder. It tore him up.

She moved her head slightly.

"Wonder what that noise is behind us. Sounds like something walking in the snow."

"I heard it, too," he answered. "We're probably just edgy from everything that's happened today."

She nodded.

"Ada, I'd give anything if we had today to do over. Why couldn't the little SOB who tried to torch my trailer wait until next week?"

"Don't say that. I'm glad I was here when it happened." She lifted her head from his shoulder.

"You were right. Something is definitely going on down there, and it seems to circle around you. Come on. It's freezing! Let's go sign in. I'd like some hot cocoa."

The registration desk was located in one corner of the lobby. At another end of the big room was a huge stone fireplace with logs that had been burning for some time; they were red hot and almost white. Tom looked around. Only a few people were in the lobby. He knew that the snowfall in recent weeks hadn't been great, and that might account for the lack of guests and cars outside. But one of the owners of the motel where he had stayed in Pinetop inferred that the lodge couldn't seem to make a profit, that it lacked an experienced manager.

Tom signed them in at the registration desk, still embarrassed that he couldn't pick up the luggage himself. He made himself pick up the pen and hold it between his thumb and forefinger, where it hurt least. At least, he could do that. Ada had come in with him and went immediately over to the fireplace where she began to warm her hands. She had put the two bags down next to her. By this time both of them were hungry. There hadn't been time to think about dinner before now. Tom asked the clerk about food, but she said that the restaurant was closed for the night. His frustration showed in his face. When she saw his bandaged hands, the clerk said,

"Let me see if I can ask the clean-up crew in the kitchen to check in the refrigerator. There were a lot of good cheese quesadillas and beans tonight. I know. I ate some myself," laughed the receptionist. "Would that be all right?"

"You bet!" called out Ada by the fireplace.

Within fifteen minutes they were sitting by the fire, bags by their side, wolfing down the food that had been brought to them on trays, along with a couple of cups of hot coffee. Tom noted that during the half-hour they had been there, no one had entered or left the lodge. That was fine with him. Ada cut up his food as if he were a baby and even helped put it in his mouth. Somehow, he didn't mind. She held the coffee cup up to his lips as well. The quiet was blissful, the cheese melted to a soft yellow, and the fire warmed their feet. The chairs in which they were sitting next to the fire were big, brown and leather with footstools that directed their feet toward the flames. They didn't need anything else, not even the cocoa Ada had mentioned earlier. Tom felt himself falling asleep, but he forced his eyes to stay open.

Even the pain in his hands was not quite so bad now. He had been given a pretty strong pain pill by Roxy before they left. They sat there like an old married couple, but underneath Tom kept thinking that this special night he had planned was ruined. Ada had no idea that he had intended to ask her to marry him, well, he hardly knew it himself. Unlike his old self, he had no doubts about his feelings this time; he just hoped she didn't either. They hadn't been together that long. Maybe that's what she would be thinking. He squared his shoulders. It was a chance he was determined to take, putting his feelings on the line. It had all happened so fast. But now with his useless hands.....

She seemed to read his thoughts.

"Please don't worry about tonight. I just want to be with you. You need a little care. Will you let me do it?" He nodded reluctantly.

"You're going to need to take another pain pill before we turn in." She said it matter-of-factly, as if it didn't mean anything. He was reading into her statement a whole other scenario.

She watched his expression.

"Tomorrow we'll see how you feel. No skiing for sure – thank goodness!"

He couldn't help but laugh at the thought of the two of them trying to ski.

"We'll have a quiet day, and I don't want any protests from you!"

He retorted, "What do you think you are, my superior officer or something?"

"Yes!" She laughed.

He was glad in a way that she was taking charge. He did muster himself enough to ask the clerk to get someone to take their bags to their room. A young man appeared, lifted up the bags as if they were nothing, and they followed him to the elevator and up to their room. The locked door opened to reveal a large double bed, a high wooden ceiling and a window that looked out into the black of night.

Ada closed the door after the young man left. She walked over to Tom and kissed him on the cheek.

"No shower for you tonight. I hope you didn't buy any fancy pajamas for tonight, either. Just sleep in your undershirt and shorts."

He gave in without a murmur, let her put his cell phone on its charger, used his mouthwash, and did exactly what she told him. He crawled in beneath the sheets. She had to get him to sit up to take the pill. As he took it, he tried to apologize again, but she stopped him, tucking the covers over him. In two minutes he was asleep, even snoring.

As soon as he was settled, Ada showered, got ready for bed and was about to lie down next to him, when Tom's cell phone went off. She looked at her watch. It was only about 10 o'clock. Tom was dead to the world. She picked up the phone and answered it. It was Sergeant Waylon Pinal.

"Sorry to bother you, ma'am."

"No, not at all. Tom is asleep, pretty exhausted from his injuries. Could you talk to me instead?"

"No problem. We just wanted to let you know that we believe that we have caught the boy who started the fire."

"Great!"

"We'd like you to bring Doctor Collins by the police station tomorrow morning. The boy has been talking, says he didn't mean to hurt anyone. He's got a story Dr. Collins should hear."

"I'll talk with him tomorrow and have him call you, but I'm pretty sure we'll be down in the morning."

"Thanks. Sorry to disturb you."

"That's all right. Good night."

She hung up. Tom would be upset. Their weekend alone would be pretty much over. She put the phone back on the charger and lay down next to Tom, careful not to touch his hands. She kissed him lightly on the top of the head. He murmured something. She was so glad to be able to be with him at this time, when he needed her most.

It was hard for her to get to sleep. There were strange noises, a strange bed and millions of thoughts. She could have sworn she heard footsteps outside, beneath their window. Slow down. You're not on duty now.

XXXIX

The next morning came quickly. Ada hadn't been able to sleep well in the new surroundings, and she woke up every time Tom moaned in his sleep.

The sun was just beginning to light up the icicles that hung outside their window. When she got up, put on her jeans, new boots, sweater and vest, she took a second look in the bathroom mirror. Her hair was faintly wavy, and it curled up on the back of her neck. She was ready for the day. Tom was beginning to move his arms and legs. A few minutes later he called out to her in a hoarse voice.

"Could you stand to kiss a man before he's brushed his teeth?"

She grinned. "I kissed a camel once in Afghanistan. It can't be any worse than that."

She knelt by his bedside and kissed him on the lips, thinking, as she did, that she'd better break the news to him now about the phone call.

"They called last night while you were asleep."

"Who?"

"The police. They caught the boy."

"Great." He rolled over and put his feet on the floor, grimacing as the blood rushed to his hands.

"The thing is, they want you to come down this morning. Apparently, he's been talking."

He turned toward her.

"Oh, no," he groaned. "I thought we'd have at least one day to ourselves."

"I know. But best to get it over with, so we can do what we want after that."

He got up slowly and went to the bathroom. It wasn't easy to brush his teeth holding the toothbrush with two fingers. His thumbs weren't hurt, thank God. He threw off his old underwear, gingerly grabbing clean shorts and shirt from his bag. A mean, hot pain hit the palms of his hands. He stood still until it subsided. She didn't need to know how bad his hands felt.

"Hey, Honey," he asked. "Should I take a pain pill?"

"Yes, and the antibiotics, too. I'll get them for you."

In another quarter of an hour, they were both dressed and headed down to the restaurant to eat breakfast. The sun had appeared in full force, changing the appearance of the lobby from dark and cozy to multi-colored, with its woven rugs of red and black that hung on the walls. Brown chandeliers made of antler prongs dropped down from the ceiling.

They went into the dining room at seven o'clock. It was early; only six or seven people were taking advantage of the breakfast buffet. Maybe they were the only guests in the whole place. He saw two men across the room, maybe father and son, who were dressed as if they were going hunting. A few feet from the father and son were another two men who were more formally dressed, as if they were on business. There was one man by himself. He couldn't figure him out by looking at him. He was Apache, and he wore the biggest boots Tom had ever seen. That left a young couple, blond, blue-eyed, who were talking to each other in low tones. Every once in a while Tom and Ada could hear them say something about skiing.

It was the kind of breakfast for big men. There were bacon slabs, eggs, even tamales, sitting next to big pieces of Texas toast. A round pot of oatmeal simmered,, sending out bubbles of steam, and next to it on the warming tray lay links of pork sausage. They were hungry; they ate and ate until everybody else had left the room. The pain pills helped Tom to use his fork himself this morning, and he took full advantage of it. When the little Apache teenager came over to clear off their table, they finally got up to go.

Tom had booked the room for one more night. Leaving their belongings upstairs, they set out for Whiteriver, down to the warmer climate. They drove directly to the police department behind the tribal building. It was small. Two police cars were parked in front. They walked in the building under the tribal seal above the front door. Sergeant Waylon Pinal ushered them into a small room. He looked at Ada.

"You're welcome to stay if you want."

She looked at Tom. He nodded; she said thank you.

"Well, this kid, Dusty Lupe, is in our holding cell. He's about sixteen, and he's got a record with us, selling drugs, petty robbery. But attempted arson is something he hasn't done before, at least, not that we know of."

"Did he say why me, why he picked my trailer?"

"That's the part I want you to hear from him. I'd like to bring him in here. I want to hear him tell the story again, in front of you this time."

"Let's do it."

In a few minutes Dusty Lupe was brought in, hands cuffed in front of his body. He hung his head down after Waylon set him across from Ada and Tom. His dreadlocks were dangling down on either side of his head. The boy glanced up once at Tom's bandaged hands, and then looked away.

"All right. Let's hear what you told me, Dusty. Start from the beginning – and hold your head up when you talk to us."

Dusty reluctantly raised his head, looking at Waylon, not at Tom. He spoke like a boy trying to sound like a man who wasn't afraid.

"I never meant to get nobody hurt. I just needed the money."

"Go on."

Dusty's voice was low and sometimes cracked.

"It's like this. My mom rents a mailbox at the post office. Don't know why. She don't get that much mail. Costs money, too. Anyway, a letter came for me, which was weird because I never get any. It was printed with something like a crayon, like a kid done it. Said there was money in it for me if I could do a job – just scare somebody."

He finally looked toward Tom.

"Nothing in the letter about who it was from or nothing. Said all I had to do was set a fire near his" – he pointed to Tom -- "front porch. I was to burn the letter first. There'd be twenty-five dollars for me if I did it, sent to my mom's mailbox." He looked down. "It was a black crayon, like they use in school."

"So, nobody forced you to do it," said Waylon.

"Yeah, but see, I needed the money real bad. See, I've got a little drug habit. My hands is shaking right now. Somebody needs to do something for me."

"Go on."

He sat up taller.

"Anyway, I got a can of gasoline from the back of our house. We use it for barbecues and stuff like that. I figured that nobody would see me late in the afternoon, up on that hill. If he" – he pointed to Tom -- "hadn't gone out to that hospital lot, I woulda had the money and nobody would have gotten hurt. What a screw up! Nobody's going to give me money for a job I didn't get away with. And, here I am, locked up in here."

He was angry now. "It's his own fault anyway, that Anglo, for trying to put out a fire when he don't know how."

"Yeah, yeah," said Waylon. The boy looked perturbed.

"O.K. That's enough," said Waylon. "You're going back to the cell."

"Wait, just wait a minute. I got something else to say." He shot it all out.

"The one who wrote me that note said something else, said they knew about something else I had done, and they'd report me if I didn't do what they said. So, see, I didn't have no choice."

The deputy took Dusty back to the cell.

Waylon turned to Tom and Ada and said, "That last part's pretty interesting. I've got a feeling he's connected to that fire that started up the hill. It was too odd for a fire like that to start in the winter."

Ada looked at Tom

"I'll tell you about that later," he said, as they left the station.

Waylon stood at the door, watching the two leave. He turned to his deputy and said,

"That Dusty kid, he's like the old saying – what goes around, comes around."

The deputy replied, "Witches around here say the same thing."

He hurried back to his desk before Waylon could answer him.

XL

It was puzzling, Ada and Tom agreed later. No proof of whom was behind it. Apparently, even Dusty didn't know. But whoever it was, they knew all about Dusty, enough to reward him and hint at blackmailing him at the same time. That could be just about anybody around here, Tom told her. And why would anybody hate him enough to pay someone to scare him? Did they think it would make him leave here? Was it Bessie again?

He decided to tell Ada about the stolen files that had not turned up. The only reason he told her was to discuss it with her. It was not something that was directly harmful to him. He was going to make sure she didn't have more things to worry about.

Ada and Tom had gone back to the ski lodge and were sitting in the car where no one could hear them. She reminded Tom of how strange Arlene had acted at the time of the fire, saying that it was all her fault.

"Did you get any more out of her while I was with Roxy?" Tom asked her.

"No. She left the office soon after that. Something's definitely going on inside her, though. You surely don't imagine that she would instigate Dusty to set the fire, do you? If so, she doesn't need to be working with you."

"That's always the issue. I never know for sure who is behind what's happening around here. I'm stymied from acting because I have no proof of anything. And, even if I did, what could I do – go to Waylon Pinal and say that someone should be arrested for tampering with people's minds? Now, the fire is another story. If I knew who sent that letter to Dusty, then that would be a crime that could actually get someone punished. But, even Dusty doesn't know, he says. There would be no reason for him to hold back that information to the police unless he could use it to help him get out of jail later."

By the end of their conversation Tom reminded himself that he had numerous leads to follow when his hands got better. He was going to have a long talk with Arlene and find out what she meant. He was going to sound out Shirley again about the possibility of her husband trying to get even with him. There should be some way to find out where he was laying low. His hands were hurting now. He held them up so that the blood subsided in them. They felt better.

He had never gotten back to Bessie after his threat that he would bring her into his office if he had to strong arm her. He was also going to ask Roxy whom she suspected. He had to do something about Ronnie for his own personal reasons; and he would find out, maybe from Dusty's mother, if Dusty had actually kept the letter from whomever sent it to him. It was possible. And finally, he was going to have that long talk with Rev. about their working together. Even Tom had to admit to himself that all these leads might lead to nothing. It would all take a lot of work, with his not even able to drive for some time because of his hands. There were so many things happening that he would have to leave the theft of the files up to Ben to deal with.

At least they were alone now, up here in the wilderness, he thought. Tom and Ada got out of the car and took a long walk in the snow, toward Hawley Lake. It was still; only a few birds called out, and the wind was making the smallest effort to stir up the bare trees. The air was the cleanest he had ever breathed. It froze the little hairs inside his nose. The lake was silver like mercury, completely frozen. It looked clear and smooth, but full of dangers should one trod upon it. Just like Whiteriver, thought Tom. Well, we won't do that. They turned around and headed back to the lodge, to get ready for dinner at the Alpine Inn in Pinetop that he had scouted out earlier. After that, they were not seen again until Sunday morning by anyone at the lodge.

Before Tom put her back in her car in Whiteriver to head back to Huachuca on Sunday morning, Ada was wearing a silver locket on a chain that had belonged to Tom's mother. He had thought about introducing her to Rev that Sunday morning at church, but she had to get back to the post that afternoon. Maybe another time, he thought.

Yes, she had said yes. That was all he could think about on Sunday night after she had gone back to Huachuca. Even the pain in his hands was muted when he thought about her. He had planned a romantic dinner at the best restaurant in Pinetop, a perfect setting for him to give her the locket.

She was thrilled by the place. There was snow on the ground, and a winding sidewalk beckoned them into the wooden building with a beg wreath on the door. It didn't matter if it were after Christmas; it was Christmas for them. There was a big fire in the fireplace, candles on the tables, even tablecloths. Weiner schnitzel, potato pancakes, purple cabbage, even apple dumplings for dessert. The wine was actually German, also. He broke his rule and had a glass with Ada. Some kind of oompah music was coming out of a speaker in the ceiling.

The restaurant was small; only a few tables were filled. They would go back to the lodge that night and face whatever would be coming tomorrow and in the days ahead, but tonight was theirs. After finishing off the big apple dumplings and topping it off with the best coffee he had ever tasted, it was time. Then reality hit. He realized to his chagrin that he was unable to make his fingers take the locket enclosed in tissue paper out of his pocket in order to give it to her.

"Ada, this is not the place I had in mind for what I am going to do."

She was puzzled.

"What's that?" she answered.

"Would you go into my right pocket and pull out the tissue paper carefully?"

She frowned but did as he asked. The older couple at the next table were watching, too.

"Open it."

She did what he asked, sat back down, and folded back the creased tissue paper until the newly cleaned silver locket and chain were exposed. He had been proud of himself for cleaning it last week. It shone in the candlelight.

She finally figured it out. She smiled. It was for her, but she didn't know what was coming next. He spoke.

"It was my mother's. I didn't want to buy an engagement ring until you were with me. Nothing has turned out like I wanted it to."

She said nothing, prompting him to add quickly,

"If you aren't ready for this, if I have misread......"

Her eyes grew wide, her smile wider.

"You haven't asked me yet."

He had the courage to say, "Please say yes. I can't lose you."

The older couple were a little hard of hearing, but they could figure it all out without hearing it.

She couldn't hold Tom's hands, but she got up from her chair, put his face in her hands and kissed him. She whispered yes. That was enough for him. The word 'love' finally escaped from both their lips.

The older couple reached over, holding each other's hands.

Tom and Ada didn't know and probably didn't care that the waitress and the bus boy were watching also, and decided that the table didn't need to be cleaned off until later.

XLI

In the days ahead, it was frustrating to have his hands so useless. He could tell they were healing, though. The really bad pain had gone, and he was off the pain pills, but they were still sore and tender. Thank God it hadn't been worse; there had been no blistering. Tom had been forced to give up the computer for the time being, except for a little hunting and pecking, and he was just beginning to steer the car again by using mostly his right hand, which had been less injured.

The following week after the fire, the first person he talked with who was on his long list was Shirley. He called her into his office. She was the easiest one on his list to reach. She also might be the only one to have no hidden agenda. He didn't waste words or time.

"Shirley, I need to ask you something."

"Sure, Mr. Doc."

"This is not about you." She looked relieved.

"Do you think there is any possibility that your husband could have gotten Dusty Lupe to set the fire? Maybe to get back at me?"

She didn't look upset. She answered rapidly.

"To be honest, no, I don't. I'm not saying this to protect him. But, my cousin heard that he's been seen in the bars in Tucson. She says he was drinking and trying to get money out of his friends and relatives. When he starts doing that, that's all he's thinking of."

She was still wearing her shawl, but it had dropped off her shoulders, exposing the yellow marks on her arms. The bruises seemed to be healing, and the scabs from the cigarette burns had been replaced by two red marks. She went on talking.

"Besides, you told us that somebody had been offering to pay Dusty, and I don't think my husband has had anywhere near twenty-five dollars for a long time. He's mean to me, Mr. Doc, but I don't see him doing something that complicated." She brushed off her skirt.

"Really, if he wanted to do something to you, he would have just come running over here and yelled at you, not much else. You see, he's kind of a coward around men. He only picks on me and the kids."

Tom felt relieved. He thought she was correct.

"I just had to ask. Sorry to bring it up. How are you and the kids doing?"

"Pretty good. We're back home, and my sister Rose is with us. She won't take nothing from anybody. We've both got cell phones now, so in case he comes back we can call the police."

She went back to her desk, as Tom thought to himself, "Well, I might as well get the next chore over with also."

Arlene had just come in from East Fork and was writing a note in one of the new files. She looked up when he called her name. There was a change in her. She didn't look as upset as she had been during the episode of the fire, but he was never fully comfortable around her. He never knew what her next mood might be.

"Can you give me a few minutes in my office, Arlene?"

"Sure."

Ina's ears had perked up as Arlene went into his office and sat down. When she saw that Tom had closed the door, she went back to her phone call.

Tom spoke firmly to Arlene.

"Just to let you know. I am going to get to the bottom of a lot of things that have been happening. I have asked Shirley if her husband could have been able to pay Dusty Lupe to set the fire near my trailer. She gave me good reasons why not. Now, I've got to ask you -- Why did you say the fire was your fault?"

She seemed to want to talk for a change.

"I didn't realize you had heard that. I was really upset. Well, I had some bad thoughts – about you – but you already know that. And I got to thinking after Big Boy was gone – I got to seeing things right for the first time. I got to seeing that you didn't have any part in what had happened to Big Boy."

"You mean about my being used in witchcraft?" He was going to bring it out into the open.

For a second, she looked as if she were going to close down again, but she went on. Her eyes narrowed, but she answered him calmly.

"Well, I got to thinking that Rev would have been surprised if he knew the way my thoughts were going. I had strayed from the way he wanted me to be."

She wiped her eyes on the sleeve of her dress. She did look genuinely sorry to Tom.

"I know how bad I've been to a lot of people, and I can't help thinking that all of these things that have happened – my boy, you, the bad stuff on the rez – I'm thinking that God is punishing me by hurting me and everyone around me! It's God that is doing this to me, not a witch."

Tom wanted to slam his hands down on the desk; he was so frustrated with her. He needed to get his temper under control.

He said firmly, "It sounds like your thoughts are going in the same old way you always have. Why do you always think someone, even God, is out to punish you? Why couldn't it be some action you have taken, something you believe, that has caused so much trouble for you? Why couldn't it be that you have made some mistakes? Why couldn't it be that no one caused Big Boy's death?"

She looked at him with the old anger creeping out; she didn't understand what he was saying at all. All she knew was that he was challenging her, and she didn't like it. She hadn't liked him from the beginning. He was trouble. He was upsetting her life.

"You probably need to have a talk with Rev," said Tom, now trying to cut the interview short. She nodded, holding in her anger, bowing her head down. It was as if he were using Rev to control her. She couldn't help being scared of Tom, being threatened by him.

"I know, I know," she answered quickly. "Anyway, I want to tell you I'm just sorry if I caused you any trouble."

"It's O.K." he answered.

He breathed a sigh of relief as she left his office. He had gotten absolutely nothing out of that interview.

So did she breathed a sigh of relief. She couldn't take this much longer. She was going to have to see what she could do about him, she said to herself.

XLII

Tom had promised himself that he would deal with Bessie next. If there were any humanly possible way to get her to his office this time, he would do it. But she was not coming to the door today when he knocked loudly. He knocked even louder again. He could hear the children somewhere in the back of the house, so she had to be there. But she wouldn't come out. She wasn't the type to leave the children alone. Tom was getting more frustrated by the minute, but there was nothing he could do about it.

He had a sudden thought. Maybe she was actually afraid of him instead of the other way around. He worked at the hospital. Maybe she was afraid that he could see that her grandchildren would be taken away from her, if he reported her to Social Services for some of the things she had done. Funny, it had all started by her trying to scare him. Now, just maybe, the tables were turned; he wasn't scared any longer.

He finally stopped knocking, turned and went back to the car. He couldn't make her come out, but this was not going to be the end of the matter. He was going to see Rev today. He was back in town after escaping to the South for a while. Tom wished now that he had made more effort to introduce Ada to Rev when she had been up here. The next time she came up, he would do it. This time there would be no excuse, no delay. They had a wedding to plan, and Ada kept asking him questions that he couldn't answer. But, when he saw Rev this time, there were a lot of questions that he himself needed to have answered, and they weren't going to be just about the wedding, by a long shot.

What could he do next, with Bessie unavailable? There was Roxy. He had a question to ask her – to find out whom she thought was behind all of this. She had said once that she had an idea about it, and she had never gotten back to him about it after they had gone to see George and Sheena that day. He knew that she was in her office today doing some paperwork. That was where he found her – alone, stooped over a box of meds, sorting plastic cylinders and putting them on the shelf above her. She smiled when she saw him.

"Hi, Tom. Come on in. I've been trying to go through these things for over a week now. Maybe I can postpone it a little longer!" She grinned at him.

He sat down in the only chair in her office as she talked and half-heartedly kept looking through the box, sorting meds, moving items onto shelves. She finally stopped.

"That reminds me. Time to look at those hands again. Change the bandages, too."

She reached up on the shelf behind her for scissors, bandages, and medications. Turning to him, she took off his bandages.

"Looks pretty good. No infection. Seems to be on the mend. You're lucky it wasn't any worse. What in heaven's name made you think you could put out that fire?"

"Just crazy," he replied, not really thinking about what she said.

"Say, Roxy, I wanted to ask you whom you thought is behind all of this. Is there one person you suspect, or do you think it is a series of random incidents? I need to know what you think. You said you had some suspicions about who was scaring George and Sheena."

She put down the scissors and bandages, and let out a sigh. She went over to close the door.

"I know I said that I suspected someone, but I didn't tell you more because I decided it wasn't anything but an unfounded suspicion." She folded her arms across her chest.

"See, years ago my mother and Ronnie Kane had a thing going -- before she met my dad. It didn't end up well - but, that's a lot of past history you don't need to hear. She told me about Ronnie, what he was like. She said that power over others was his driving force in life. That's why she didn't want to have any more to do with him. He was trying to control her also."

"Go on," said Tom.

"She said he thought he was descended from chiefs, and he believed that people here owed him their loyalty. He told her once that he'd get that loyalty one way or another."

She waited for a few seconds, then resumed.

"This all sounds so ridiculous, things that happened years ago. But, I have never trusted him because of that. You can see that none of this can be proved. But, I just think he'll do anything to get the best of them."

"So you think he's behind some of this?"

"I really don't know what to think. I have no proof at all, just this feeling. It's possible he could have tried to exercise his power over Sheena, guilty as she feels." She corrected herself immediately. " No, not likely. She is so sure that Bessie did it, and she's probably right. And, as to George, I don't know why Ronnie would try to hurt him, unless it was to show Bessie that he is more powerful than she. The two of them have this kind of rivalry going."

She scratched the top of her head.

"This is beginning to sound far-fetched."

She thought for a minute. Tom didn't interrupt her.

"Suppose, just suppose that Bessie and Ronnie were rivals for the power position around here? Wouldn't that make sense?"

Tom shook his head. "I don't know, but it's a thought."

Tom told her about the incident with the tarantula, which she hadn't heard before. She was surprised.

"It could have been him. It could have been. He must be feeling some sort of rivalry with you, because you were a military man. He's capable of doing something like that. But even if he did such a stupid thing, that doesn't mean he was behind the fire or frightened Sheena, or any of the other things that have happened."

She looked straight at him.

"Believe me, I'd be the first to blame him if I could. I just don't trust the man farther than I can throw him. But the plain fact is that I don't have any evidence at all."

There was nothing Tom could say. She finished up with his hands, and he left. She didn't know it, but her remarks merely added another piece of information that made it all the more puzzling. Instead of cleaning things up, Roxy had inadvertently made it more confusing. She had kept Ronnie in the mix.

He needed to see Rev today. He couldn't rule out anybody, even Roxy. He was almost ashamed to think it could be she, after all she had done for him. There was absolutely no reason to suspect her that he could think of.

XLIII

March was finally here. Rev told Tom that he didn't mind the weather up in Whiteriver now, because there was the hope of Easter and spring in the air. He and Hilda had come back home; the hard days of February were over. He didn't mind working all summer, but the winters seemed interminable, even when the snow had been less, as this year. Maybe, he said to Tom, he was just getting old, and you know how old people like the sun. He gave a little chuckle.

Nevertheless, he told Tom, he loved coming back to the place where he was born, to the house of his parents, and he loved the people here. They had walked with him through death and agony, misery and happiness. Their incredible endurance and courage in the face of difficulties had never faltered. They had survived. He felt right here.

Hilda Herz had unpacked and was organizing the groceries that they had picked up on the way back, when Rev told her that Tom had called and was on the way over. She inwardly balked at her husband's quick resumption of his duties, but she had gotten used to such things over the years. She made coffee, put the cups on the kitchen table and headed for the back bedroom. It was a good time for Hilda to talk with her sister in New Mexico. She was laughing with her when Tom's knock was answered by Rev. Herz. Tom was truly glad to see him.

"Nice to have you back, sir."

"Tom, my boy, the coffee's made."

Tom was now to be welcomed into the inner sanctum of the kitchen. He was no longer a dining room visitor, Rev told him with a laugh. He started to shake Tom's hand, then stopped.

"Say! What's happened to your hands?"

"That's part of what I want to tell you," Tom replied.

Rev frowned.

"Come round to the kitchen. Hilda's on the phone talking to her sister, so you may never get a chance to say hello to her. They're like two hens in a hen house. Let me hear what you have to say."

He looked rested from his short California trip. He had acquired a slight tan, and the lines around his eyes seemed diminished. A young deacon from St. Louis had been glad to take over for him during the couple of weeks he had been away, but he was equally glad to leave, Rev said ruefully.

They sat in the chrome chairs, drinking weak instant coffee in mugs. Some talk had to be made about the weather, the craziness of L.A., the car's performance on the way back home. Then Rev got to down basics, even before Tom could talk about his concerns.

"What's been going on here? Tell me first about how you got those hands hurt. I'm surprised someone hasn't told me already. I haven't heard the gossip yet, even from my wife."

He looked seriously at Tom, seeing his grim face and his bandaged hands. "Has something happened while I was gone?"

Tom put the mug down carefully, cradling it between two of his good fingers. He told him about the fire and Dusty Lupe and about Ada's coming up. He told him he wanted Rev to meet her, that he wanted to marry her. They were hoping he could marry them this spring. Rev got up from his chair and patted him on the back. There was a big grin on his face.

"I'd be delighted, Son. I'll look at my calendar and you take a look at yours and Ada's. Ask her when she's free to come up for counseling, too."

Tom looked surprised.

"Only a few sessions, Boy. Don't get yourself in an uproar!"

Tom had to laugh. There was so much he wanted to tell him besides this, so he added,

"No, no, I'm sure we'd be happy to do it. But, well, I'd also like your opinion about a series of events which occurred while you were gone, some even before you left, actually."

"Sure. So they caught Dusty Lupe. Good. He needs a good hiding, in my opinion. Guess I'm just old fashioned, but that's what we used to do around here. That kid's going to do more harm if we're not careful. I'd better talk to his mother. Or, maybe it's best if I go over to the jail first."

He slapped his hand down on the table, rattling the cups.

"Say, do you remember that forest fire we saw on the way back down from Pinetop? It makes a lot of sense that somebody like Dusty started it instead of my believing it was some kind of spontaneous combustion – not this time of year."

Tom agreed. Rev took a big gulp of coffee.

"Must be important, what you have to say, and your coming here right when I got back.. You didn't waste any time coming to see me."

Tom looked embarrassed.

"Just a joke, Son," said Rev. "Go on. Tell me."

Tom continued, telling Rev about Arlene's statements that she made about his part in Big Boy's death, on to Bessie's gift of the card, Sheena's feeling she was being hexed, George's fear of someone before his death, even the wake of the baby, and Bessie's words to him that night. He went into more detail about the fire and told him what had happened to Shirley. Finally, he even told Rev about his suspicions concerning Ronnie.

It took a full fifteen minutes to describe everything, including the theft of the office files. Tom talking non-stop while Rev said nothing. He always seemed to being doing it around this man. As he was talking, saying it aloud, Tom suddenly felt this was all ridiculous, a figment of his and everybody's imagination. He had been suckered in like everyone else to believing that there was a giant conspiracy theory afoot. He said so. Rev took a last swig of the coffee and looked directly at Tom.

"You are not imagining things. Such things do happen here. I've seen and heard about them since I was a boy. Some people, especially Anglos, are never aware of any of this. You sure got right into the fray!" He looked somber.

"So, I presume that the reason you came right to me instead of someone else is to know from a preacher if witchcraft exists here, if spells are concocted – and maybe how someone in your profession can handle it. And that last part – the dealing with it – is the hardest."

"I don't like it when you put it in those words, but, yes, that's it."

Tom was grateful that he didn't have to spell it out any further.

"I want to know what I'm up against. I want the truth from an expert."

He smiled a half-smile.

"O.K." answered. "Then, first you have to understand that my being a Christian minister doesn't mean that I have to deny that witchcraft happens. The Lord himself certainly had experiences with soothsayers, seers and false prophets while he lived. He was definitely against it. I've read a batch about it myself.

All over the globe, even today, people have experienced fear, even terror, caused by others who try to manipulate people for their own purposes. They take the beliefs inculcated into their society and use them for their own purposes. That belief which they make use of is what is called animism – believing that spirits separate from bodies and can get into human beings, spirits getting into trees, owls, whatever, all for the purpose of causing evil."

"I don't understand. Are you saying that someone like Bessie can cause death and hurt people through her mind – through this animism?"

"I'm saying this," he said flatly. "It's a powerful mind tool that someone can develop and learn how to use over others. This so-called witch or sha-man or whatever you want to call them, uses clever strategies to get people either to hurt each other or to conclude that the witch is the originator of the bad things that happen, or sometimes even good, for that matter.

For example, I have known Arlene for a long time. I baptized her, but I also know what runs under the surface here. In her agony over her boy, she looked for an answer as to who caused this evil. She doesn't know that I am aware that she is capable of using the old ways to get what she wants. I'm not as naïve as everyone around here thinks."

He looked at Tom. "You didn't think I just learned about this from you, did you? No, of course you didn't, or you wouldn't be coming to me for answers. Forgive that remark. As to Arlene, I know she's a strong young woman, bitter because she hasn't been able to use the potential God gave her. Big Boy's illness and death seemed to heighten these feel-ings within her. She's like a lot of people around here – living in cycles that go round and round, not able to get out. It's no wonder they turn to the old ways, to anything they feel can give them some control."

He paused. Tom waited.

"I suppose you need to know the Christian answer. Maybe you think we don't have one either. There is one, but the Judeo-Christian answer, Job's answer, isn't enough for many people, both here and everywhere else. There's no magic to it. Suffering happens, and that's it. But that doesn't mean that we, as Christians, don't do everything in our power to overcome it."

"You happened to come along at the right or wrong time, depending on how you look at it, and you an outsider. So, you must have some of the blame, Arlene was thinking. It sounds to me like Arlene convinced herself of this, maybe to take away any of the guilt she may have felt – we know Our Lord had other ways of dealing with this, but the old ways took over instead. Anyway, I'm glad to hear that she is seeing things differently now."

It was Tom's turn to frown. Rev noticed. He slowed down.

"Just watch her, Son. She's capable of turning on people. She doesn't think I know it."

"I will," said Tom grimly. He had to ask the next question.

"Are you saying that Bessie had nothing to do with any of this – that she didn't scare George to death?"

"I know it's confusing. What I'm saying is that Bessie feeds on the fear of others, so in that sense she has a lot to do with what happens around here. She only has the power that people allow her to have. So, my answer is no, not directly. George was in the terrible position of being afraid of her, and she took advantage of it. But Bessie is also capable of preying on these kinds of fears, and she is guilty in her intentions. It gets her an exalted position, maybe even some money from it. She's raising the grandchildren without any help. Bessie's clever and careful. That's why she gave you that card, I think. She knew Shirley and Ina would interpret the card for you. It would scare them and make you wonder also. I think she sees you as a rival, like she does me. And, as for it being Ronnie instead of Bessie, I'd put my money on Bessie. She has a lot more need for power than even Ronnie. He's not poor, and she is. That's her driving force, I think. But I've been around so long that she knows she can't get to me. You, maybe. You're young, and not so established in your faith. Am I correct?"

Tom looked embarrassed. He nodded.

"But what about the others, George and Sheena, and all the rest? Are you sure about Ronnie Kane?"

"Well, I'm guessing, making some assumptions here, but I have a lot of experience in backing up my guesses. Poor Sheena. So many bad things have happened to her that she needs a cause, a scapegoat, just like Arlene did. But most of the horrific occurrences – the abusive, philandering boyfriend, the crash, the aspirin overdose, were caused by means that involved her own choices. It was all horrible but true, too true to accept." Rev shook his head.

"Maybe you don't know how many presents of food, diapers, fire wood and so on that Bessie has received from Sheena's mother?" He smiled. "There's not much I don't know about over time."

"But, Ronnie," said Tom. "Am I crazy to think that he harbors bad feelings toward me?"

"I think Roxy hit the nail on the head. He does want to exercise control over others, and like Bessie, he has his own little way of getting it. You came in, young, military, and he wanted to see you knocked down a peg. I'll bet he got a big kick out of seeing you jump away from that snake. He's probably told the story a lot. But, he just took advantage of what happened to make himself look braver than you. Although, I wouldn't put it past him to have put that spider on your desk, either. That whole episode, the way you describe it, was just a little too coincidental for me."

Rev pulled his chair back from the table, and stretched his legs out under the table top.

"The one most able to carry out fear tactics for gain, however, is Bessie. From everything you've told me, she is the most potentially harmful person of all those we have been talking about today."

"This makes more sense than anything I've heard since I got here," said Tom slowly. "But what can be done about it, about her, in particular?

I can't see the police coming to get her when they have no concrete evidence. Does this mean she can go on forever?"

"Good question. From what you've been telling me, the worst act she committed was causing George to die. I feel especially bad about George. I should have spent more time with him. Could we take this case to the police with proof? I don't see how. What proof could we ever have? Not even George can testify against her now."

Rev paused, and then went on.

"Now, George was a perfect example of what Bessie could do to a weak, poor soul. He was an outsider, exiled from his own people. He believed completely in her powers. He was probably more vulnerable than everyone else around here. Maybe he was grasping for help when he gravitated toward you, Tom."

"I wish I had known. I was stupid. I should have spent time with him."

"How could you know about all these underground eccentricities? You had just gotten here. I'm the one who should have sought him out, defended him against her. I should have had my ear to the ground; I should have found out what she was up to.

This is one act I'd blame Bessie directly for. She used him as an example of what she could do. She wanted him to talk about it. That's wrong, and that's evil, but it's like the old story of the emperor's new clothes: Everybody here pretended the truth was not the truth. That is, I think everyone had some sense that Bessie was just an ordinary person, but everyone was afraid to say so, just in case."

"Me, too. I found ways to avoid it. I didn't want to deal with it either."

"I share the blame more than anyone else, believe me. In fact, after talking this out with you, I see now that I have allowed this witchcraft to go on for years without really confronting it. I told myself that it was disappearing. My fault. I have told myself for years that I would preach the Gospel, and that would drive the witchcraft underground. I have been focusing on helping people in need, but I failed to see what their real needs were. I see now that I haven't been direct enough. Well, that will change soon, I assure you."

Rev sat up straight in his chair.

"Now that we're talking," said Tom, "I can see clearly what was happening the other night at the wake for the baby. I'm sure people had worked themselves up to believe she had the power of life and death, that she could make the baby live if she chose to. She reveled in it and used the wake as her stage. When she told them the baby was dead, they immediately fell into line."

Rev said, "Tom, you had the courage to come to me. You must be quite some strong young man to be attacked by our best witches!"

He laughed, but said seriously. "I'd say that says a lot about you and your strengths."

Tom didn't know what to say. Could that be he whom Rev was evaluating in such a positive way? He had the weirdest picture of something he hadn't thought of since leaving Arlington – the regimental flag. In his mind he could see himself as the color bearer for a regiment, something that had never entered his mind before, not even in his wildest dreams. It was an egotistical thought, but he couldn't help liking it.

Rev frowned. "I'm so sorry for my lack of action about all of this. Tom. Well, the emperor isn't wearing any clothes, and I am going to point it out."

He didn't say how he intended to confront the issue, and Tom didn't want to ask.

"Now back to this fire by your trailer. If I were you, I'd still keep a sharp lookout. Bessie may very well have tried this trick through Dusty, and she could try to harm you again."

Tom replied, "Maybe I'll have some outdoor lights installed, maybe even one of those cameras they have up at the hardware store in Pinetop. But, you know, I have a feeling that if Bessie instigated it, she's smart enough not to try the same thing again."

"Probably. But getting those technical gadgets sounds like a plan, just in case. And it wouldn't hurt to ask Waylon and his guys to check out your place when they can."

The last thing Rev said to him before he left was:

"Tom, boy, I've got a feeling you can be a real wildcat if you choose to!" Rev laughed. "And, I don't mean just the way you drive!"

Tom left Rev, feeling exhausted. He went home and slept for a full hour. He woke up with Rev's last words to him in his mind. It sounded like an honor to be called a wildcat. Waking up refreshed, he walked back to the hospital from his trailer, wondering what would happen next, but glad that a burden had shifted off him by talking with Rev. He saw that he had been carrying around his own burden of guilt, taken in by the thought that he had some blame in hurting people here. Arlene had done her work well. He wondered if she really had changed after all.

Unfortunately, as it turned out, not all things have happy endings. Tom was correct to question Arlene's apparent change for the better.

XLIV

A week after Tom had spoken with Arlene privately, all remained quiet in the office. But what Tom had no way of knowing was that Arlene had other plans. A few days later, dressed in black, she went to see Ben Altaha, the administrator. She didn't tell Carla why she wanted to see him, but there wasn't much about what was going on in the hospital that Carla didn't know eventually. Ben often left the office door ajar when he was talking with someone.

After Ben ushered Arlene in and left the door slightly open, she instead of sitting in one of the chairs, stood up in front of Ben's desk. She used her soft voice, saying she wanted to complain about Tom, that he was interfering too much in the personal affairs of people. She said that she wanted Ben to know that Tom was overstepping his bounds as a non-tribal member. He looked up at her, waiting. She said that she couldn't prove it, but she thought the community was in agreement with her. In her opinion, she said she believed that someone stole the files because they didn't trust him with private matters.

"I feel that he should be transferred somewhere else in Indian Health Service, maybe some place like Phoenix, where he could work away from any reservation." She lowered her eyes. "Of course, I wouldn't want to see him without a job."

Ben was surprised at what she said, but he was not a stupid man. He had dealt with many relationship issues in his role of hospital administrator.

"Can you give me examples of his interference?" he asked her.

She stumbled a moment before answering.

"Well, I feel that would be a breach of privacy. I do have a lot of information, but II wouldn't want to tell anything confidential that has to do with other people. That would be doing the same thing he is doing." She paused for a moment.

"And I consider myself a professional in my job. I might not have the schooling, but I am a professional. I would never repeat what my clients have told me."

"All right. You have made some serious accusations. I'll make some inquiries with others," Ben responded to her.

"Thank you so much!" Arlene turned to leave.

"I trust you will help our people." At her last words, Ben ushered her out, noncommittal.

After she left the office, Ben did as he said he would do. He asked around, speaking quietly to Roxy, Dr. Lang, the head nurse, even Sheena. All were supportive of Tom. No one had seen or heard anything negative against Tom. Ben was left with no proof of misdoings on Tom's part; even Arlene did not give him specific examples. Given the comments from others, he made the decision to take no action, but to tell Tom at his earliest convenience about Arlene's accusations. Perhaps, he considered, he might bring in a consultant to see what was going on in that department.

However, Tom first found out about what Arlene had said to Ben through the grapevine. Carla told Shirley after she heard Ben talking on the phone to Roxy; Shirley told Ina. Carla told Shirley to promise not to tell anyone, but Shirley and Ina took matters into their own hands.

The next day while Tom was out of the office, they confronted Arlene openly, not behind closed doors, but in the middle of the department. Ina started the confrontation, but Shirley wasn't far behind.

"Arlene, what's this you've been telling Ben?"

Arlene looked surprised, but she answered them right away.

"The truth. I'm telling the truth. I'm the only one around here with the courage to say it."

She folded her arms across her chest, standing her ground.

"You two are cowards. You fall for any stranger that comes in here to run the office."

Shirley, no longer draped by her shawl, came to the forefront.

"You're not telling the truth, and you know it. We know what you're really up to. Power. You want it back like the old days, when you could control us, make us afraid of you. We know it, and we can tell everyone what you're up to. We know what you pretend to be and what you really are."

Shirley had never spoken like this before, not to anyone. She liked herself.

"Yeah," said Ina. "You've got a job and good chances to get ahead. Keep on, and we'll see that you are the one who'll lose everything. If you try anything, we'll speak up against you."

Arlene didn't know what to say. She grabbed her jacket and left the office; Ina and Shirley hugged each other, laughing. They had broken her power over them at last.

After they thought over what they had done, they decided to tell Tom, to make sure to warn him. When he returned to the office, they both tried to talk to him at the same time. Tom finally grasped what they were saying. He frowned.

"It's all right, Mr. Doc! Arlene lost. She tried to get you, but Ben saw right through it," said Shirley.

"Yeah," added Ina. "And she can't get us anymore either. That's never going to happen again."

Tom still looked grim.

"I'm going in to see Ben right away."

He turned to them.

"I really appreciate your loyalty."

They looked at each other.

Ina said, "Us Apaches, we always stand with the right side."

XLV

As a member of America's post-Christian society, Tom had really meant to go to the Lutheran Church on Sunday, but he didn't set his alarm. It was well past noon when he awoke. So, he never heard the actual words of Rev's sermon, and Rev certainly wasn't part of the generation that taped sermons. But word of mouth, the old Indian smoke signals as everyone called them, came Tom's way bit by bit over the next week. Shirley and Ina were eager to tell him what Rev had said.

They reported that Rev began his sermon by reading Psalm 6, a prayer for help in time of trouble, a plea from David to keep evil men away from him. People were on edge at this beginning, but it got even more direct. Names were called out and challenged, both the believers in witchcraft, and the supposed shaman, Bessie, who was not present. Others, Rev said, who had ambitions to go the old way, needed to straighten themselves out. He told them it was about time that they made a choice for which way they intended to go in this life. He said that he realized now that this was the purpose God had kept him in Whiteriver, and he was going to do his job.

Tom heard from another source that some people had said that they would not come back to church, but that the majority listened and heeded. Many, even now, didn't want to talk much about what happened that day. Shirley and Ina repeated as much as they knew, but it was Roxy, however, who had heard it all as well, and she reported it to Tom with great glee, especially the part where Arlene was directly challenged to come back to the faith, and Ronnie was mentioned as well, as an example of one who grasped at power at the expense of others.

"This wasn't your proper Eastern kind of church service," she said animatedly. "It was a real fight against evil. Whoopee!"

A few days after Rev's sermon, Bessie, it was said, disappeared from her ramshackled house with her grandchildren, finding a half-sister and went away to live with her in Cibecue. The spells that had been so carefully crafted fell apart. According to gossip, people were no longer afraid to talk about Bessie, and they made up for lost time by talking with great glee. All kinds of jokes about old ladies were dragged out of the closet and repeated.

Ronnie Kane, who had been mentioned by name as well in the sermon, found himself spending more time on his land; it was said that he liked to watch old movies, old cowboy and Indian movies. The hospital found it unnecessary to use his services any more. Roxy reported to Tom that he seemed to look more like an old man now than a chief.

In one way, though, Tom wasn't satisfied with the outcomes. Bessie was not prosecuted. He understood that nobody would have known how to do it anyway. Still, for George's sake, he would have liked to have seen her publicly punished, to have had her arrested. But, then there would be no one to take care of the children. What Tom didn't realize, however, was that the most powerful weapon that was used against Bessie was carried out by the people themselves. It was humor. They laughed at and about her, made jokes, and with this simple action, she became weak.

All in all, Tom told Ada on the telephone, things were being resolved pretty well. At least, that's what it looked like on the surface, he said.

But, what was happening on the surface was never the whole story around her, he told her later.

XLVI

Tom hadn't realized that the funeral arrangements for George would be so complicated. He had promised George he would see that he was buried near his people, but after talking to others about Hopi burial beliefs and customs, and to Hopi people as well, he had found it difficult to carry out his wishes. He didn't know what clan George belonged to or if he had any relatives whom he could contact. Tom had found that George had not named anyone as his next of kin in any hospital records. Nobody around here seemed to know either. Roxy said that George had left Hopi over twenty years ago.

It looked as if he were going to have to rely on the funeral home, after all. Somehow, he had secretly hoped he could find a personal connection for George. But how? The funeral home wanted some specific directions. It had to be done right away. There was nothing to do but fall back on the home.

Let's give it one more chance, thought Tom. He went on the internet. Tom sat in his office and pulled his chair up to the desk and began to search. The eerie, gray light of the computer flooded the office as he began to search. It surprised him how quickly he could pull up information on Hopi Indian burials. Someone named Goddard reported that when an adult Hopi died, the nearest relatives by blood took care of the body and performed the necessary rituals, carrying it to one of the nearby graveyards in the valleys near where the dead person lived.

Well, Tom thought, that's out of the question, since we don't know the family. What was he going to do now? I don't want to turn his body over to strangers, even if they are Hopi. In his frustration, he opened his desk drawer, looking for a box of mints he had put there especially for times when he needed a pick-me-up. His hand touched George's cap at the back of the drawer. No matter what, the promise he had made to George had to be carried out. A thought came to him. The funeral home had even told him they could do it, but for his own egotistical reasons he had delayed in taking up their offer. He popped open his cell phone and called the Raymon Florian funeral home immediately. They'd have the answer. They had even told him they could do it. He'd bet they knew more about Northern Arizona than he would ever know. After all, they were the professionals. They were just waiting for him to make up his damn mind.

A woman's voice answered.

"Mr. Florian, please. This is Tom Collins."

She asked him to wait. It wasn't long.

"Dr. Collins. We were hoping you'd call."

"Sorry I've taken so long. I really do need your advice in making the burial arrangements for George. As you know, he was Hopi. I can't figure out how to carry out his wishes when we don't know exactly where he was from or who his relatives were. Is there some place he can be buried where he can be near some of his people?"

"Oh, yes, sir. I'm sure we can find out the answer. My nephew Sam, he knows a lot about that part of the state. His wife is Hopi."

He sounded embarrassed.

"Actually I already told him the problem. I thought that was what you wanted when we met in Pinetop?"

Tom had to agree. Florian went on.

"He suggests we take the deceased to near Tuba City. There's a memorial park not far from a Hopi village, southeast of the city. Do you know Tuba City?"

"Not at all, but I'll take your word for it," answered Tom. "Maybe that's the best we can do for a man who claimed no relatives. When do you think the body can be moved?"

"I'll call up there – I've got a friend who is director of that park. You know it's a pretty long trip from here? It might cost a little more."

"That's all right. Just let me know when. I'd really like to see the grave. And I'd like to make it up there and back in the same day, if I can."

He got off the phone feeling a lot better.

That night he got out a map. Tuba City was on the edge of the Painted Desert and only about fifty miles from the Grand Canyon. The internet told him that Navajos, Hopis, all kinds of people lived there, mostly Navajos. That would have to be all right with George. It was as close as Tom could get for George to be near his people.

XLVII

The day for his drive up to Tuba City was planned for the next Friday. The funeral car was to go up the day before. George's coffin would be buried, and directions to the site would be left for Tom at the front gate of the memorial park. It was going to be a long drive.

That Friday morning Tom left Whiteriver early, stopping almost halfway toward his destination in the town of Winslow for a burger in a café near the train station, as he watched a long passenger train stop, with faces looking out of windows. They were heading for California, people probably afraid to fly, or maybe they just wanting the adventure of seeing part the Grand Canyon on the way. They were looking at him as if he belonged in Arizona. He did.

Maybe he and Ada would do that someday, if they could get their lives in sync. There would have to come a time, soon, when they would need to figure out what they wanted to do, where they wanted to live, and what careers they wanted to pursue. They couldn't just drive up and down through the Salt River Canyon all of their married lives.

He had enjoyed leaving Whiteriver early in the morning, with the first rays of the sun. George's kachina, sitting on the kitchen table at Tom's, had seemed to know he was going with him. He was almost smiling through his mask, Tom thought. The funeral director had called Tom the night before, assuring him that the body had arrived at the park and was already buried. He gave Tom the number of the grave.

Sitting here in Winslow, he realized that he didn't really have to make this trip, but in another way he did. It was a duty. It was going to be a long trip, up there and back, and he wanted to make it back home in one day, even if it were late at night when he arrived.

It was a dry, cold day, but it wasn't snowing, even up here in the North. He left Winslow after he wolfed down the burger and started driving Northwest through Navajo territory, through miles and miles of Coconino County. The pink layers of horizontal rock in the Painted Desert were passing quickly by the car. He had no time to stop. He saw flocks of sheep, hogans, a corn field full of dried stalks, shepherds guiding their sheep. The high desert brush seemed to go on forever. And the funny thing was, that he felt that this was foreign territory, that he belonged back in the land of the Apaches.

He followed Georgette's directions carefully this time. Hours passed, giving him time to think, then all of a sudden he had arrived. The sun was slanting differently now as he drove up to the memorial garden. Afternoon had come. The cemetery hadn't been hard to find; nothing was hard to find out here after Washington, D.C. He could have done it without the GPS.

He got out at the front gate and knocked on the door of the little office. No one answered. That was all right; he had the number of the grave, and there couldn't be many new graves that had all been recently filled. He scanned the area. He was looking for the newest graves, for the upturned earth that would mark the spot, for the newly placed temporary marker with the name and number on it. Memories of Arlington Cemetery flooded back. The graves, the six families. Why was he always at grave sides? Why was he always at wakes?

He drove slowly around the circular, tarry driveway. It wasn't a big cemetery. The grave site wasn't hard to find, a little away from the others, its piles of chunky red earth mounded in a rectangle. No need to cover up the grave with rocks as at Fort Apache. The green grass in the memorial garden seemed out of place, artificial, Anglo. On the grave stones were names of all kinds, Navajo, Hopi maybe, Anglo, Hispanic, and who knows what else. They were all resting together, finally in harmony. George would have liked that, thought Tom.

There it was. George's grave lay alone, apart from the others. A metal marker about a foot high was sunk into the earth at what was probably the head of the grave. It bore a number on the metal plate, a number like the one Tom had written earlier on a scrap of paper, the number that the funeral director had given him. This was the temporary marker that would be replaced by the headstone that Tom had ordered. It was to be finished within a month, they had told him. His name, date of death, and his tribe would be carved on it.

A metal bar. George had a metal plate in his head, the sign of an old wound. But, right now, all that was left of George above ground was a number on a metal bar tamped into the soil. Arlington Cemetery also had numbers for veterans, he remembered. He wondered if George had been a veteran; it wasn't likely. He was a veteran of life. No flowers, no mementos would be laid on this grave. Tom would be the only one who would ever visit it. He reached his hand into his left coat pocket. Found Face, George's kachina, came out. Tom placed it upright at the top of the grave for a minute. All was silent around him.

Tom reached into his other pocket and took out a pen. On his knees in front of the marker and the kachina, he took out a piece of card-board he had brought with him. He wrote carefully on it –GEORGE DEWAKUKU – in square letters. Next, he jabbed the pen's point into the cardboard, and inserted a piece of string into the hole made by the pen, string he had brought from home. He tied the string into a circle, from which the cardboard dangled. He carefully put the string and cardboard around the metal marker. It fell to the ground and lay there. George had a name; he was somebody. There was a little space left at the bottom of the cardboard, where, without thinking, he drew a small black cross. He got up, dusted off his knees and, almost as a second thought, picked up Found Face and put him back in his pocket. The kachina had found a new home. Tom didn't come from a culture where you leave the dead person's most precious things with the deceased.

When you're born you get a name; when you die, you need one also, he said to himself, as he headed back to the car that would take him back to Whiteriver.

XLVIII

Tom arrived back home after midnight. He was glad to see that the bright light that had been installed on the trailer after the fire was illuminating the whole front of his home. He stumbled tiredly up the partially new steps and pulled out his key to open the door.

Boy, it was good to be back. He flipped on the light switch and the thermostat to start the heat pump. A humming noise and a slight stirring of air moved through the trailer. It ruffled a piece of paper lying on the floor next to the door. He must have stepped over it as he entered the trailer. Tom reached down and picked it up, holding the small of his back with the other hand. His back was killing him. Tom stood up and turned the paper over on both sides. Maybe it had blown off his desk. It was folded in two. He was really worn out from the drive. He rubbed his eyes before squinting at the paper again.

He opened the fold of the paper as he sat on his bed. Suddenly, he sat up straight. This was weird, really weird. The paper didn't belong to him; perhaps it had been pushed underneath his front door.

It read: "I need to see you as soon as possible. I'm afraid. Meet me Sat night midnight at Kinishbah. Alone to be safe. Need your advice. I trust you. Help me, please. Don't tell anyone. They are out to get me."

There was no name at the end. The print was large and all in caps. The spelling was all right. He looked at his watch. It was late Friday night; that would mean tomorrow night. Whom did he know that was so afraid? It had to be someone he knew well, not a stranger. Damn it. This was all supposed to be over. He could not think well right now. He was worn out. Why would anybody choose a deserted ruin like Kinishbah for a meeting with him? The only reason he could think of was to get him alone or to be so afraid that they couldn't let others find out about the meeting.

He got ready for bed and fell into a fitful sleep. He awoke once, thinking he heard scratching on his front door. His dreams weren't any better. He dreamt of a silver-scaled snake with the head of a cobra.

When he finally awoke, it was after eight o'clock in the morning. The night hadn't cleared his thinking; he still didn't know what he was going to do. Was it some kind of trap? Should he tell someone, ask what to do?

Two cups of coffee later, he felt more in control. The daylight always had a way of making him see things in his head more clearly. He looked at the paper again. Who knew that he had gone up to Tuba City, leaving the trailer unoccupied? Otherwise, it would have been too risky to leave the note. Almost everyone knew, he had to admit. The paper was ordinary, the size of a piece of computer paper. It had been folded in half neatly. The writing was large and the print was square. It was as if the person who wrote it was trying to disguise their handwriting. Why wouldn't they sign their name if they were on the up-and-up? They didn't tell him to destroy the note, however. Someone out to do him harm might have done that, to get rid of the evidence, as Bessie had told Dusty to do. Maybe they knew he wouldn't have been that stupid, anyway. Could this be Bessie again, up to her old tricks?

He didn't recognize anything about the writing. Nothing yelled out at him. Naturally; it was disguised. Whoever did it seemed to have used an ordinary ballpoint pen, the inexpensive kind used by half the world. Why would someone with sincere motives disguise his writing?

Why wouldn't someone who wanted his help just come to him and ask him? Bessie wasn't any longer a problem; at least, that's what everybody thought. Whom were they afraid of? And what use could he be? There were Shirley and Sheena. They needed help, but would they have chosen a place like Kinishbah to meet him? Not a likely spot for a woman to choose. As for Sheena, since Bessie was out of the picture, there was nothing more he could do for her. She couldn't get out there in a wheelchair, anyway.

If it weren't a woman, what man would do this? George might, if he had been alive. There was Dusty Lupe, but he had been controlled by Bessie who was gone. Dusty probably wouldn't want to have any more to do with him. There would be no reason. He was probably still in jail anyway. It couldn't be Ronnie Kane, having another joke, or could it?

It all kept coming back to Bessie. Maybe she still wanted to get even with him, and Cibecue, her new home, wasn't that far away. If he did go out to Kinishbah, he'd better make sure he told someone he trusted exactly where and when he was going. He knew who that would be. He'd tell them to call the police if Tom hadn't called them by 12:30 p.m.

He slowed down his thoughts. He hadn't realized it, but he had already decided to go and to go alone. Jackass. Here he was, putting himself on the front line of battle again, the infamous imbecile line. Should he take a weapon? He didn't own a gun anymore. All he had was a knife, and a Swiss army knife, at that.

Those damn rattlesnakes. Do they sleep during the night? He'd better take a flashlight and wear his heaviest boots again. His stomach was quivering, even as he thought about it. But, someone was asking him to protect them, supposedly. The more he thought about it, the angrier he got. The ancient Greeks called courage a 'fire in the belly.' His anger was overcoming the little quivers in his stomach. Now, it felt like he had acid reflux, a burning sensation that was taking over from the quivers.

Too much coffee. Not enough food. Enough of this. The first thing he would do this morning would be to go get a big meal at the Pinyon Restaurant, and see what that would do to the fire in his belly. Next he would go to his chosen confidant, telling them to call the police if he hadn't called by twelve -thirty. He'd tell them where and when he would be at Kinishbah, just to be on the safe side.

He was at the restaurant early for Saturday morning. It was just nine o'clock, but they were open. Several men were eating big plates of food. He didn't recognize any one. There was no music playing at this hour of the morning. He ordered a platter of tamales, sausages and another cup of coffee. Afterward, he sat back with a sigh. Actually, he found himself feeling pretty good right now. But, just to be sure, he reached into his pocket and pulled out a single Tums, washing it down with a glass of water. He reminded himself that George was resting near his people; at least one problem was solved.

Now, on to another one. He had no idea if he were doing the right thing by going out to Kinishbah, or if he were being stupidly rash. Guess I won't know until it's all over, he thought. The waitress offered him a plastic box of toothpicks. What the hell, he thought. Might as well live dangerously. He took a sharp one from the box and put it in his pocket.

XLIX

Evening came early. Tuba City, George and even the pink of the Painted Desert had faded into his memory after the anonymous note of last night. He was determined to be prepared for tonight; his confidant was told, and the batteries were charged in his flashlight. He had also charged his cell phone, even taken out the Swiss Army knife and checked its acuity. He would keep it open when he put it in his pocket. Next, he pulled his Army boots out of the closet. They were still tough and strong, still protection for him. No snake would be able to get at him as he walked toward Kinishbah.

He was going to plan this all out, to be ready for no matter who showed up tonight. What if it were Ronnie, ready for another chance to get at him? The best defense against him would be to be prepared. He had plugged the phone number of the tribal police into his cell phone. If it turned out to be Ronnie who wanted to play another trick on him, he'd call the police immediately. A good questioning by Waylon Pinal might shine a light on Ronnie's activities. Maybe he had only been laying low after Rev's sermon chastised him; maybe he was waiting to try something else as a form of revenge.

As to the other possibilities, he wasn't afraid of them. It wasn't likely that Shirley's husband was back or that Dusty Lupe would be a match for him if he were out on bond. He didn't have time and didn't want to ask Waylon Pinal if Dusty were out of jail. His question might generate curiosity in Waylon. But, what if it were Bessie? She was an old lady; he could handle her. Anyway, her tactics would more likely be of the frightening kind, like casting a spell on him. She was not known to harm anyone directly. And, as to her supposedly casting a spell, that was the last thing he would be vulnerable to.

But what if it really was someone who needed help as they said in the letter? The only ones that he could imagine who would want to meet him in a secret place would be Dusty or Sheena, for some weird reason. He was working with a lot of alcoholics. Maybe one of them wanted to see him.

No, none of that made any sense. It came down to three or four possibilities: 1. Someone wanted to rob him; 2. Someone wanted to hurt him; 3. Someone needed his help; 4. Someone wanted to humiliate him. The first two were dangerous; number three was what it was; and number four would need others around in order for him to become the butt of a joke.

He ruled out the first one. A robber would go to his trailer, not out here. He would have a better chance of stealing valuables in his trailer while he was away. Better make sure he locked his door while he was gone tonight. It just didn't seem likely, though. He needn't worry about number three. That would take care of itself, and he'd figure out how to help them when he saw the problem. So, he reasoned, he needed to plan what to do if someone wanted to hurt or humiliate him. He had already thought about the latter; if it were Ronnie, the police would take care of him.

That left the possibility that someone wanted to hurt him. He couldn't think of any more to do to prevent that than he had already done. He could have brought someone with him, he supposed, someone hiding in the car, but he ruled that out. Besides, who could he get to go with him and stay hidden? He couldn't even ask that of Rev. The police don't operate that way, either.

He remembered that his gas tank was almost empty from yesterday's trip. He'd better fill up before it got completely dark. He drove over to the only gas station, located down town. The station was empty of people. Later, no one could say when they had last seen him that day, except for the guys at the restaurant that morning. His mind was leaping onto every scenario he could think of right now.

While filling up his tank, he had a second thought. Maybe he should have brought a gun with him. Too late now. He didn't have time to go to Pinetop to buy one. What if he just didn't show up? That would make him a coward one more time, and one more was too many.

L

Night came, and with it the cold and the dampness. There was a smell of wood fires. Not many people were about. The Saturday night drinkers had either gone to the Melting Pot up in Pinetop, to the bar at Blueberry Hill, or inside their houses to hide their beer cans from others. God help any children who might be vulnerable. It came out as a prayer. Tom didn't realize what it was until it came out of his mouth. Well, he thought, I might as well give another quick one for a good outcome for tonight, as long as I'm doing it.

"Lord, keep me safe," he added quickly.

He left the gas station to wait out the evening at home. Time was going slowly. He didn't feel like turning on the TV. He looked at Ada's picture. He had called her earlier, saying nothing about what he was going to do tonight. There was no need to give her another reason to worry about him. He looked at the two pictures of Geronimo again – the bronze faces, the lines. This evening would have been nothing for him.

Finally, at half past eleven, he went to his Jeep in the parking lot. He had on his boots, his gloves, jacket, and, as an odd, last minute gesture, he had put George's old cap on his head. He had taken it home from his office, washed it and put it in his bedside table drawer. He would have looked unrecognizable to anyone seeing him without his Jeep.

Flashlight and knife in his pocket, he drove slowly out toward Kinishbah, knowing that there could be horses crossing the road or a drunk in a car coming home. There were no street lights, and only a few houses back from the road still had their lights on. He hadn't been back to Kinishbah since he had been there with Ronnie. Nobody at all was on the road now.

Soon, ahead of him was the turnoff to Kinishbah on the right. The rusty metal gate that said "Kinishbah" was easy to push open. Did that mean that no one had been there before him? Not necessarily. He decided to leave the gate open, almost as a sign to announce his being there. The road was rutty, but dry. The car made it easily down toward the rendezvous site. He had a momentary thought that his greatest danger might be from a bear or a wild cat looking for prey. He hadn't considered that before.

He slowed down. The only other time he had been here the sun had been burning bright and the rocks hot enough to entice the snakes. But, now it was almost midnight by his watch. There was no light visible anywhere. Even the moon was being elusive, coming out for a moment from the night clouds, then hiding again.

He had turned his bright lights down to parking lights just as the stone buildings showed up ahead. Maybe he would turn his car around before he stopped. That would mean he couldn't see the building from the car, but it would be a safe tactic in case he wanted to leave quickly. He would leave the doors unlocked also. He was beginning to feel that hot spot in his belly.

He turned the car around, careful not to run over any big rocks that would hurt the tires. But before he turned it around, he scanned the buildings. He couldn't see any sign of a light or a person. They would have to have gotten here by vehicle. The moon, however, was behind the clouds. Maybe he would be able to see more if it came out again.

He turned off the motor, facing the road going out. It was quiet. He rolled one window down. An owl hooted to another one who answered back. Was it really an owl or the old Indian tactic of communicating? Quit the crap. Don't let your nerves take over. That's what Ronnie would have liked. He rolled the window up and opened the car door, leaving his car keys on the seat. He put his boots down on the dry earth. Nothing happened this time— no snakes ran at him. He had the sudden feeling that he knew how those wounded warriors had felt trying to escape the explosive devices they knew were out there waiting for them. But, the IEDs didn't sleep at night like the snakes did.

His flashlight in his left hand, he held onto the knife in his pocket. Nobody knew that he didn't have a gun. Walking slowly, he proceeded toward the biggest stone building, with the sharp edge of the canyon behind him.

Suddenly, as the moon rolled out from behind the clouds, he had a brief glimpse of something metal toward the side of the building, something that might have been a vehicle. As if flirting with him, the clouds quickly covered the face of the moon, leaving Tom to rely only upon his flashlight.

LI

He walked steadily toward the entrance of the building in front of him, toward what had once been a rectangular door, but now was only a gap between the stones. He played his flashlight around the perimeter of the opening. Nothing. What sounded like a coyote called in the distance.

He needed to do something, to confront the quietness, to make it his own. That car he glimpsed hadn't appeared magically without a driver.

"Who's here?"

His voice sounded loud to him. It echoed against the inside walls, stirring up a noise like the wings of bats. If was as if a hundred little birds were flapping their wings. Suddenly, above the fluttering wings and squeaks, came a small, feminine sort of sound.

"I'm over here, to your left."

He had heard the voice before, but it was a whisper and hard to identify. He didn't move but turned his light in the direction of the voice.

There before him was Arlene, but an Arlene he had never seen before. She had on a black dress, shapeless, long, and her hair hung down as always, but now it looked unkempt, uncombed. There was something about her eyes, a wild, feral quality that made her look more like an animal than a person. Could it be drugs, the peyote he had heard of? She came toward him and stopped a few feet in front of him.

Tom was astounded. His fear had turned into puzzlement. If she had wanted to talk with him, she could have easily done so in private at work. He quickly regained his guard again. This was the woman who tried to get him transferred, who had lied about him to Ben Altaha. Of all the people he had suspected of sending him the note, he had never considered her as a likely possibility, perhaps because she worked in the same office; perhaps because he saw her every work day.

She spoke again, still in her small voice.

"I didn't think you would come."

He was annoyed, now that his fear had dissipated somewhat.

"Why go through all this rigamarole – why not talk to me at work, Arlene?"

She shook her head.

"I couldn't. Too many eyes and ears in that place. I want to explain it all to you."

She moved a little closer to him.

"I'll give you ten minutes; then, I'm leaving."

All of a sudden she let out a long, wailing sob that startled him, stirring whatever creatures who were in the building to act as a background chorus. It was as if she were playing Medea in a Greek tragedy. She had to be nuts.

She suddenly left off wailing and faced him directly. Her mouth was open, her teeth white.

"You listen to me for a change! You don't know how it feels to lose your son, to know that there is a power stronger than you waiting to destroy you."

This was insanity. It was as if her mind had slipped away to another place.

"Go on," he said, wanting her to talk.

"Bessie, she knew I was her rival. She knew I was younger and that I would grow stronger as she grew weaker, so she made up her mind to get me, to scare me into losing my power by attacking my son."

She paused. He said nothing.

"Then, you came along, you with your education, your refusal to believe in the spirits. At first I was happy you were there, because Bessie found you a stumbling block."

She was a foot away from him now, his flashlight shining on her face. Tom found himself grasping the knife in his pocket. What time was it? He had to make the call by twelve -thirty.

She continued talking.

"So when I discovered that Bessie was clever enough to use you to get at Big Boy, I knew that something had to be done. You helped my boy die! Don't you understand?" Her teeth were bared toward him like a wild animal. "But you're not going to get your hands on anybody else. You'll never be able to use the information in those files now. They're burned, up in flames! Don't you finally understand? I did it. It was me!"

"No, I don't understand," he said firmly. I did not help your son to die. Such a thing is not possible. Bessie tricked you into believing that she had the power to do that, and you fell for it."

"No, no!" She yelled out at him, but suddenly she stopped, as if she had returned to normal.

"You are wrong. You don't see what has happened. Bessie's power is gone now, but that leaves me. I'm here, taking her place. People will have to be afraid of me now – everyone – my husband, you, even Rev. I've got the power now. I don't have to pretend any longer."

He wasn't going to listen to this craziness from her. He had had enough.

"I'm going to leave, Arlene. If you decide you need some help getting out of the witch business, I'll try to find someone who can work with you. The way you are right now, there's no way you can help others. You're going to need some time away from the office."

She laughed as if it were all a joke.

"No, you can't take my job away from me." She laughed again, but spat out:

"My job is mine. You're the one who will be leaving. What a fool you are. Leave if you want, but I'll tell the police that you lured me out here and tried to rape me. I'll say you made up that note yourself as a cover. Ben Altaha will testify that I was concerned about you."

She reached out her hands to touch her black dress and started pulling on it, pushing her strong, thin nails into the material.

"Leave, but your tire tracks are here. My dress will be torn when I go to the police. An Anglo attacking an Apache woman. You'll be the one who will lose your job."

She had found a weak spot in her dress; she was ripping it, working herself more and more into a frenzy.

"You did it! The saintly Mr. Doc! You tried to rape me! But I strug-
gled to get away from you. The police will like that story."

She started yelling, "Help! Help! Don't rape me!"

There were crescendos of noise all over the ancient room. Bats were
moving, and moths came forward toward Tom's flashlight. Scurrying
sounds were emitting from the creatures living in the earthen floor. A
cacophony of crickets, creatures of all kinds seem to stand with Arlene
against him.

He found himself standing stock still, not knowing what to do or say.

Suddenly she pulled out of her dress pocket a pair of tiny scissors,
nail scissors. They weren't for him. They were for her. She started slash-
ing at her arms and her black dress. Making red lines on her arms, even
lines across her face. It was a hideous sight.

She had him trapped.

"Come on, come near me! You killed my boy. Try to hurt me! Let's
see how brave you are now!"

As if to provoke him to attack, she lunged at him with the little scissors. She couldn't kill him; that wasn't her aim. She wanted to implicate
him, to set him up.

He took his hand away from his own knife and dropped the flashlight. It still glowed against the wall from the floor. He had to get her
away from him and leave. She was not a big woman. He pushed her
with his two hands. She fell back, tripping on her long dress. Giving a
surprised yelp, she fell upon the rocks on the ground. Oh, God, he must
have hurt her. Her scenario was coming true. But, suddenly there was
another noise.

The rattling sound was no stranger to him. Arlene must have heard
it also. She was trying to get up. She issued a grunting sound from her
open mouth, then fell back on the floor. With a swish, something slid in
front of the flashlight's glow and disappeared.

A snake. It was a snake. She had been bitten. Forgetting all caution,
he retrieved his flashlight and went over to her. She made no protest. She
was holding her left ankle above the spot where two dots of blood lay,
almost like a tattoo, on the upper part of her ankle.

He had to do something. But what? Old westerns showed people cutting into the snake bite, sucking the poison out.

"Oh, God," he heard himself yelling. "What am I supposed to do? Help me!"

Suddenly, his right ear picked up a sound, a rumbling sound like that of a big vehicle. It could have been thunder, but it wasn't. Rays of lights were now penetrating the doorway, like a search light. Arlene was moaning. He forgot about the noise and the lights; he reached in his pocket for his knife and cut at her ankle where the little holes were. He started sucking at her ankle, tasting the rustiness of the blood in his mouth.

LII

The lights that Tom at last was able to focus upon were not coming from his little flashlight. Its beam was thrust into the corner of the floor where Arlene lay. She was curled up in a ball now, weakly pushing at Tom as he kept his mouth clamped onto her ankle.

"They're coming. Someone's coming," he kept saying to himself. "She got me after all. They'll think I tried to attack her. That's what she'll tell them."

He sat up and spat the blood out of his mouth. Maybe it wasn't the right thing to do. Maybe it only made the poison kill her more quickly. Before he could think further, there were voices, doors slamming, lights arcing through the dark. An engine was rumbling outside.

"Tom!" yelled out a voice. He knew it was a good voice, but in his confusion, he didn't recognize it. His senses didn't seem to be working right.

"Over here!" he made himself answer.

Within seconds Waylon Pinal and a younger man in a uniform, his deputy, stood in the doorway silhouetted by the moonlight.

"Here. Back here," Tom yelled again.

They ran toward his voice. The noise from the bats escalated once more. Waylon arrived first, bent down, looking at Arlene who wasn't speaking, eyes closed.

"What happened?"

"She was bitten by a snake, I'm pretty sure. Or maybe a spider. But I think I heard the rattle. She needs help fast."

The young policeman started stamping his feet on the floor, to ward off any creatures nearby.

"Come on, Johnny," said Waylon. "Let's get her out of here and up to the hospital pronto."

The two men picked her up and headed for their police car, leaving Tom standing alone. Waylon, trying to talk and carry Arlene at the same time, looked back toward Tom.

"You sure you're O.K.?"

Tom nodded.

"How about your car?"

"Yes."

"Come up to the hospital, so we can get a statement from you."

Waylon made a gesture with a nod of his head.

"Come on out of there. There's someone here you need to thank."

Tom walked slowly outside, no longer caring or thinking about snakes. He didn't even ask them how they knew he was here. He was drained out. Suddenly, all he wanted badly was a candy bar. At the doorway, he shielded his eyes against the lights of the police car. Before he got his vision back, a long arm grabbed him around the shoulder, giving him a big slap on the back. Carl Herz was a strong man for his age. He shook Tom by the shoulders.

"Boy, you sure do get yourself into a mess. Thank God you told me where you were going."

Seeing the look on Tom's face, he pulled him toward the jeep.

"Come on. Let's sit down. Get your breath and tell me all about it. I've got a thermos of sweet tea in the car. You need something."

Tom didn't protest. He tried to look at his watch, but his eyes couldn't see the dials.

"What time is it?"

"Almost one o'clock. You said if I didn't hear from you by twelve-thirty, to call the police. Well, I did call them, but I decided to call them at midnight instead, and I decided to go with them."

He couldn't help grinning.

"But, first, I told Hilda I'd be back – she went nuts, not so nuts that she didn't make me this thermos of tea – and by 12:10, I called the police, and I didn't bother to wait. I went to the police station. Too hard to explain it all on the phone, anyway. They didn't waste any time getting out here. Haven't had a ride like that in years!"

He was clearly enjoying himself.

All Tom could say was, "Glad you did." He couldn't put into words how grateful he was.

"You able to drive?"

Tom sat up straight, nodding. He started up the Jeep, turning up the heat to full blast. He was freezing, even wearing his jacket and George's cap. The gloves had been lost somewhere back there, and he wasn't going to get them, now or ever. They had served as protection for his healing hands; he couldn't remember how they came off.

Motor running, he made no effort to drive.

Rev said quickly, looking at him, "Let's sit here a minute before we go to the hospital. Can you tell me what happened?"

"O.K." First, Tom took a big swig of the tea from the thermos that Rev had offered him, before he began to speak slowly to Rev. The tea washed away the rustiness in his mouth.

He explained his shock at seeing Arlene, her appearance, her belief that she was a witch and destined to take Bessie's place. As he was telling the story, it all seemed too crazy to be true. When he came to the part about her attempt to set him up as a rapist, Rev couldn't help but let out a big "What!"

Tom wanted to tell someone, tell them everything. He told him about the snake bite, his stupid way of trying to save her. He kept on until he couldn't talk anymore.

"Let's go back, Son. Let's get out of this godforsaken place and into the real world again. Give me that new-fangled phone of yours. I'd better tell Hilda what's up."

Tom started the car. He didn't want to look at Rev. He had to get his emotions in check.

"I might even tell her we've taken some territory back for our side tonight. That would keep her guessing," smiled Rev.

Tom couldn't help laughing. He surprised himself. His laughter was loud, surging out from the depths of his body. He felt warm now, even though his still tender hands were now tingling.

Rev looked suddenly somber. "And I need to see Arlene. She's still part of my flock. Let's get up to the hospital."

Tom's momentary laughter had disappeared.

"She'll tell them I tried to rape her."

"What if she does?" retorted Rev. "You told me ahead of this mess about the note, and you still do have the note, don't you?"

"Yeah. Of course."

"We, including the police, are all witnesses that she was in a weird state of mind. And, my guess is that it'll be a long time before she'll be able to accuse anybody of anything."

Tom let out a sigh, put the car in gear, and drove out of Kinishbah.

LIII

During the next twenty-four hours, Tom was occupied with a round of activities. He gave a written statement to Waylon, found out about Arlene's condition – she would recover, at least physically – called Ada and played down the incident, got Roxy to patch up his still tender hands, and called Ina and Shirley in to tell them the story before the moccasin telegraph went into effect. It turned out that they had already heard all about it, anyway. It was Sunday, and they were both at home, but their phones had been ringing since early that morning, they reported to Tom.

He did one more thing. He attended the healing service that Rev conducted every Sunday evening. A couple of dozen people were in the church, most of them staring at him, he felt. He was relieved to see smiles on their faces after the service. One lady invited him to a barbecue, and an older man said that maybe they could go hunting together some time.

During the service Rev's hands had touched each person coming to the altar asking for healing for himself or another person. The service was calm and soothing. But even more soothing to Tom were the greetings that the men and women gave him after the service.

It was that night that he asked Rev to do premarital counseling for Ada and himself.

"Hallelujah!" laughed Rev. "You mentioned that a while ago, and I was wondering when you were going to ask me that again."

LIV

Tom had never had the opportunity to see the Apache Crown Dancers before, and he had been told by Ina that what he would be seeing would be just the tip of the iceberg. The actual ceremony went on for four days in order to complete it. Nevertheless, he felt privileged that he had been invited by Sheena, Ina and Shirley to watch.

The women told him that the Crown Dancers are the spiritual ancestors of the Apache people, to show them how to walk a holy life. The dancers evoke blessings and ward off evil.

"This is our healing ceremony," explained Sheena. That's why we wanted you to see part of it." Tom was honored. He watched intently as the four dancers representing the four sacred directions came out to dance. Their bodies were painted black and white, decorated with animal motifs and lightning designs. A fifth dancer was painted gray. There was so much healing that was needed, thought Tom, both physical and mental.

The drums and the singing began and the dances started. Tom was mesmerized. He was hardly aware of the time passing, until the dancers stopped.

Ina and Shirley walked him to his car. What a day it had been.

He had no way of knowing that when the Crown Dancers were to perform the whole four day ritual, Arlene would be there, sitting quietly with her mother and children. No one looking at her and not knowing her would have ever realized what turmoil lay beneath her exterior surface. Everyone in the community prayed that their spiritual ancestors would help her. Sheena was present also, walking in on her crutches, hoping for the same thing. There was one certain thing about the ceremony: the community was one, the community wanted each person to be healed and cleansed.

LV

Early spring, the end of March, finally came. The land was beginning to wake up. The leaves inside the bravest of trees began to thrust out, and patches of snow cringed and hid in the shadows. At this time of year, Apache girls reaching maturity are honored by the tribe with the Sunrise Dance. The dance celebrates the enduring women who are honored as they dance almost continuously for several days. Friends and godparents help, and songs are sung. The girl is not permitted to falter. It is an important ceremony, for it honors the resilience and continuity of the women and the community.

Bells on leather straps rattle and jingle on their elbows, knees and ankles. Prayers are given to the Creator, as the girls run and dance toward the four directions. There is healing in this sacred ritual through the giving of gifts and blessings.

The healing poured over the bad winter and blotted out all iniquities. Rev had also offered days of atonement during the season of Lent. Many people went to both the Sunrise Dances and the Lenten and Easter services. Life could begin anew. Two cultures joined together to give prayers to the Creator and to the resurrected Christ. Almost in response to the efforts of the people, Spring seemed to bring new life. Sheena's strong feelings about movement in her right toe were corroborated by the specialist in Phoenix. There was hope for her.

And Ada, who had consented to marry Tom that winter, had gone into a flurry of planning for the wedding that was to take place in Whiteriver at the Lutheran church. She took over the job of calling his relatives and hers, picked a decidedly non-military wedding dress, and even got adequate leave arranged for herself. Among her chores, she found time to chastise Tom for putting himself in danger that night at Kinishbah. But, she had other things to do as well, and so he got off fairly unscathed. She had some special surprises for Tom that she was working on also.

For their April marriage ceremony, the Lutheran church wore its Easter regalia and Rev his vestments, and everyone in the community was invited to attend the service. The church was full. There were young and old sitting in the pews, the women dressed in everything from the old fashioned camp dresses to the latest Phoenix styles. Long, silky black hair adorned almost all of the young women, and there was turquoise and silver jewelry, beaded hair clasps, long earrings, even a couple of little boys wearing bow ties. One all dressed up was little Willie, the fetal alcohol child, running back and forth outside the church, with his mother nearby.

Ada had asked Shirley and Ina to be her matrons of honor. It was the first time Tom had seen Ina wearing a dress. Both women wore bright yellow, a color of hope, with sunflower corsages brought in from Phoenix. Ada's best friend had been deployed to the Mid-East, and she sent her regrets at not being able to be with them. She also sent a bouquet of tulips, Ada's favorite flowers, that had to be taken out of a hot house in Phoenix and flown the 200 miles to a florist in Pinetop, then driven down to Whiteriver along with the sunflowers that were meant for Ina and Shirley as corsages.

But the best wedding present for Tom that Ada organized was kept secret until the very hour of the wedding. As Tom stood at the altar waiting for Ada to come down the aisle, he looked over to the side, expecting to see his father who was to be his best man. Instead, he was sitting in the front pew with his wife. Tom was about to go over and remind him to stand next to him at the altar. But, his elbow was nudged gently from the side. He turned and looked. Wayne Pasternak was standing by his side; his wife Sandy and little Cody were sitting close by. Wayne had Ada's ring in his pocket, and was prepared to give it to Tom during the ceremony, using both his hands to pass it to Tom. One big tear passed down Tom's face, over his lips and ended at his chin. Tom's father understood, and nudged his new wife.

Roxy was prominently seated with Tom's dad and stepmother and Ada's mother who flew to Phoenix, rented a car and drove the 200 miles over the Mogollon Rim, to her own great amazement that she could accomplish such a feat. Ada had one more surprise for Tom. His old friend Dempsey, the military lawyer, sat with Sandy and Cody during the service, grinning broadly.

After the wedding, the hospital, thanks to Ben Altaha, hosted a beef barbecue of enormous proportions. It was still cool in April for the outside event, and Ada wore her woolen coat over her wedding dress for the occasion held in the parking lot of the hospital. Anyone who was patient enough to wait for the chunks of beef and the bread, the pots of food of all kinds, was invited to attend.

The smell of roasted beef permeated the whole area. Music by Johnny Cash was heard coming out of a pickup truck nearby. The beef, the fry bread, sunflower cakes, and beans kept being brought out from the hospital. There was a deep purple berry stew, corn soup and cases of cokes provided by the tribal chairman himself, who was young, ambitious and looking forward to another term of office. Ina and Shirley had organized a dozen women who took their allotments of commodity flour given to them once a month and turned it into the perfection of warm, crusty circles of fry bread.

Neither Ada nor Tom had thought about a wedding cake, but Roxanne got Croziers' up in Pinetop to provide an enormous sheet cake topped with a sugary white icing so sweet that it burned one's throat if not washed down quickly by a coke. Sheena, beautiful in an orange dress the color of the Indian paint brush flower, leaned against the table as she stood up for a few minutes to cut the cake. Rev's father was sitting in one of the nearby pickup trucks. He wasn't able to stand with the others for the food, but Hilda Herz and a very old but mobile Indian lady brought him a plate piled high. Old Rev. Herz assured everyone that nothing was wrong with his teeth, as he plowed into the beef.

Tom was awed by the generosity. Silently, he gave a prayer for Big Boy, remembering those low days of winter, and a prayer for all the people he had grown to love. He introduced Cody, Sandy, Wayne and Dempsey to everyone who came near.

He and Ada had a lot to work out in terms of where they would live and where they would work. Blending two lives was going to take a lot of maneuvering. They weren't quarrelling about it, but they had reached a roadblock. For the present, they had decided to let things remain the same; Ada would work at Huachuca, Tom at Whiteriver, and they would take turns making the Salt River Canyon trip on weekends. Both knew that this couldn't go on forever. But each one didn't want to ask the other to give up his choices for the other.

Tom and Ada did go to Rev for counseling before their marriage. Carl Herz was pleased.

"Well, you two," he announced at the first session. "I usually divide this discussion into four areas: sex, politics, religion, and money. Those are the biggest issues of contention that you will probably face. Which one do you want to tackle first?"

"Religion!" they both answered simultaneously.

"But don't include witchcraft," Tom added. They all laughed.

Epilogue

At the wedding ceremony of Tom and Ada, Rev. Herz put gold bands on the fingers of Tom and Ada, symbols of the completeness of marriage, but also the Apache symbol of the circle, the life path of all creatures. Somehow, Tom thought, both Geronimo and Chief Alchesay would have understood both worlds.